BLUE WOLF BOOK FOUR

D1607581

BLUE VENOM

BRAD MAGNARELLA

ISBN-13: 978-109790-330-6

ISBN-10: 1-097-90330-3

Cover design by Ivan Sevic

Cover titling by Deranged Doctor Design

Wolf symbol by Orina Kafe

THE BLUE WOLF SERIES

———

1

I watched the dim light of the quarter moon play over Yoofi's coat-draped form as he hunkered in front of the library door. With each word he murmured in Congolese, another finger of dark energy seeped from his bladed staff to explore the door's seams.

While my magic-user performed his spell work, I remained back in the shadows of the manicured lawn, my gaze climbing the library's stone facade. The little building in the quaint Massachusetts town had been an 1800s schoolhouse once. It still featured a bell tower. But the historical site, not to mention the entire town, had seen drastically fewer visitors in recent months.

The spate of disappearances had a lot to do with that.

Beneath the bell tower, light glowed from an arched window. A single figure moved inside, casting shadows against the glass. I smiled tightly, muscles bunching around the hinges of my wolf jaws.

End of the line, you man-eating bastard.

The air underwent a change in pressure, and I dropped my gaze back to Yoofi. He gave a thumbs-up to indicate he had removed the ward from the door, then stole off under a cloaking spell until I could no longer make out his outline or hear the faint clinks of the flasks in his coat pockets.

Adjusting my large grip on my MP88, I approached the door from the side. When a shadow passed through the projection of window light onto the lawn, I slipped into the library and swept the main room with my weapon. Orderly bookshelves, computer stations, and a comfortable-looking reading area radiated softly in my wolf vision. Nostrils flaring, I pulled in the lingering scents of the day's patrons, which hadn't been many.

Only one scent dominated now—a fusion of wool and pipe smoke—but beneath that something rotten stirred. It was coming from the second floor, where I heard footsteps and the occasional riffling of paper.

Leading with my weapon, I eased past the polite sign announcing that only library personnel were permitted beyond that point and made my way up a wooden flight of stairs. The door to the second-floor office was ajar, releasing a spill of light. The sounds were coming from inside, but I made a circuit of the upper floor to ensure the other rooms were clear.

Back near the office, I activated a button on my collar. A computer-generated hologram of my human head sprang to life around my wolfish one. One of Centurion's latest high-tech toys. It glitched from time to time, but it was a huge improvement over the flight helmet I'd had to don my first six months with Legion.

I drew in my breath and kicked the office door the rest of the way open.

Mr. Hinkley was hunched over a desk, a sheaf of papers held to the chest of his forest green sweater. Pressed khakis and gleaming loafers completed his wardrobe. The elderly man with trim white hair and a lean build jerked upright, spilling half his papers. He blinked at me from behind a pair of bifocals. Now that I knew what he was, I could see all the little things about him that weren't quite right. The faint blue of his lips, for example. He removed a wooden pipe from them and frowned.

"Working late, Mr. Hinkley?" I asked, stepping inside.

"Is it late?" He glanced at his watch.

"Unless two in the morning is considered normal office hours."

"I accidentally omitted our audio-visual needs from next year's budget. Tomorrow's the deadline to amend, and I've been gathering what receipts I can find to bolster my case. Even municipalities like ours can be, well … *grudging* with their money, to put it diplomatically. The time must have escaped me."

When he chuckled, a rotten scent I'd earlier mistaken for cancer leaked from his mouth. He stooped and gathered the spilled papers. The much-loved Mr. Hinkley had been the head librarian since half the town could remember, making him the perfect host for the fae creature.

"Funny," I said. "Those don't look like receipts."

Composed now—*too* composed under the circumstances—Mr. Hinkley smiled in a grandfatherly way as he set the papers on his desk. "Well, Miss Doddington took it upon herself to organize my office last week. Between us, it looks like someone took a snow blower to the drawers. She meant well, of course, but darn it if my papers aren't scattered from here to Maine." He glanced at my weapon, still aimed at him. "How is your search going … I'm sorry, was it Captain Wolfe?"

"It's about wrapped up."

"Is that so?" he asked, leaning back against the desk and puffing on his pipe.

I nodded at the papers behind him. "Which means you don't need to study up."

Mr. Hinkley's brow beetled in pretend confusion. "Study up?"

Under Sarah's direction, the community newsletter had run an announcement that we would be performing mandatory interviews of town employees as part of our investigation. The emphasis would be on past work history. As an Oni, the fae creature in front of me had access to Mr. Hinkley's recent memories. Beyond that, he didn't have squat. The creature had come tonight in search of something he could review before sitting down for the interview tomorrow, where he no doubt planned to put on the same folksy act that had fooled everyone in town for the past few months.

"It's over," I said.

Mr. Hinkley set his pipe in an ashtray on the corner of his desk. "I'm afraid I'm not understanding you."

But as he spoke, his pupils were turning pale. Strange energies warped the air around him, their threads writhing toward me. No doubt one of the last things his twenty-two victims had experienced before being devoured. And that term, *devoured*, was apt. Onis left nothing of their victims.

"You're wasting your magic," I said, holding up the protective charm around my neck.

The lovable old librarian snarled, his pupils glowing white in eyes that had suddenly gone the color of midnight. The creature pounced. I met his attack with a sidekick to the stomach. The superhuman blow sent the old man flying over his desk and crashing through the second-story window.

"He's coming down," I radioed, rushing to the blown-out window.

"We see him," Sarah radioed back.

The Oni had landed in the yard. No sooner than he gained his feet, gunfire sounded, and a fusillade of iron-forged rounds exploded into him. I took aim and unleashed a burst from the rifle barrel of my MP88. The Oni, still in Mr. Hinkley's form, staggered this way and that. We were hitting him from four sides now—Sarah and Olaf from the ground, me from the window, and Takara from the library rooftop. We had known the magical creature would be able to withstand heavy-duty damage, but damn.

With a primal roar, the elderly Mr. Hinkley began to morph into the Oni's true form. A pair of nub-like horns punched through the skin high on his forehead. His body swelled and stretched, shedding what remained of his clothes, while his hair bloomed into a shaggy mess, turning coal black. When the Oni straightened, he was an eight-foot ogre, enormous muscles bulking beneath his blue skin.

That just gave us a bigger target.

"Full auto!" I shouted into my radio.

My teammates complied until the Oni was a lurching mass of mini explosions. Ejected casings hit the bookshelf beside me and tumbled down in a smoking cascade. I paused to change mags, slamming a fresh one home. We were expending a crap-ton of ordnance, but every hit was taking another bite out of the creature's protective magic.

Before long, the Oni's form began to waver.

"Hold fire," I ordered. "He's going gaseous."

As the gunfire tapered, the Oni transformed into a serpentine-like mist that snaked toward the forest north of the library. Lowering my head, I crashed through what remained of the office's window frame and landed in the yard where the creature had been. The hologram around my head flickered on impact. Another glitch to work out. I took off after the Oni, the rest of the Legion team falling in behind me.

"Yoofi," I prompted.

"Yes, I have him," he answered.

The air rippled with energy, and the Oni's mist, which had been turning transparent, flashed with little glittering sparkles, making him easier to track. Still, he was pulling away. Fortunately, we'd mission-planned for that too.

"I've got eyes on him, boss," Rusty radioed.

The drone overhead changed pitch as my tech wiz tracked him through the forest. Like the half-dozen missions the Legion team had been called to since the wendigo job in Canada, we had identified the culprit systematically, quickly, and without any real surprises. The only hiccup with this mission was that while we knew our Prod 1 derived his power from a holly tree, we hadn't been able to determine *which* holly tree. The town was full of them. The solution was to get the Oni to lead us to his.

Weakened, he didn't have a choice.

"He's stopping," Rusty radioed.

"At a tree?" I asked through harsh breaths.

"Oh yeah, and it's a mother-honker. Whoa, now we've got a light show."

The Oni had already begun drawing power from the tree to restore himself.

"Take it out," I ordered.

"You got it, boss."

As the rest of us took cover, Rusty fired the drone's mini-Stinger missiles. Explosions flashed through the trees ahead, their booms rattling the earth. The Oni released a pained cry. Smoke rushed past our position.

"Wipe out," Rusty radioed. *"Nothing left of the tree but a crater, and a very disappointed looking creature."*

I ordered the others to cover me as I moved forward and entered a small clearing. Sure enough, the Oni had taken form again. But the hulking creature appeared smaller and less substantial than he'd been at the library. He was staring at the smoking hole where the holly tree had been, arms hanging at his side.

"Tough break, bud," I growled. "But you fucked with the wrong plane."

The Oni turned toward me. Though his black claws and gargantuan teeth more than rivaled mine in size and frightfulness, the creature wore the slack face of something that knew the jig was up. He didn't even try to run when I aimed my weapon. Though the wolf in me was disappointed at the lack of fight, my captain's mind steeled itself.

Just finish the SOB.

I curled my finger over the trigger for the grenade launcher and squeezed once. The golf ball-sized round punched into the creature's defenseless gut. The ensuing explosion spattered the surrounding trees with Oni parts. An arm landed in front of me, the limb already oozing and turning to a lifeless gas.

I prodded it anyway as the rest of Legion came up behind me.

I lowered my MP88. "Nice job, gang. Mission accomplished."

"Woo-hoo!" Rusty belted through our feed. *"Can I bring Drone 1 back home?"*

He was referring to our operating base just outside of town.

"Go ahead," I said. "We'll be heading there ourselves in a few."

"Very good, man," Yoofi said, switching his staff to his other hand so he could clap my shoulder. He appeared to think about doing the same to Olaf, who was scanning the clearing through his night-vision ocular. But with a nervous giggle, Yoofi backed away. It was clear he was still uncomfortable around our "non-living" teammate—or zombie, for short. In Yoofi's defense, Olaf remained about as readable as a boulder. Though I'd thrown him a lifeline back in September, ordering him to tell me if he ever wanted out of Legion, he'd remained silent. He continued to excel as a soldier, though.

"Well done," I told him.

"Coming through," Sarah announced in her clipped voice.

Olaf and I stepped back as our medic and chief investigator knelt beside the Oni's arm. She filled a test tube with the ooze, capped it tight, and labeled it. She then crossed the clearing to collect samples of the holly tree Rusty had blown to shit.

"These are getting too easy."

I turned to find Takara standing on my other side. Her midnight hair whipped around her ninja leathers in the chill New England breeze as she appraised the scene without the use of artificial night vision.

I followed her gaze, wondering how we would have handled the Oni when we were just starting out—half the team raw and Takara barely following orders. We'd come a long way in the ten months since. A lot of credit went to Takara for not only learning to work as part of a team but for helping me to control my wolf nature.

"Or maybe we're getting more proficient," I replied.

"Perhaps, but I would like a challenge. Is it wrong to want to test yourself?"

When she faced me, red crescents flashed around her black irises. That could have been her dragon talking, because the wolf in me felt the same. It had been too long since Legion had been seriously challenged. But two months from the end of my term with Legion wasn't the time to court more danger.

"No," I grunted. "But be careful what you wish for."

2

The sun was just cresting the desert horizon when we arrived back at the Legion compound outside Las Vegas. The wrap-up back in Massachusetts had gone smoothly. With a team of Centurion suits taking care of the post-mission details, we only had to break down, load up, and jet off—and we'd accomplished all three this mission in record time. Eight missions had a way of streamlining your processes. Sarah and I filed our reports on the ride back.

Now, as our solar-powered personnel carrier pulled to a stop in front of the barracks, I shook Rusty awake.

"I didn't know she had a husband!" he blurted, eyes popping wide.

That drew a snort of laughter from Takara, which didn't happen very often.

I got Yoofi's attention and signaled for him to remove his earbuds. "All right, everyone knows the procedure. Unload, unpack, and then take the rest of the day to R&R. We'll convene in the meeting room at twenty-hundred for debriefing. Can you have the drone footage downloaded by then?" I asked Rusty.

"Will do, boss." He completed a yawn and scratched one of

his muttonchop sideburns. "But could someone wake me up around nineteen-hundred? I always seem to sleep through the durned alarm."

"I can poke you with one of my blades," Takara said.

Rusty bounced his eyebrows up and down. "Ooh, you know what I like."

Takara turned away with a frown, but it was clear Rusty had finally grown on her. Takara had even begun to exchange little bantering jabs with him. I wondered how much of her loosening up in the last months had to do with Biogen possibly zeroing in on a cure for her as well.

"Sarah," I said. "Do you have anything to add?"

"No," she replied curtly, her thick lenses aimed at her tablet.

In contrast, Sarah had managed to remain largely impersonal—something I'd come to accept.

I looked around at my five teammates. With the hologram collar turned off, they were seeing my wolf face.

"Before we go our separate ways for the day, I just want to say that I'm damned proud of how you handled what could have been a really challenging mission. This is what I saw when I took the command position. Everyone executing at maximum strength and effectiveness in a team framework." I still had two months until the end of my term, but I felt a small catch in my throat. Was I already getting nostalgic? "This is without a doubt the most unique group I've ever worked with, and you're also one of the most capable. I'd put Legion up against just about anyone or anything at this point."

"Hell, yeah," Rusty drawled, pumping a fist.

"And we are honored to be on your team, Mr. Wolfe," Yoofi said. "You have made us what we are."

Olaf nodded, though it could have been a reflex.

"I wasn't fishing for compliments, guys. I just wanted—"

"Yoofi's right," Sarah cut in, her gaze still locked on her

tablet. "We wouldn't have attained a level of effectiveness so soon had it not been for your command. If you're going to commend the team, it's only appropriate that your team reciprocate." She gave the tablet a final tap and looked up at me. Though often inscrutable, her eyes now suggested approval, or something close to it. Not knowing how to respond, I simply nodded and opened the carrier door.

"Conference room at twenty hundred," I reminded them.

———

Back in my suite, I pulled off my gloves and boots and removed what I referred to as my *collar*. In fact, it was a little more complex than that. A single transparent wire came off the back of the thick metal band, arcing above the crown of my head while two thin extensions wrapped around the sides of my face.

I looked over the contraption with its multiple micro-lenses. It really was an impressive piece of engineering. Inside, cameras, computer chips, and mini projectors worked in concert to create the illusion that I possessed a human head, one that blended seamlessly with my surroundings. Only very close examination, or preternatural senses like Takara's, would suggest something different—or even pick out the contraption itself. Centurion was using it on me as part of their R&D, which justified the expense.

I collapsed the collar, plugged it into a charger, and stepped out of my jumpsuit. In the mirror over the sofa, a seven-foot, four-hundred-pound wolfman with blue hair crossed the living room and dropped the suit into a hamper with the rest of my dirty clothes. I'd been headed to the shower for a good scrubbing, but now I stopped and faced my reflection.

I studied my lupine eyes … peaked ears and lethal snout … the mass of muscles that gave me superhuman strength and speed. As impressive as the collar was, the blend of mystical and physical engineering in front of me was on an order far greater. It was mind-blowing, really. And now the thought of giving it up drew a twinge from my gut. I quashed the feeling before it could form into thought.

You're committed to someone now, I reminded myself. *You have responsibilities.*

I dropped my gaze to the wedding band nesting in the thick blue hair of my chest. Too small to fit on my transformed finger, I'd threaded the band with a cable chain and hung the chain around my neck.

I picked up the ring now. Not one to carry mementos into the field in the past, I had worn it on every mission since Dani's and my wedding. It was like carrying my vows to her with me. Setting it back against my chest, I decided the shower could wait and pulled the private sat phone from my bag.

"How's my favorite East Texas gal?" I asked when Daniela answered.

"Just East Texas? Do you have gals in Lubbock and Odessa I don't know about?"

I chuckled into the phone. "Not anymore, apparently."

"Good answer."

"Hey, I'm back on base."

"How did it go?" she asked.

"Honestly? A breeze. I've got a solid team around me."

"Did they get the package I sent?"

She was referring to the huge tin of homemade walnut chocolate-chip cookies she'd mailed through Centurion's secure system. "They did, and they loved them," I assured her. "Thanks, Dani. That was really sweet."

"If they're hankering for anything in particular, just let me know."

"Well, this one guy's always talking about his mother's Kentucky bread pudding with bourbon sauce..." I told her, thinking of Rusty. "But I'm not sure how you'd ship something like that."

"Let me worry about the hows. If he's got my baby's back, I'm taking care of him."

"You really are a saint."

"How are you?"

My smile straightened. Back in the fall I had shared the generalities of what had happened to me in Waristan, from the old woman marking me to leaving the military for my current position in exchange for a cure. But I hadn't been able to tell her about my physical transformation into the Blue Wolf. A being so massive I had to stoop to see my lupine face in the mirror. Dani knew I'd left out key parts—I could hear it in her voice every time she asked how I was—and it raked my guilt.

But I'd sworn to myself I would tell her everything when this was over.

"I'm good," I replied. "I mean that—I'm feeling better than ever." My sessions with Takara were helping. I hadn't come anywhere close to the kind of control loss I'd experienced in Canada when I'd had to give up command. "And by all accounts we're not far from a cure," I added, which was also true.

"I'm really happy for you, Jason." She fell quiet for a moment, which allowed the sentiment to sink in. "And hey, I've got some good news too."

"What is it?"

"The owner accepted our bid."

"No shit? I mean, no kidding?"

Daniela didn't like it when I swore.

"It's ours for the taking," she said, letting my transgression go this time.

I thought about the house we'd decided on when I was last home—and human—a month ago. Dani and I had bid low because of the work needed, but we liked the walnut floors and high ceilings, and there was enough square footage that we'd never have to move, even after we'd had our three or four little monsters. Also, the house backed up to a hundred-odd acres of wooded county land, where I planned to teach the kids to hunt. And not just small game. Now that I knew what lurked in the dark corners, I was going to ensure my family could protect themselves. It wasn't the world I wanted for them, but it was the world we'd inherited. Which meant our clan had to be more Winchester than Walton.

I switched my thoughts back to home-buying.

"So I guess the next step is the inspection," I said.

"Already scheduled someone for this coming week."

"You're amazing."

"If that goes well, we're looking at six or so weeks to closing."

The thought that in two months' time I could be wearing a tool belt instead of a tactical one and beginning the renovations on our new home sent a dizzying wave of happiness and unreality through me.

Also a little fear. Could it be that easy?

Seeming to pick up that thought, Dani said, "This is really happening."

As much as I hated to, I needed to ground expectations—for both our sakes.

"Let's not get too far ahead of ourselves," I said. "A step at a time, remember?"

"Oh, you're such a party pooper."

"Hey, I was trained to be cautious."

"Anything on the horizon?" she asked tentatively.

When I'd counseled caution just now, I was thinking about my cure, but Daniela's thoughts were on future missions. She had done the math. If the averages held, she knew I had about two missions remaining. And Waristan had taught us that the final mission could change everything, regardless of planning.

"Well, we're always monitoring situations," I replied, "but I've had no official word on anything imminent."

"Don't military-speak me."

"Sorry," I laughed. "No missions that I'm aware of."

"Better." I could almost feel her relax a little through the connection. "Just…"

"Be careful?" I finished for her. "I will."

"You promised a spring reception," she reminded me, her voice teasing again. She was trying her hardest to be a trooper. "Not that our courthouse wedding wasn't everything I dreamed it would be, but it'll be nice to include family and friends."

I thought about that late September day, me in my best suit, Daniela in the gorgeous bridal gown she'd picked out months before. The ceremony was presided over by a judge with permanent smile lines and attended by her parents. The smallness of the ceremony hadn't bothered me; in fact, I'd liked the intimacy. The judge's wife even put together a little floral arrangement for the lectern. To be honest, while Daniela and I exchanged vows and rings, I wouldn't have known if there had been six of us there or six thousand. All that existed was my love for Daniela, a love mirrored in her shining eyes.

"I want your teammates there too," Daniela said, breaking up the memory.

"My teammates?" As close as the team and I had become, I couldn't quite picture them sipping cocktails and doing the Macarena. "That, ah, might be a little tricky with the confidentiality and everything. But I'll see what I can do."

"And tell your friend I'll start on the bread pudding today."

"He'll be over the moon," I said, knowing how stoked Rusty would be.

Turning from my massive blue reflection, I clutched our wedding band in my fist. I suddenly felt bad about shutting down talk of the house. This was my wife, our future. To hell with grounding expectations.

"Hey," I said. "It's going to be an amazing house."

I didn't have to see Daniela's face to know she was beaming.

"It will be," she agreed.

3

I arrived at the conference room early for the evening's debriefing and found Sarah already seated at the table, papers and folders spread around two open laptops. She was still wearing her digital camos from that morning, the chemical pattern trying to blend her into the room's plain surroundings.

"Didn't you rest?" I asked.

She glanced up, the strain beyond her glasses answering my question. "I received a call from Director Beam this morning. We have a new assignment. I wanted to review and organize the information."

"Why didn't you get me?"

"You hadn't slept in two days."

"Yeah, well, neither have you now."

But this was how Sarah operated. Knowing that Beam's office was sending info over, she wouldn't have been able to idle down her brain enough to sleep. For a while now, I suspected at least mild OCD.

I came around behind her. "Another Berglund case?"

Berglund had been our client in Canada. Upon the mission's successful conclusion—which involved recovering his girlfriend from a wendigo—Berglund was so overcome with appreciation, he set up a multimillion-dollar hardship fund. The fund helped finance missions for cash-strapped clients. Our last five missions had been so-called "Berglund cases," including the one we'd just finished in Massachusetts.

But Sarah shook her head. "No."

"A paying client?" I grunted in surprise. "Who, another hedge fund CEO?"

"A country," she replied. "A kingdom, more accurately."

"A kingdom?"

"New Siam," she said. "It's between Thailand and Laos. Rich in minerals and gems."

That explained how they could afford us. I looked at the map Sarah pulled up on one of the laptops. "Southeast Asia," I remarked.

"Ever been?"

"Not to New Siam. I spent a month jungle-training in Cambodia. You?"

She shook her head, then began typing on the other laptop.

"What kind of case?"

"Disappearances," she replied distractedly.

Disappearances had become Legion's bread and butter—not that I minded. We had a solid record of finding and recovering survivors while ending the Prod I that had snatched them. The Oni case was one of the few where there had been no survivors. Fortunately, pure devourers like Onis weren't real common.

"How many vics are we talking?"

"Five."

"Not bad," I remarked. Five vics was five too many when dealing with the disappeared, of course, but that beat twenty or thirty. I looked over the material on the table in search of their profiles.

Sarah stopped typing and blinked up at me as if her mind was only now registering our most recent exchange.

"I'm sorry, thousand. Five thousand."

My heart clenched into a tight fist before releasing.

"Five thousand," I repeated to make sure I'd heard her.

Nodding, Sarah zoomed in the map. "They lived in this town on the edge of a jungle. Two months ago, the entire population vanished. I have the information here." She began to reach for a file folder, but I stopped her.

"If you're ready to present, why don't you lay out the mission for the entire team."

———

Fifteen minutes later, the rest of the team began to file in. Takara was early, while Olaf arrived at exactly twenty hundred hours per my order from that morning. That was typical. Yoofi showed up a minute after, alternately sucking on a flask and puffing on a thick cigar: his offerings to Dabu. Rusty took up the rear five minutes late, wearing a sleeveless hoodie, and muttering his standard excuses. Also typical.

"I did get the drone feed loaded into the system," he said as he sat down.

"We're actually going to hold off on the debriefing," I said. "We have another assignment."

Waving a hand through his smoke, Yoofi peered at me and giggled. "Already?"

Rusty slanted his eyes. "Are you putting us on, boss?"

Takara shushed them and nodded for me to continue. I sensed her keenness for the challenge she felt we'd been denied in our previous missions. With five thousand missing in New Siam, I suspected she would be getting her wish.

"Sarah's going to present," I said, taking a seat beside Olaf.

Sarah took another minute to organize her material before standing. Using the controls on her tablet, she dimmed the lights and activated the wall-mounted LCD screens. The map we'd been looking at a moment before appeared on the middle screen, showing the small country on the Indochina Peninsula.

"Last week the Kingdom of New Siam contacted Centurion," she began. "They claimed to have lost an entire population in their northern province. The town is Ban Mau." She zoomed in further to show a small community made up of a neat grid of streets surrounded by acres of irrigated farmland.

"Someone from New Siam's central government spoke to the town's leader on a Monday," she continued. "He reported nothing amiss. The following day, the same leader could not be reached. No one in the town could. The kingdom sent soldiers from a nearby army outpost to investigate. They arrived in Ban Mau to find it completely abandoned. Not a single one of the five thousand plus inhabitants remained."

"Geez Louise," Rusty said, rubbing a wiry, freckled bicep. "That's the entire turnout for Friday Night Motocross in Maysville."

"Any sign of conflict?" Takara asked.

"None. It appeared that the people packed their belongings and left voluntarily."

"In vehicles?" I asked.

"The vehicles remained, so presumably on foot. The neighboring towns reported no sign of them on the roads, however." Sarah swept the areas to the west, south, and east of Ban Mau with her laser pointer before indicating the dark green expanse to the north. "That suggests they went into the jungle."

"If they are still on this plane," Yoofi pointed out.

Sarah nodded once in agreement. "The kingdom has no idea what drove them to leave the town or where they could have gone. Military patrols turned up nothing, and the jungle is too vast and dense to search effectively by air."

"What did our investigative team find?" I asked.

Centurion liked to insert a team ahead of our arrival to gather additional info and ensure we were dealing with a Prod 1. Not that their assessments were always accurate. More than once they'd sent us down a false trail. But important intel often came out of their efforts, even if it took a little mining.

"Nothing," Sarah replied. "The team's entry was denied."

"Denied?" I repeated.

"New Siam is a closed country. Its king is paranoid, some say to the point of delusion. Perhaps from age-related dementia," Sarah added in her clinical voice. "It wasn't King Savang who contacted Centurion, in fact, but his oldest son, Prince Kanoa, who goes by Ken." Headshots appeared on the left and right screens. One was an elderly man with thinning gray hair and a face whose severe lines made him look despotic. Prince Ken couldn't have appeared more different with his thick black hair and large, sociable eyes.

"Ken said that no one outside the kingdom would have known Ban Mau disappeared if his father had his way," Sarah went on. "The king doesn't want to appear weak. He's paranoid of attacks by neighboring countries. Ken feared that bringing in an advance team would raise his father's suspicions, and then Legion would never get access."

Alarm bells sounded in my head. "So this is going to be a covert operation in our client's own country?"

"And did you mention an army?" Yoofi asked.

"Yes, but Prince Ken has contacts inside the military," Sarah said. "We won't have to worry about them."

Frankly, I liked the sound of that even less. In closed countries, leaders wielded absolute control over the armed forces. It was what kept them in power. That the son had military contacts loyal enough to operate behind the king's back suggested an overthrow in the planning. And the last thing I wanted was to bring my team into the middle of a politically explosive situation. Been there, done that.

"Why Legion?" I asked. "How is Ken so sure this is a Prod 1 case?"

"He's not," Sarah answered. "His older sister urged him to consider supernatural causes for the disappearance. Ken is an admitted skeptic, but he doesn't want a repeat of Ban Mau. There are other towns in the area, and the provincial capital is only twenty miles to the south, a city of more than a hundred thousand. He is worried about them."

"And Beam is giving us the green light?" I asked. For someone as risk-averse as Director Beam, it seemed unusual he'd send us into an unstable theater mined with unknowns.

"I'm assuming the offered payment is enough to offset the uncertainty," she replied.

Sarah had no doubt nailed it. With its mineral wealth, New Siam's royal family could probably splash out money like it was water. I looked over the printed information arrayed across Sarah's end of the table, much of it background material on the kingdom and ruling family.

"What did the Prod database come back with?" I asked.

"The query data is lean. All we have is a location and the disappearance of a large population without apparent struggle. Based on that, the strongest hit is for a faerie lord. It's not very strong, however," Sarah added. "Fifty-two percent probability. There are no known portals to the faerie realm on the peninsula. Neither is there recent evidence of fae activity, and certainly not on that scale."

"What are the runners-up?"

She looked from me to one of the laptops. "Demon at forty-four percent. Master vampire at thirty-two. Sorcerer at just over thirty. From there the candidates fall into the twenties and teens."

Fifty-two percent for the top hit was pretty crappy, almost as if the database was throwing darts.

"Could we be looking at human tribute to a god?" Yoofi asked.

"New Siam is predominantly Buddhist," Sarah said, "but many of the rural communities also practice a kind of folk religion. Around Ban Mau, the people worship a maternal goddess called Noma. She represents the earth. There are no records of human sacrifice to her—or to any of the holy figures in New Siam."

"How about the skunk work?" I asked, referring to the database in which Prod is had yet to be verified.

"There's an old legend of 'Snake People' in the area," she said.

"Ooh, I do not like snakes," Yoofi said from his cloud of cigar smoke.

Takara glared at him.

"*Khon ngu* they were called," Sarah went on. "According to the stories, they were an old tribe that lived deep in the jungle. They built underground colonies and bred venomous snakes for meat and poisons. It seems that's where their name came from. Area tribes traded with them. Their toxins were highly coveted for hunting and tribal ceremonies. But as tribes left the jungle and began clearing land for cultivation and settlements, the exchanges seem to have stopped. Whether the snake people left too, no more was said of them. Of course, there is no hard evidence that the *khon ngu* existed in the first place, or they would be in the main database."

"Any information on what they were like?" Takara asked.

"Shrewd traders, allegedly," Sarah replied. "Some stories

claim they were manipulative as well. No accounts of conflicts, though."

"And no recent sightings?" I asked.

"Nothing documented," Sarah answered.

I looked over the material on the table again. Knowing Sarah, she had already given it an exhaustive pass.

"What's your read on the client?" I asked.

"There are a couple of items of concern. Two years ago, the kingdom waged a campaign against a local insurgent group. Whether the group was real or imagined is up for debate, but King Savang was convinced villages in the country's far east were aligning against him. He sent in the army and wiped them out."

A feverish burn rippled through me. Three years before, I'd seen the smoking aftermath of a state-sponsored massacre in a Central Asia town, the military not sparing women or children. It was the closest I'd come to breaking down in front of my men. I suppressed the growl building in my chest now.

"Do you think this is what happened in Ban Mau?" Rusty asked.

"Possibly," Sarah answered.

"Then why contact us?" Takara asked.

"Damage control," I cut in with a raw voice. "If they were worried that word of the king's latest civilian massacre had gotten out, they could have shifted the blame to a Prod and called us to make it look legitimate."

Meaning the prince wasn't trying to undermine his father, but colluding with him. That also meant the story about keeping the disappearances hush-hush so as not to appear weak to neighboring countries was bullshit.

"So they're using us for a freaking cover up?" Rusty asked.

"It's something we should be asking ourselves," I said, furious the possibility hadn't occurred to Director Beam. Or maybe it had, but he saw it as an easy payday. Legion goes in, finds nothing, leaves. Meanwhile, the Kingdom of New Siam gets its cover story, and Centurion's balance sheet grows a little fatter.

I was speculating, but the thought that it was even possible made me want to give Beam a violent shaking. I tried to center myself, like Takara had taught me. When I looked up again, I caught Sarah watching me. It had been a long time since I'd lost my cool like this in front of the team.

She cleared her throat and looked over the room.

"The other item that could be problematic has to do with succession. With the way the rules are written, Prince Ken and his older sister, the one who urged him to consider this a supernatural case, would both have claims to their father's throne. There are rumors of infighting between them." The image of the king changed to a headshot of a woman with a pale, sculpted face and intense green eyes. "Her name is Princess Halia."

"I was sorta hoping it would be Barbie," Rusty said. "You know, Ken and Barbie?"

I tuned him out. "So even if the prince isn't undermining his father, he could still be trying to undermine his sister."

"Correct," Sarah answered.

One thing I'd learned in spec ops was that when you were invited into a politically unstable situation, the person doing the inviting often saw the foreign support as a means to strengthen his or her position. Regardless of whether that was true in this case, the uncertainties were piling up.

"Was there anything else?" I asked.

"Those were my main findings," Sarah answered.

Her efficiency was one of the many things I'd come to like about her, but I had a hunch I *wasn't* going to like her answer to my next question.

"When does Beam want us to move?"

"He understands we just returned from a mission, but Centurion needs to start coordinating with Prince Ken for our insertion. Director Beam is asking that we have a mission plan prepared by midnight."

Breaths began blasting hot from my nostrils again. "A mission plan based on no advanced intel, low-probability leads, and a secretive kingdom with a history of violence against its own people?"

Sarah stared back at me, eyes firm behind her glasses. Except for a surprising moment when she'd defied Beam in Mexico, Sarah had followed his mission directives to the letter since. I could tell she was prepared to do the same in this case. My teammates looked between us as if waiting for us to arrive at an accord.

"So what are we going to do?" Takara finally asked.

Still holding Sarah's gaze, I said, "Nothing before I talk to Beam."

4

I hadn't spoken directly to Director Beam in months. Since the mission in Canada, where I had ordered Rusty to circumvent Beam's control over our equipment, the director and I had reached an uneasy truce. My helping to secure the Berglund Fund had no doubt helped. We conducted most of our exchanges through official reports, or else Beam would communicate with Sarah. That way everyone got along.

But for this, I wanted to speak to him directly. I wanted to see his face.

It appeared shortly on the monitor in my office. Though nearing forty, Beam had the smooth and slender appearance of someone fifteen years younger. He'd gelled his hair into its standard slick part.

"Captain Wolfe," he said.

"Beam," I responded.

The dimple in the director's chin deepened for a moment, probably because I had omitted his title, but the wolf in me refused to mark him as a superior. "Have you had a chance to go through the mission info?" he asked.

"I have, and there's a lot I'm not comfortable with."

I was prepared for Beam to say something dismissive, which was the way these conversations had gone in the past. His mandate was to make the Legion Program a profitable arm of Centurion, and from his standpoint I was little more than a hired gun: a meathead with blue hair who could handle big weapons. He surprised me, then, when he nodded.

"Let's hear them."

I studied his face for a moment. Though the muscles around his jaw indicated impatience, his eyes suggested a willingness to listen. "Well, for starters, King Savang has a history of attacking his own villages," I said. "Wiping them off the map. How do we know that hasn't happened in Ban Mau?"

"We don't," he answered.

"Good, so we're on the same page so far. If that *is* what happened in Ban Mau, has it occurred to anyone in your office that the kingdom might have requested our presence to give legitimacy to their Prod 1 story?"

"It has, in fact."

"And what, the money was right?"

"After an internal discussion, we decided to treat this like a Prod 1 case," he replied, ignoring my jab. "If your investigation indicates as much, you'll pursue the case per standard procedure. If not, we'll fly you home."

"Meanwhile, New Siam gets its official 'We Tried to do Something' stamp from Centurion, and the kingdom's campaign of killing continues," I growled. "If that's the plan, I'll tell you right now, I'm not going along with it."

Per a stipulation in my contract, I had the authority to refuse missions that felt sketchy.

"Even with five thousand missing?" Beam posed the question as if he were dangling a piece of raw steak above my jaws. He knew I had a weakness for innocents, a sentiment foreign to him.

"Not without an assurance."

"And what's that?"

"If we take this mission and find evidence that the kingdom is responsible for the disappearances, we don't bury it. We report the crime to U.S. authorities and all relevant international bodies."

Beam smirked.

"Something funny?" I snarled.

"Just your presumption that we haven't considered these factors. I know you see us as a for-profit conglomerate staffed by scoundrels in suits, but give us *some* credit. Look," he said, holding up his hands to indicate the sniping was over. "In our international work, Centurion is obligated to report evidence of war crimes, crimes against humanity, and humanitarian crises. We're integrated into a system of rapid-response channels for the specific purpose. That obligation supersedes any nondisclosure agreements we make with any country in which we operate. New Siam is no exception."

"So if we find something, it would be reported?" I asked, watching him closely.

Beam's steady eyes seemed to meet my gaze through the monitor. "Yes, Captain. And if that's what's happening, you'll keep a poker face until you're out. We'll report your findings." His tone turned stern. "You're not to engage the kingdom or its officials in any way, shape, or form. Are we clear?"

Everything I observed of Beam's face and voice suggested he was telling the truth. Even if he reneged, I still had military channels I could report through.

"Sure," I agreed.

"Anything else?"

"Yeah, there is. If this is a legitimate Prod 1 case, the prince appears to have key members of the military in his pocket. For all we know, he could be working to undermine his father's rule or even boot him from the throne. If the king learned there was a paramilitary force in his country, it could trip off a civil war. And that's not even getting into the potential shitshow between Prince Ken and his sister."

"In which case we'd evacuate you," Beam replied.

"Sort of hard when the reaction force is a country away."

Beam sighed. "It's the best we could do under the circumstances."

I didn't want the team to end up pinned between warring army factions. That's how things went FUBAR: fucked up beyond all repair. But if a covert mission was necessary to keep King Savang in the dark, the prince couldn't risk a greater presence in his country beyond the six of us. In which case, Beam had a point.

"All right, when does the prince want us there?"

"As soon as reasonably possible. How much time do you need?"

The question surprised me. Usually we were ordered when to be somewhere and were left to work out the planning details. I thought about the team. We'd had our day of R&R, but I wanted another day to review jungle tactics. Save for our first mission in Mexico, we hadn't operated in anything close to jungle conditions.

"We can be ready Wednesday morning."

"Excellent, I'll set up the flight schedule."

Though Beam kept a straight face, I picked up a hint of smugness in his eyes, like he'd brought me to heel. I could feel the wolf in me bristling at the suggestion. I went back to my breath control, my training.

"Sounds good," I said in a thick voice.

Before I could end the call, Beam said, "Hey, I know we come at these assignments from different angles. You're focused on the mission, and I tend to be more attentive to the bottom line.

That's the way it should be," he added quickly. "We've hit some bumps, but I respect what you do and how you do it. Now that we're relaxing some of our non-disclosure provisions, word of Legion's effectiveness is starting to get around. Moneyed interests are taking notice. How do you think Prince Ken knew to contact us?"

I watched warily, not sure where he was going with this.

"You brought up the payment earlier?" he said. "On this one, both of our interests are covered. You'll have as much latitude as you need to complete the assignment." He was telling me I didn't need to worry about him shutting us down for cost reasons. I'd definitely welcome that, but he was getting overly friendly now, and that felt weird.

"All right," I said abruptly. "We'll keep an eye out for the flight plan."

"We'll get it to you by midnight. Goodnight, Captain Wolfe."

I hesitated for a beat. "Director Beam."

Why not? I thought as I killed the connection and stood. *He gave me the reassurances I needed.*

With my main concerns addressed, my mind turned to the five thousand disappeared. I was already thinking tactically, but I could feel my protective instincts kicking in, muscles swelling, pulse quickening.

Prod 1 or king, we were going to find the son of a bitch responsible.

I left the office to inform the team it was mission on.

———

That night, I woke up with the acute sense that someone had entered my suite.

I shot upright, ears peaked, nostrils scouring the air for an intruder's scent. For several moments, all I could hear was my own heart booming in my chest. I was reaching for the pistol I kept beneath my bed, when someone called from the living room.

"Captain Wolfe?"

I recognized the voice, even as a raspy whisper. I finished drawing the pistol and eased toward my bedroom door. When I peered around the doorway, my wolf vision filled in the shadowy figure of Reginald Purdy.

"Apologies for the intrusion," he said, a night vision ocular covering his right eye.

"Ever heard of knocking?" I asked in a raw voice. I was not happy about my room being breached in the middle of the night, even by Centurion's Director of Program Development, the man who had hired me. And this was the first time I'd seen him in months. I maintained a firm grip on my weapon.

"Again, my apologies," he said.

"What are you even doing here?"

More importantly, how did he get inside without me hearing?

Purdy removed his ocular and snapped on the living room light. I shielded my brow so I wouldn't have to squint. Instead of a pinstripe suit, Purdy was dressed in one of Centurion's black coveralls. Some versions had noise-suppressant technology, explaining how he'd slipped in. He was also carrying a satchel on a strap across his body. Though my nose wasn't picking up obvious weaponry, I tensed when he reached inside it.

"Your new and improved collar." He produced the piece of tech for creating a hologram of my head and swapped it for the one I'd plugged into my charger earlier. "You reported the last one malfunctioned when you landed from a two-story jump? This one is supposed to address that with improved shock absorption."

I relaxed slightly and looked the collar over. "Since when do you do parcel delivery for engineering?"

"When I need to talk to you discreetly." He opened a hand toward the living room. "Shall we?"

His breathing was calm, his pupils slightly dilated from having just been in darkness. No stress on his scent, either. I motioned for him to go ahead, and he took a seat on the couch. I angled the plush chair toward him and lowered myself onto it. He hadn't slipped into my room to evade my detection, I realized, but Centurion's. I leaned my elbows on my knees, a flicker of curiosity replacing my earlier caution.

"Why discreetly? What's going on?"

He interlaced his dark fingers and regarded me for a moment before replying.

"This mission in New Siam? You need to reject it."

"Reject it?" I said "Why?"

Purdy pulled a neatly folded handkerchief from a pocket and dabbed the corners of his mouth, something he did frequently. He then gave his thin mustache a quick pass before replacing the kerchief in his pocket.

"This one is beyond Legion."

I bristled at his words. "What do you know that I don't?"

Beyond his vague title and the fact he had recruited me, I knew almost nothing about Purdy's role at Centurion. He would disappear from my radar for weeks or months before reappearing, acting as though he'd never been away. The one constant was that he usually seemed at odds with Director Beam over the Legion Program.

"What I know," Purdy began in his old-time lawyerly voice, "is that certain officials are allowing the proposed payment to cloud their good judgment. Viewed objectively, the mission is as I've stated: beyond Legion."

My defensive reaction was muted this time, but it was still there.

I glared down my muzzle at him. "Is there something Beam didn't tell us?"

He frowned toward the ceiling, seeming less to consider the question than how to word his response. "Let's just say he was hasty to accept. It's what he doesn't know that's at issue."

"And what's that?" I demanded, tired of the circular talk.

"That's where things get tricky, Captain Wolfe. Let's assume someone witnesses a murder while committing a robbery. If he reports the first in detail, he confesses to the second. The solution for the conscientious robber, of course, is to report the murder anonymously. That way everyone is satisfied."

"Is that what this is?" I growled. "An anonymous tip? Well, maybe I want the details."

"Understandable. But you have the essential information, and that's all that matters."

"So you're saying you've obtained info through suspect means that suggests the New Siam mission is more dangerous than the suits realize? Too dangerous even for the Legion team?"

"To be clear, I said no such thing," Purdy replied cagily. "I'll simply repeat that you need to exercise your clause and kill the mission."

"And what reason would I give?"

"The one you already did: political instability. You were correct to raise it as a concern. That situation alone should have been grounds for Centurion to conduct a more thorough assessment, but the payment being in the amount it is..." He waved a hand as though to suggest he'd done all he could. "Clouded judgments, Captain."

I sat back in the chair and watched Purdy over the knuckles of my left fist. He had never misled me—not that I knew of. But he also straddled several departments at Centurion and carried a "political operator" vibe. Given his power struggle with Beam, his warning could have nothing to do with the safety of Legion.

If he could convince me to cancel the mission, Legion would miss out on a massive payment. That would put serious corporate pressure on Beam, maybe even leading to his ouster.

But would Purdy jeopardize five thousand lives for a political payoff?

He watched me watching him, his eyes seeming to glint with knowledge.

"I can't kill the mission," I said. "Not without at least going in and investigating."

"But it wouldn't stop there, would it?" Purdy asked. "You would want to know what happened to those five thousand disappeared. And you would pursue and pursue, even unto Death's welcome mat."

"That's our job," I snarled.

"You see?" Purdy grinned as if I'd just made his argument for him. He dabbed his mouth with his kerchief. By the time he replaced it, he'd turned serious again. "I admire that about you, Captain. I do. It's why I wanted you to lead Legion. But not this time. Not this mission. I'm asking you to trust me. Please."

"Does this have anything to do with you and Director Beam?" I asked.

Purdy hesitated a second too long. "We've had our differences," he admitted. "But no, that's not what this is about."

"Give me something concrete then."

Purdy chuckled without humor. "What's concrete, Captain? You know as well as anyone that this world is nothing if not porous. But all right. I see things that others don't. I think that much is obvious from our talk so far. I'll also add that this story has played out already. With tragic consequences."

"How? I need details, *dammit*."

The Director of Program Development stood, telling me the meeting was over.

"I'd kill the mission myself if I could, but I don't have that power," he said. "You're two months from completing your term," he reminded me as he walked to the door. "And we're hearing encouraging things from Biogen."

He didn't mention Daniela, but he didn't have to. I knew exactly what he was saying: listen to him, play it safe, and I'd be back home with her before I knew it.

"Tell me," I repeated.

"Let this one go," he said, and slipped out.

6

With the jungle growing thicker, I signaled for Rusty to come up a little. He grunted as he hustled forward in full gear, his face dripping sweat. Sarah, Olaf, and Yoofi tightened in behind him, while Takara watched our rear.

"Are conditions really gonna be like this?" Rusty whispered.

"Close enough," I answered tersely. "Now zip it. Live exercise."

Rusty typically manned the support drones, but I'd wanted him on the ground for the exercise. I pushed aside a thick vine with my MP88's barrel, impressed with what Yoofi had been able to manifest with some *tumba* seeds and an animation spell. Like the rest of the team, he'd upped his game in the last eight months. Partly why I was having a hard time accepting Purdy's assessment of the mission from the night before.

This one is beyond Legion.

I hadn't brought his visit up with the team. I needed time to process what he had said, to consider his motives. I also wanted to assess my team one more time. They were under the impression we were practicing movement and communication in jungle terrain, but I'd planned a surprise for them.

I made eye contact with Yoofi and nodded. His white teeth flashed back at me.

We arrived at a clearing—the central square of the mock town on our training campus—but now dense growth blocked out the surrounding buildings as well as most of the sky. Ours had to be the only tropical jungle in the Nevada desert.

I stopped and signaled to the team that we were entering a potential danger area. Sarah and Olaf broke off to take left and right security positions, while Takara signaled that she and Yoofi had the near side. Jerking my head for Rusty to follow, we started across the clearing to secure the far side.

I might not have noticed the subtle wave of energy ripple past if I hadn't been expecting it.

The only warning for the rest of the team was a chorus of low groans before the edges of the clearing sprang to life in giant rustling piles of vegetation. Ten-foot creatures shambled forward on vine-tangled legs, thick arms taking form and swinging beneath featureless heads. I didn't realize Yoofi had seeded so many of them. There must have been a dozen of the damned things.

He'd done well.

"Contact!" I called.

Gunfire coughed from Sarah's and Olaf's positions. Splinters and shredded leaves burst from the creatures. Single shots began popping from Takara's weapon as she aimed at where the animating magic twisted into thick ganglions. Rusty looked wildly around and brought his M4 to his shoulder.

"Watch your field of fire," I reminded him, hefting my MP88.

Though we were packing salt rounds and wearing full armor, I didn't want anyone getting hit.

While my teammates ripped into the shambling giants closest to them, I began cutting down the ones on the clearing's far side. My automatic fire blew off the entire top halves of creatures, the salt explosions breaking up the magic giving them life. When their magic failed, the animations collapsed into debris piles.

"Help!" Rusty bawled.

I spun to find him in the grip of one of the animations. The thing lifted him toward a mouth of bark-like teeth. My MP88 thundered and ripped apart the thing's legs. It staggered to the equivalent of its knees, but the spell-work held fast, maintaining the animation. With Rusty flailing, I didn't want to risk a higher shot.

He hollered as his upper half disappeared into the foliage. The animation's teeth crashed down, breaking around Rusty's armored torso. At my command, Yoofi could withdraw the magic and end the exercise, but I didn't want this to be an easy walk-through. I wanted a true-to-life simulation—as much to test myself as my teammates.

Drawing my 16-inch Bowie knife, I launched myself at the animation. My serrated blade twisted and tore as I hacked my way inside. The foliage responded by swarming around me.

"Is that you, boss?" Rusty cried above me.

I could just make him out beyond thick tangles of vines, branches, and leaves.

"Close your eyes!" I shouted.

I pulled a salt grenade from my vest, armed it, and thrust it into the animation's core. The foliage collapsed around that too. As I turned my face away, the grenade detonated. Salt hit my suit like a sandblaster. It also blew through Yoofi's magic. The animation came apart, and a couple hundred pounds of vegetation collapsed over me. Rusty landed beside me with a groan. I stood from the debris and dug him out.

"You all right?" I asked.

"That hunk of jungle tried to eat me."

"So will most Prod is." I pulled his M4 from the pile and pressed it to his chest until he took it. I peered around the smoke-blown clearing to see how the rest of the team was faring. Most of the animated creatures were down. Takara, Sarah, and Olaf concentrated their fire on the remaining two. I'd instructed Yoofi to hang back and focus on maintaining the spell, and he was doing just that.

Time to kick it up a notch.

As the final creature came apart, I gave Yoofi another signal.

Dark energy began to circle his raised staff, growing outward until it felt like we were standing in the outer rings of a cyclone. Rusty staggered from the force while I hunched low, my massive quadriceps bulking through my suit. The others used trees to brace themselves.

As the magic gathered strength, it amassed the debris from the fallen animations into a heap the size of a house. Appendages sprouted out, writhing and thickening, until they looked like tentacles, and the heap, a giant octopus. One of the tentacles lashed toward Sarah. With the energy from Yoofi's staff still bombing around the clearing, it was all Sarah could do to keep her grip on a tree.

The tentacle whipped around her leg and jerked her from her hold. Olaf managed to bring his MP88 up one-handed and fire, but the cyclone forces batted his weapon around, throwing off his aim. Salt rounds blasted everywhere.

Meanwhile, I'd gone to my belly to lower my center of mass. With one hand clamped around Rusty's leg to keep him from flying away, I took aim with my other. I wasn't reacting well to Yoofi's magic, and this newest animation wavered sickly in my squinting vision.

Narrowing in on the tentacle dragging Sarah, I squeezed the trigger. Salt rounds punched through the appendage and broke it apart. Sarah fell to her stomach and, teeth gritted, clawed for cover.

"You sure this is just an exercise, boss?" Rusty shouted.

As more tentacles lashed out, I squeezed off a burst of grenade rounds. They punched into the center of the thing and exploded with low thuds. Shredded foliage rained out like confetti. The creature shuddered as the salt broke through the magic, but Yoofi was sustaining a steady current into his animation.

If I couldn't break up the magic, I would have to incinerate the material it was animating.

"Hold on to my leg!" I shouted, shoving Rusty down until his hands were clamped around my right boot.

Belly-crawling forward, I shot up any tentacles that reached toward us. Olaf, who had managed to wedge himself between a pair of trees, resumed firing. Sarah took up the attack shortly, legs anchored inside a tangle of growth. When I didn't hear Takara's weapon, I glanced around, but she'd slipped off somewhere.

Ten feet from the animation, I switched triggers and squeezed. A flame roared from the MP88's bottom barrel and lit into the massive pile of foliage. Its appendages flailed wildly as its body erupted into flames that billowed black smoke.

I was backing out of the thing's range when the cyclone ceased, and the animation collapsed into a burning pile. I rocked onto my elbow to ask Yoofi what had happened—I hadn't ordered a halt—and found him in Takara's embrace. He sagged, staff falling to the ground, as she released him from a sleeper hold.

The jungle shrank, and desert light rushed in. Within moments, we were back in our mock town, the square littered with the *tumba* Yoofi had used to seed his creation. I gained my feet and rushed across the square.

"What are you doing?" I asked Takara.

"Basic execution," she said defensively. "Any time there's magic in play, you eliminate the source."

She was right, of course, but that hadn't been the point of the exercise. Yoofi didn't appear hurt, in any case, and was already coming to by the time I reached them. Takara waited until his legs were supporting him before releasing him.

He stared around. "Did I faint?"

"Someone snuck up on your six," I said, deciding to use Takara's attack as a teaching moment. "Even when casting, you need to be aware of what's going on behind you. We won't always be there to cover you. Nice casting, though."

"Yeah," Rusty said, bracing the right side of his ribs as he staggered up. I could see where the animation's teeth had left impressions in his armor. "Make believe or not, that thing had some serious pounds per square inch going."

"I asked Dabu for something extra special," Yoofi said, retrieving his staff with a giggle.

I nodded at Takara to tell her she'd done fine, then looked over at Sarah and Olaf, who were approaching from the sides of the square. Their camos had already shifted from the jungle green to the plain sandstone of our surroundings.

"How's everyone feeling?" I asked.

"Like I was just thrust into another mission," Sarah answered, adjusting her glasses. "But good."

Olaf grunted in what sounded like agreement.

"That was the point, of course," I said. "I wanted you to experience an actual engagement in jungle conditions. Everyone showed good discipline, and we succeeded in putting down the threat."

Sarah nodded. Even an über-planner like her could appreciate the importance of surprises in training.

"When do we leave for New Siam?" Takara asked.

I gestured for the team to gather around. Olaf took a knee and stood his large weapon beside his right boot. Rusty leaned an arm against Olaf's shoulder. The other three congregated on either side of them, Yoofi removing his helmet.

"You heard some of my concerns yesterday during the briefing," I said. "When I brought those concerns to Director Beam, he said that if our investigation showed the kingdom was behind the disappearances, Centurion would share the info with the appropriate authorities. If not, we're to proceed with this as a Prod 1 case. Centurion will monitor the political situation and extract us if needed."

Rusty looked around to make sure he hadn't missed something. "Sounds like still game on then, right?"

"Well, I received another communication last night."

"From whom?" Sarah asked, concern lines creasing her brow.

"A senior official with Centurion." Sarah could figure out the rest without me outing Purdy to the others. "He claimed to have information suggesting the case was beyond Legion's capabilities."

"Beyond *us*?" Rusty asked indignantly. "Man, screw that."

Takara narrowed her eyes. "What reason did this official give?"

"Honestly? Not much of one. And that's what I'm struggling with. He just said this story had played out already and that it hadn't ended well. He recommended I reject the mission. Strongly," I added.

"You can do that?" Yoofi asked.

"Technically, yes," Sarah answered for me. "But he needs to have *clear* cause." The challenge in her voice felt like a small shove, probably because I hadn't shared Purdy's visit with her before now.

"The political instability could be enough," I said, holding firm. "Especially with the reaction force a country away. We're equipped for Prod 1s, not a foreign military."

In tensing her jaw, Sarah was showing more emotion than I'd seen in months. "If it came to that, we would only need to evade the forces until our extraction," she said. "Yoofi could help us accomplish that with deceptive magic."

When I turned to Yoofi, he nodded. "It would not be difficult."

Good, I thought. *This is the kind of discussion I was hoping for.*

"But what if this official isn't talking about the political situation, but the Prod 1?" I asked the team.

Sarah answered again. "We've handled Prod 1s that, by any objective measure, would have been considered beyond us. The Chagrath in Mexico, for example. The Wendigo in Canada. A *primal* Wendigo," she added. "And in both cases we recovered the survivors."

I looked from her to the others. "How do the rest of you feel?"

"Like I want to tell that official he doesn't know sheepshit from Shinola," Rusty said, his face still red from the suggestion we weren't up to the challenge.

"Sarah's right," Takara said. "We've handled difficult cases before."

"Yoofi?" I asked.

In the past, he was usually the one to shuffle his feet, fearful of this or that, but now he stood tall with his staff. He'd had his cornrows redone in the last month, and they gripped his scalp in an intricate pattern. His billowing coat completed the look of a potent magic-user, the kind you wanted on your team.

"I would like us to go," he said.

"Me too," Olaf echoed, ever the good soldier.

We could proceed with extra caution, I told myself, back out if the threat appeared too great. My team's reasoning was sound, jibing with both my captain's logic and my wolf's instincts. Especially with five thousand people missing.

"All right," I said. "We leave at 0400 tomorrow."

7

"Approaching the LS," our pilot announced.

Our formation flew in so low that the skids were nearly skimming the jungle treetops. Having every helo dark gave it the added feel of a nighttime raid. But this was how Prince Ken insisted we enter New Siam: quietly.

Ahead, the jungle ended at a pasture. A cement building stood alone beside a dirt road. Several military vehicles were parked beside the building, including an armored personnel carrier. Our landing site.

I shook Rusty awake and met Takara's gaze. She nodded back, her eyes as primed as I felt.

Our escorts descended to establish a security perimeter. Minutes later we touched down, the helo carrying the other half of Legion landing beside us. At my signal, we disembarked with our weapons and hustled through the flattened grass and humid night toward the building. Per our plan, Takara used the darkness to slip around toward the building's rear.

Ahead, a pair of doors opened at the front of the building and two New Siam soldiers in olive-green uniforms appeared. They carried automatic rifles, barrels aimed groundward. The soldiers motioned for us to enter. I signaled back for the Centurion team to start unloading our mission containers.

The New Siam soldiers awaited us in an anteroom and opened a second set of doors. With Yoofi's protective magic humming in the air, we stepped into a large windowless room that ran the length of the building. Moths batted around lanterns that had been placed on several wooden tables. A man whom I recognized from the mission info approached us in plain clothes.

"Welcome," he said, extending a hand. "I'm Prince Ken."

I made a quick inspection of the rest of the room. Two more soldiers stood at either end. There were four doors at the back, though I couldn't smell anyone beyond them. My gaze returned to the prince, and I gripped his offered hand.

He was young and handsome with the same stylish hair as in his photo. Though dressed in a basic black shirt and pants, the well-built man carried an air of royalty. It wasn't forced—he wasn't trying to dominate the handshake or impose himself physically—but more a feature of his general bearing. Intelligent, charismatic eyes worked to read mine. All he could see, of course, was the hologram.

"Captain Wolfe," I said, releasing his hand.

I introduced him to the rest of the team. Sarah stood beside me, while Olaf and Rusty took up flanking positions. Yoofi remained behind, covering the room with his magic. Prince Ken greeted each in turn in the cordial way of a host.

"I'm very pleased you've come," he said in an English accent. "And I do apologize for the secretive nature of your visit. I trust your organization explained the situation. It's ... well, it's the way we have to handle this, unfortunately."

I nodded, studying his face and scent for deception. The prince was nervous—the muscles around his eyes coupled with his sweaty tang told me that much. But whether it was because he was undermining his father's authority or conspiring with him to cover up a mass killing, I couldn't tell.

That's what the investigation would be for.

"I trust this will be suitable as a base of operations." Prince Ken gestured around. "It served as a community building for Ban Mau. There are rooms to store your equipment, and we've placed several military cots in that room behind me. You can set them up wherever you'd like. The water in the bathroom runs off a manual pump."

"What about electricity?" Rusty asked, lantern light flicking from his face as he peered around.

"The electricity to the sector has been shut down," he replied apologetically. "I would prefer to keep it that way rather than suggest any new activity up here. The king's formal investigation concluded last month."

"Looks like we're going nuclear, then," Rusty said, referring to our portable generator.

"And what did the king conclude?" Sarah asked, catching Prince Ken's last comment. There had been nothing about a formal investigation in the info Beam had sent over.

Prince Ken lowered his eyes. "That the people left for richer work opportunities being offered in the kingdom's new economic zone."

"All at once?" Sarah asked.

The prince gave a humorless laugh. "Perhaps now you understand why we have to handle it in this way."

The official explanation lined up with his father not wanting New Siam to appear weak. So far the prince's account was consistent, anyway.

"I understand there's a military outpost nearby," I said. "Should we expect any trouble?"

"I have a trusted officer commanding that outpost. He's suspended patrols until your work here is complete. If any other units are deployed to Ban Mau, we'll have plenty of warning. Right now, the army's attention is on nearby villages and the provincial capital."

The eyes of the hologram disguising my head were programmed to track my own. When the prince saw them cut to the soldiers at the ends of the room, he said, "I chose them for a reason. You don't have to worry about anyone leaking news of your presence."

On that question, I sensed he was telling the truth.

I signaled for Rusty to start bringing containers inside, and he nodded.

"So what do you think is really going on?" Sarah asked. "How did five thousand people disappear?"

The prince's shrug looked apologetic. "I honestly can't say. That's why I contacted Centurion."

"But your sister has some ideas?" Sarah pressed.

At mention of her, the prince's face darkened. "Yes. Well, general ideas. My sister and I are quite different. I studied at a boarding school in England while she was sent to school in Japan. While there, she developed an interest in folk divination and the esoteric. Following the Ban Mau incident, she consulted what she called *Himitsu* paintings." He said the word dismissively. "She insisted there was great evil at work. Supernatural evil. It's not where my own thinking would have led, but I told her I'd consider the possibility. After speaking to your representatives, I understand such things aren't as outlandish as they might seem. I also understand you've had some success with the supernatural?"

"The first step is to determine if that's what we're facing," I said.

"Of course," he replied, seeming to grow nervous again. "What will you need?"

"Once we set up our base of operations, we'll want to take a look at the town."

A line of Centurion soldiers led by Rusty entered with our containers and began stacking them at one end of the room.

"Of course," Prince Ken said. "Ban Mau is just south of here. We've closed the roads to the town to keep people out, but I'd still prefer you not travel on foot. There's a personnel carrier for your use."

I glanced over at the New Siam soldiers. "A carrier that *we'll* command?"

"Yes, yes," the prince assured me. "You'll have complete autonomy while you're here. I just ask that you do nothing to draw attention to your presence." He regarded our soldiers for a moment, then consulted his watch.

Centurion had agreed that the helos would be on the ground for no more than twenty minutes, and we were approaching the fifteen-minute mark. As the support team brought in the last of the containers, I cleared them to return to our base just across the Thai border. The prince, overhearing the exchange, relaxed slightly. He didn't know the helos would actually remain in New Siam's airspace for the next two hours, in case we required air support or quick extraction. Caution was the name of the game.

"We understand there were community members away at the time of the disappearance," Sarah said.

"Yes," Prince Ken replied.

"I'd like you to put me in touch with some of them."

"That would be, ah, difficult. You see, they've been ordered to repeat the official story."

"I'd like to talk to them anyway."

Sarah and I had discussed this during mission planning. The accounts of those community members were vital to our investigation. But as the helos outside began lifting off, the prince dragged a hand through his hair.

"Look," he said, "I'm not trying to impede your work. I *want* you here. I'll do whatever I can to help you. But no one else can know of your presence." His eyes verged on pleading. "Talking to them will create problems. And I assure you, anyone I put you in contact with will only repeat what they've been told to say."

"That their families and neighbors moved to the economic zone?" I asked.

"Yes, and trust me when I tell you they will not deviate from that story."

Probably under threat of some kind, I thought.

As the helos thumped into the distance, a chorus of insect sounds filled the void. I glanced at Sarah, who looked back with compressed lips. She was ready to keep pushing, but there was no point. Whether or not the prince was telling the truth, we weren't going to be talking to anyone from Ban Mau. I changed tactics.

"In the weeks before the disappearance, did anything unusual happen up here?"

"Nothing that I know about. If anything had occurred, the mayor would have reported it to the outpost."

"The mayor had a good relationship with the military?" Sarah asked.

"He wouldn't have hesitated to communicate trouble to them, if that's what you're asking."

We had to tread carefully. If the prince thought we suspected a massacre coverup, he could order us out. I watched his shoulders stiffen, but when Sarah nodded to indicate he had answered her question, they lowered again.

"I understand there's a legend about snake people in the area," I said.

He looked at me in surprise before chuckling. "Ah, yes, I've heard the stories. They're like your boogeyman, I imagine. A way for parents up here to get their kids to eat their vegetables and go to sleep at night."

"Any recent reports of sightings?" I asked.

"Of snake people?" He looked between me and Sarah as if we were putting him on.

"Or any tribal people in the area?" Sarah amended.

"There are no more tribes in the jungles of New Siam. They migrated to the towns many years ago." He consulted his watch again. "I apologize, but I do need to return to the capital. You have a direct line to my secure phone. Call me about anything, and I'll see that it's addressed. Besides the outpost commander, you shouldn't see anyone out here. Contact me immediately if you do. Do you have any other questions before I leave?"

"What haven't you told us?" I asked him.

The prince reacted as if I'd punched him in the chest. "Excuse me?"

"It's the last question we always ask," I lied.

To the prince's credit, he didn't turn defensive. Instead, he composed himself and nodded. "I see why you might have the impression I'm hiding something. I'm edgy, I admit it. I can't begin to know what happened to the people of Ban Mau. And I feel like I'm alone in trying to find the answer."

"What about your sister?" Sarah asked.

"Halia? We had a falling out. In fact, she said something about hiring her own team."

I stiffened. "There's another team out here?"

"No, no," he said quickly. "Well, that is, I don't know that she actually followed through."

If he meant to console me, it didn't work. I was thinking about the wendigo case, where our disgruntled client had gone off and hired a group of bushmen for the same job. His team ended up wounding an asset and nearly boning the entire operation. I wasn't about to go down that road again.

"Who are they?" I demanded.

"Someone met with Halia last week. A large man. The name 'Ban Mau' was overheard."

Great. Sounded like the prince had spies on his sister, underscoring my suspicion that we'd walked into a power contest.

"But I don't know who he was," he finished.

"I thought you hired us at her request," I said.

"Halia and I disagreed over who *exactly* to hire. I wanted a modern force, and she was insisting on something more traditional. That was partly what led to our not speaking. In fact, I haven't seen her in over a week."

"And you have no idea who this person was?" I asked.

When he shook his head, Sarah pressed, "What did he look like?"

The front doors opened, and the New Siam soldiers showed Takara inside. We made eye contact, and she nodded once to indicate she'd completed the security check of the building, the vehicles, and the immediate surroundings. If there had been a threat, she would have found it and alerted me.

"He looked a little like her," Prince Ken said.

"Who?" Rusty asked. "T-cakes?"

Takara glared at him.

"You're Japanese, correct?" Prince Ken asked her.

"Why do you want to know?" she snapped.

"He thinks his sister might have hired another team for the same job," I explained. "She was seen meeting with someone who apparently looked like you."

"Allow me to clarify," the prince said, switching on a smile. His accompanying scent told me he'd taken an interest in Takara. "My sister has contacts in Japan, and that was the language she and her guest were speaking. Though the large man's face was covered, he was wearing an outfit similar to yours."

He reached toward the sleeve of the billowy black attire Takara often wore over her leathers, but she drew her arm back sharply. A change had come over her scent too. But unlike the prince's, hers suggested discomfort.

"Was there a band on the left sleeve of the outfit?" she demanded.

The prince blinked and lowered his arm. "Well, now that you mention it, yes. A red band. How did you know?"

But instead of answering, Takara's face went masklike.

The prince looked at her for another moment before consulting his watch for the third time. "I really do need to be going," he said, a note of nervousness returning. "Is there anything else I can do for you?"

"A couple things," I said. "One, find out if there's been any new activity in this area. Drilling, mining, jungle-clearing, anything. Two, make nice with your sister and find out if she did hire someone. If so, tell her to cancel the contract."

The prince nodded but without conviction.

"I'll do everything I can."

"You guys know the drill," I said after the prince and his soldiers had left. "Olaf and Rusty, clear the building. I want a complete scan. Then set up the computers and commo. Estimated time to full security?"

"Twenty minutes, boss," Rusty answered.

"Good." As he and Olaf moved off, I turned to Yoofi. "How are we looking?"

"No magic in the building, Mr. Wolfe. I'll ready the *lingos*," he said, referring to the protective wards.

"I'm going to set up an office down here," Sarah called, unpacking her laptops and files at one end of the main room.

"Outside security," Takara said.

"Hold it." I caught her arm before she could leave. "It sounded like you knew Princess Halia's visitor. Something you want to tell us?"

"There are groups in Japan who take jobs like these. It might be one of them."

"Any idea which one?"

"Not without more information."

"Are you sure?"

"Why wouldn't I be?" Red crescents gleamed around the edges of her midnight irises, and her scent sharpened. She was holding something back, but instinct told me now wasn't the time to push.

"All right, just let us know. We'll split when we finish here," I said loud enough for the rest of the team to hear. "Sarah, Yoofi, and I will head to town with Rusty escorting on Drone 1. Olaf and Takara, I want you here with Russ on security."

"I'm going to the town too," Takara said.

She and I had been getting along so well for the last months that this sudden relapse into insubordination caught me off guard. I didn't know what was going on, but I didn't care for it. "I need you here on security."

She lowered her voice to a hissing whisper. "Do you want me to find out who else might be out here or not?"

I could hear her heart thumping like a rabbit's. Fear?

I watched her face for another moment before turning back to the team.

"Update," I announced. "We'll go as four and leave two."

———

The personnel carrier looked like it had been pulled from an old fleet—paint-stripped body, balding tires, and a smashed rear window—but it was serviceable. Though a 360-degree turret sat on the vehicle's rooftop, I decided not to mount a gun. Instead, Takara and I took positions inside at the narrow side windows while Sarah drove and Rusty watched from Drone 1. Yoofi sat in back, catching up on his cigar and brandy offerings to Dabu.

Outside, plank homes with corrugated rooftops appeared among overgrown farm plots. Before long, the buildings tightened in, becoming brick and mortar, many with balconies. Sarah drove at a slow speed, following our planned recon route.

"Approaching the town center," she announced.

We rumbled past houses and businesses, tires heaving into and around fresh potholes. With the power cut, not a single light shone. Vehicles sat empty. Nothing stirred in the streets. Here and there, doors stood open, which made the scene appear that much more sinister.

I sniffed as we went, searching for any sign that the army had carried out another massacre, but there were no traces of human blood. That didn't mean much, though. The people could have been loaded up and carried to a remote killing field.

I turned to the back. "Yoofi?"

His eyes popped open. Our procedure had become so routine, he knew what I was asking. "Ooh, yes," he replied, already nodding. "Dabu is getting a funny feeling here. He does not like this place at all."

Dabu got a lot of funny feelings and didn't like a lot of places, so that wasn't telling me much. "Any magic?"

"Maybe ... Dabu cannot say." Yoofi closed his eyes. "He's saying this place was *manga*."

"What does that mean?" I asked.

"Poisoned."

"Poisoned?" Takara repeated.

I sniffed but didn't pick up anything obvious.

"Masks on," I ordered anyway. "Possible chemical agents in the air."

From their packs, Takara and Yoofi drew out filter units that fit snugly over their noses and mouths. I handed Sarah hers, and she slowed the carrier to put it on. Even though my regenerative abilities could handle moderate doses of poison, I donned a unit that had been specially designed for my muzzle.

"Let's proceed to foot patrol," I said.

Sarah pulled over beside a wall that bordered a small cemetery.

"I'll take point," I said, hunkering beside the carrier's door. "Takara, rear. You two flank. We may not be the only good guys out here, so use trigger and muzzle discipline. How's it looking, Russ?"

"Roads are still clear, boss," he answered through my earpiece.

"Let's go."

We filed out and covered the surrounding buildings, our weapons loaded with mixed rounds: iron, silver, and salt. The rounds cut down on the guesswork as well as the time expense of swapping ammo. An insect chorus rose and fell around us, but the sound was distant, as if they'd pulled back to a safe perimeter. Remembering what Yoofi had said, I lifted my filter enough to sniff the wall we'd parked beside. If the army had carried out a chemical weapon attack, the plaster would have soaked up the agent—chlorine or cyanide, most likely.

"Anything?" Sarah asked.

"Nothing I can smell. Why don't you go ahead and grab a sample."

While she chipped off a section of plaster, I scanned the area for munitions debris.

"Dabu keeps saying this was a poisoned place," Yoofi whispered. "Permission to cast a protection, Mr. Wolfe?"

"Go ahead."

He'd started asking following a mission in the fall in which one of his invocations had blown up a nearby power station. Holding his staff aloft, Yoofi chanted until a warping bubble of energy formed around us.

"Yes, that makes me feel safer," he said.

It only made me feel queasy, but I didn't say anything.

Sarah stored the plaster sample and took up her M4 again. Takara had moved a short distance away, eyes closed as if trying to sense something. Heat pulsed from her in waves. Though she hadn't said anything more, I could guess why she'd insisted on coming. If this group from Japan *had* been brought in, they would have started their investigation at the town too. Takara wanted to know if they'd been here.

"We'll follow the planned route," I said, tapping the flexible tablet affixed to my forearm—another Centurion innovation. By the time Takara came over, a map of the town had appeared on the screen, showing our positions. I traced the figure-eight route meant to cover the most ground in the least amount of time.

With Drone 1 providing overwatch, we passed dark house after dark house, looking for munitions and anything odd. After several blocks, though, the biggest oddity remained the absence of people.

I tuned into Ban Mau's smells. The human body shed 10,000 skin cells per second, so there were billions here, but they were all old. I wasn't picking up anything fresh. I clenched my jaw in frustration. This was our first case with no actionable intel. We were starting with practically nothing.

At a random two-story house, I signaled a stop. With Yoofi on outside watch, Sarah, Takara, and I stacked and entered. We cleared both floors of the residence, then took our time looking through the rooms. A family had lived here. Open dresser drawers and gaps in the closets suggested packing. No evidence of struggle, though. When I arrived back downstairs, Sarah was swabbing surfaces.

"Looks like the family loaded up and left," I said. "If it was under force, they didn't resist."

"There's not much in the fridge and pantry for a household this size, suggesting they brought food too."

"Unless it's all a cover," I said. "Hard to believe they fled on their own. Why would they have left the vehicles? You saw that nice Range Rover in the driveway. Someone or something compelled them."

"Two months ago," Sarah reminded me. "That's going to make evidence-gathering challenging."

I grunted in agreement.

"Do you still believe it was the military under King Savang's orders?" she asked.

"Don't know yet. Our base and the personnel carrier are clean, so they're not listening. No evidence of surveillance equipment in the area either. Seems if they had something to hide, they would have at least put ears on our investigation."

"Well, if it's a Prod, I might be able to grab something that will match to our bio-base."

As Sarah began swabbing the kitchen counter, I opened my senses again. My mother, who used to deliver medical equipment to homes, once commented that every house had a distinct smell and no two were alike. That had stuck with me for some reason. It wasn't until I gained my wolf senses that I saw how right she had been. I was getting traces of this home's scent, but with the family absent for two months, the jungle was reclaiming the enclosed air, filling it with a smell that was damp, almost swampy.

Sarah capped her Petri dish and slid it into a vest pocket. Takara entered from a back room, holding up a pink booklet.

"What's that?" I asked.

"Looks like a journal. I found it in the girl's room, behind her dresser. It wasn't very dusty. Could have recent entries."

Sarah and I walked over as Takara opened it on the dining room table. The Siamese writing was in the large script of a young hand. Takara turned to the last filled-out page, then flipped back until she arrived at the start of an entry. Using her tablet, she took shots of each page and requested a translation.

A moment later, it came up.

"'March second,'" Takara read from the tablet. "'Analu likes me. His best friend told me at school today. So why did he put sand down my dress last week? Boys are so stupid.'" Takara raised her eyes. "I think we can skim."

Sounds like a normal day in the life, anyway.

Takara scrolled to the start of a new paragraph, where she resumed reading.

"'We have temple again tonight. When I asked Father if I could stay home, he became very angry. He said everyone has to go, even Mother. She's been having bad headaches and is sleeping a lot. Probably sick of going to temple. Cleric Dao isn't looking well either. I hope it's not bird flu. That means we'll need shots and I hate needles. I always tell myself I won't cry but then I do. Why don't adults cry? Do you stop hurting after a certain age or do you just learn to deal with pain?'"

Takara looked up. "And that's where she ends it. Signed, 'Leilana.'"

"That was about a week before the community disappeared," Sarah remarked.

My thoughts lingered on the young author—musing on pain and the stupidity of boys one week and then vanishing without a trace the next. The wolf in me felt an overwhelming urge to recover her, protect her. Takara was already working backwards through the journal, capturing previous entries for translation.

"Looks like they were spending more time at the temple," she said.

Sarah came around to peer over her shoulder. "Being forced to attend?"

"Doesn't say," Takara replied. "The temple could have been trying to ward off the poison Yoofi sensed, especially if it was affecting people. Sounds like the mother and cleric were sick. There could have been others."

"It gives us a lead, in any case," I said. "Let's check out the temple."

"The courtyard looks clear from up here," Rusty radioed.

We had stacked on a gate in the wall surrounding Ban Mau's main temple and now we filed inside. While Sarah, Takara, and Yoofi covered the banana trees and overgrown gardens along the courtyard walls, I focused on the temple structure itself.

It was large with a multi-tiered roof in the Asian style. Three steps led up to a large sanctuary that could have held a thousand, easy. In the back, a ten-foot statue of Noma, their goddess of agriculture, peered back benevolently. Mold covered half of her face. In the darkness, it looked like blood.

"What are you feeling?" I asked Yoofi.

"Strange energies," he whispered back. "But that is not unusual in places of worship."

I thought back to the Chagrath case, where a shaman's ceremony had inadvertently opened a hole to the creature's realm. Prof Croft had warned that with fresh rips around our world, such things would become more common. Is that what we were looking at? Had a Chagrath or something similar come through?

"Any holes?" I asked.

Yoofi frowned for a moment before shaking his head. "I cannot feel any."

I whispered into my radio, "Keep watch outside, Russ."

"Yes, sir."

I waved the team forward, my lupine senses buzzing with energy. The temperature dipped as we climbed the steps. Straw prayer mats stood in skewed stacks along the walls of the main sanctuary, their edges chewed by rodents. I cut my gaze to the feet of the statue to Noma where hundreds of melted candles surrounded a shrine. This was where the head cleric must have led community prayer.

A door stood on either side of Noma. I signaled a split, and

Takara and Sarah disappeared through the right doorway and into the temple. The left door opened onto a narrow hallway lined with meditation cells. Yoofi and I proceeded past them to a closed door at the hallway's end.

"Feels like a tomb in here," Yoofi whispered.

I signaled for silence, but it smelled like a tomb too. The rotten odor could have come from spoiled meat or dead rats, but my gut was telling me different.

The door opened onto a small room. A simple bed with a trunk sat opposite a wooden desk and chair. I opened the trunk with my MP88 and poked through a stack of mustard-colored robes. Yoofi, meanwhile, gazed over a series of framed portraits depicting men and women with shaved heads.

"Check out the books on the desk," I whispered.

While he did that, I captured the two dozen portraits with my tablet and ordered it to translate the script beneath them.

"Prayer books," Yoofi said behind me. "They look normal. No magic in them."

I showed him the translation on my tablet. "Names and dates of service of the head clerics in the temple," I said. "Goes back hundreds of years. This last one is the cleric the girl mentioned in her journal."

Cleric Dao was an elderly man with a sweet smile. As I studied the wine-colored birthmark across his forehead, I considered why he'd started holding more than the usual number of temple services. The girl mentioned he hadn't looked well.

"Can you cast a reveal spell on the room?" I asked Yoofi.

With a nod, he lifted his staff. The dark blade seemed to draw in the room's energy before sending it back out in a flash of green light. The light broke into a swarm of locust-like creatures that explored every crack and seam of the room in chitters before burning out again. The entire spell only lasted a few seconds.

"No mystical energy," Yoofi said, lowering his staff.

I radioed the others. "Finding anything?"

"Main level is clear," Sarah answered. *"But there's a bad smell emanating from a sublevel in back."*

"We're heading over."

Back in the main sanctuary, I led Yoofi through the other doorway. Our route passed what looked like a common area bracketed by a library and dorm rooms. I followed Sarah's and Takara's scents to a pantry in the temple's kitchen. Sarah pointed out a trap door in the back of the shelf-lined room.

"Takara found it," she whispered.

The trap door was propped open, releasing the smell of decomposition I'd detected earlier, only now it was more putrid. Even with his filter on, Yoofi brought the back of a hand to his nose and moaned.

"Spoiled meat?" Sarah asked.

"I wish," I grumbled. "There are bodies down there."

"I can scout it out," Takara said.

"We'll both go," I said. "I'll cover your descent." Not liking the idea of all four of us entering the confined space, I aimed two fingers at Sarah and Yoofi. "You stay up here. We'll call if we need you."

Takara's eyes flashed as she used her powers of flight to lower herself through the trapdoor. When I heard her boots squelch into mud, I started down after her. I had to squeeze my broad shoulders in to fit through the trapdoor. At the bottom, my boots sunk several inches into the sodden ground. I peered around a large cellar space, where rats as large as my fist scurried along the walls.

Takara, who had been covering the room with her rifle, pointed to the far side. A figure half buried in mud lay face down. The scent told me corpse, but in our line of work, even corpses could be dangerous.

"Yoofi," I radioed, keeping an eye on the body. "I need you in here."

His coat clinked as he climbed down the ladder and joined us in the mud. He gagged once before recomposing himself.

"I will not lie, Mr. Wolfe. I was hoping you would not call me."

I oriented him to the body across the room. "Any animating magic?"

Yoofi held his staff forward and furrowed his brow. Though he produced no locust swarms this time, I could feel the distorting energies exploring toward the body. After a moment, he shook his head.

"It is not a zombie."

"Cover us anyway," I told him.

I may have gone against Purdy's council in accepting this mission, but that didn't mean I had forgotten his warning. I peered around as Takara and I crossed the room, the floor sucking at our boots. There were numerous other depressions in the mud, probably old tracks, water-filled and indistinct.

A mustard-colored robe wrapped the corpse. Skeletal arms and legs, barely more than sticks, jutted from the torso. The bald head suggested cleric, but the hair could also have fallen out during decomposition.

When I reached the corpse, I gripped its bony shoulder and pulled. The mud tugged back before releasing the body with a low slurp. I grunted in surprise at the preserved pair of eyes staring up at me.

Must be salt in the mud.

Pulling the hose to my water bladder from my pack, I twisted a valve and rinsed off the face. Mud slid away from the corpse's forehead to reveal the same birthmark from the portrait I'd seen in the bedroom.

"It's Cleric Dao," I said. "The one the girl referenced in her journal."

Takara squatted beside me as I finished. She pointed to a place on his neck over his jugular. "He was blood-drained."

"Vampire?"

"No, the incision is from a blade."

I saw what she meant when I spotted the clean horizontal cut. "Murdered, then."

But the precise cut didn't look like a military hit. My eyes dropped to a clot of mud over the cleric's chest. I hosed it off to find a stone amulet, a serpent carved into its face with chips of red gem for eyes. When I lifted the amulet for a closer look, a squirming sensation climbed my fingers.

I dropped it again.

"Yoofi," I called. "I think we've got an active artifact."

He was starting to squelch toward us when the corpse shot out a hand and clutched my wrist.

9

I shoved myself backwards. Maintaining his bone-mashing grip on my wrist, the corpse shot to his feet. I jammed the MP88's barrel against his chest but stopped short of squeezing the trigger. There was a stone wall behind him—the rounds would ricochet.

Mud spilled from the zombie's mouth in a vomit-like gargle as he strained his neck forward to bite me.

"No ammo," I called as Takara moved in.

Foot-long blades slid from her sleeves and extended over the backs of her fists. She brought the right blade down, cleaving the zombie's arm at the elbow. Freed, I drove a boot into his stomach, slamming him against the wall. He staggered for his footing. A follow-up blast from Yoofi's staff dropped him to the floor.

It took me a moment to realize the hand was still clinging to my wrist. I pried it off and tossed it beside the smoking body. The fingers began dragging the severed forearm back toward me. I submerged it in the mud with a boot until it stopped squirming.

"What's happening?" Sarah called down. "Do you need backup?"

"We're all right," Takara answered. "Just an animation."

"Thought you said he wasn't a zombie," I growled at Yoofi.

"He wasn't until you touched the amulet. There must have been some magic left inside."

Switching the MP88 to flamethrower, I asked, "Can you tell where the magic came from?"

"I can try." He took a step toward the cleric, then stopped and peered around. "Uh-oh."

"What is it?"

"The magic is still active. It is moving and ... and talking."

"Talking to who?" Takara demanded.

The mud around us humped up, and half a dozen corpses broke from the floor and staggered to their feet. I wheeled from the cleric and hit three of them with bursts of napalm. Their bodies went up like torches, but they continued to lurch forward. Dropping my MP88 onto its sling, I drew my knife. I could already hear Takara slicing and dicing behind me. Bolts shot from Yoofi's staff.

As the first flaming zombie came moaning in, I swung my knife in a tight arc. The blade crunched through its neck, removing its head. I plowed the staggering body aside with a shoulder and drove my knife into the next zombie's forehead. Heat bit at my face as I twisted the blade one way and then the other. When I retracted the blade, the corpse collapsed in a fiery heap beside the first zombie's head.

The third flaming zombie veered toward Yoofi. Like during our exercise the day before, my teammate wasn't watching his back. I shouted a warning, but the zombie was already bringing his teeth down where Yoofi's right shoulder met his neck.

"Owie!" he hollered.

I reached the zombie in three lunging steps and ripped my

blade through its neck. When its jaws held on to Yoofi, I punched the blade up through the base of its skull. The mouth popped open, and I flung the flaming head aside.

Across the room, Takara decapitated the final zombie. Their bodies jerked around on the floor, three of them still crackling with fire.

"Am I bitten?" Yoofi asked, wrestling his arm from his coat sleeve to look.

I inspected the area where the zombie's teeth had clamped down. "The material held," I reassured him.

Yoofi let out a trembling breath. "And the magic is gone from the room."

"Can you check him out?" I asked, nodding at Cleric Dao's body.

"Okay," Yoofi said. "But not down here."

———

I set the cleric near the shrine at the base of the statue in the main sanctuary. As Yoofi arranged candles around the body, I looked down at the amulets we'd bagged in salt. The other zombies had been wearing them too—acolytes, judging from their attire. Sarah's exam showed their jugulars had been slit like the cleric's.

She sidled up to me, glasses glowing above her tablet screen. "I'm not getting any matches for the serpent design."

"Yoofi wasn't familiar with the magic, either."

I remembered the squirmy sensation in my fingers when I'd touched the cleric's amulet. According to Yoofi, the contact had activated the remaining store of magic, sending out a signal to the other amulets. The reserve was just enough to jolt the bodies to life. Though the magic expired soon after we'd put them down, Yoofi neutralized the amulets anyway. The salt was an added precaution.

"Why do you suppose someone was controlling the cleric and acolytes?" Sarah asked.

"Maybe to get to the civilians," I said. "That would explain the uptick in temple services."

"The jugular incisions may not have been meant to kill them, then. Not initially, anyway."

I felt my wolf brow furrow. "What do you mean?"

"The weaker someone is, the more susceptible they are to being controlled."

"This is true," Yoofi called from the cleric's side.

"The incisions were small," Sarah continued. "Enough to drain blood but not enough that the platelets couldn't coagulate at the site of rupture. The perp then used the amulets as focus objects to control the cleric and acolytes. Given that the temple was the social center of Ban Mau, I agree that it would have been an effective way to influence the townspeople, maybe convince them to go somewhere else."

"And once the cleric and acolytes served their purpose," I said, "the perp sent them to the cellar to die."

"It's looking less and less like New Siam is behind this, anyway," Sarah said.

I was starting to agree.

At the statue, Yoofi finished arranging the candles and tipped a flask to his lips. He sat cross-legged behind the cleric's head. With his connection to Dabu, a god of the dead, Yoofi planned to attempt his own form of necromancy.

"Sure he's not going to get up again?" I asked, covering the body with my weapon.

"No, Mr. Wolfe. I will be focusing Dabu's magic into his mind, not his body. Whatever memories remain, the magic will shake them free, like fruit from the kola tree, and then I can see them. If this works," he added.

We needed this to work. Although we had ID'd the temple as a focal point in the attack on the town, we didn't know who was behind the attack or what the perp had done with the disappeared. All we knew was that he or she hadn't had any problem playing puppet master to the cleric and temple servants and then feeding them to the rats. That didn't bode well for the five thousand people of Ban Mau.

"I will need silence now," Yoofi said, cupping the sides of the cleric's head and closing his eyes. Takara, who had been moving through the shadows around the sanctuary's perimeter, turned her head to watch.

As Yoofi began to chant, an energy smelling of stale cigars and brandy gusted off him—the back draft from Dabu's realm. With a sudden moan, Yoofi's arms stiffened. He leaned back as if trying to break his connection to the cleric, but a glowing purple light between his hands and the cleric's temples seemed to hold him fast. I was stepping forward when Yoofi's eyes opened. Only they were voids, filled with the same glowing light. When his lips parted, more of the light radiated between his teeth.

"Yoofi," I said.

"I am having tea," he said in an eerie monotone that sounded nothing like our teammate. And the words weren't quite synching with his mouth, as if he were far away. "The tea is bitter. Too bitter. I hear something break. I have dropped my teacup. It is nighttime now. I am in a room, my arms and legs tied. Things move in the surrounding darkness. They are large and speak in whispers." Yoofi winced. "Something bites my neck. A blade. I hear liquid spilling into a bowl, and I know it is my blood."

Yoofi was describing the moment the cleric's jugular had been cut. I glanced over at Sarah. She was using her tablet to capture his words as text. Beyond her, a small wrinkle formed between Takara's eyebrows.

"I am not afraid to die," Yoofi continued in the faraway voice. "I know nothing is permanent. But this is worse than death. There is something cold and heavy against my chest, and I hear a voice. A whispering voice. And..." Yoofi's arms began to shake. "And..."

The purple light detonated from Yoofi's hands and face, blasting out the candles and knocking Yoofi onto his back. I rushed to his still body as darkness collapsed over the space.

"Hey, man," I said, sitting him up. "You all right?"

I was afraid I was going to see smoking craters for eyes—the light had blown from them too—but when he opened them, they looked fine. He blinked several times before his staring eyes found mine.

"Ooh, what happened, Mr. Wolfe?"

Takara stepped forward. "You don't remember?"

"Did you choke me again?"

"You were tapped into the cleric's memory," I said. "It sounded like you found the moment where the perp took control of him." As Yoofi listened, the confusion lines across his forehead deepened. "You don't remember drinking the bitter tea?" I asked. "Or waking up in a dark room? Feeling your neck being cut?"

Yoofi touched his throat. "Oh, no. And thank Dabu for that."

"The blood was collected," Takara said. "Do you know why?"

Yoofi squinted at her, the sudden Q&A no doubt bewildering to someone who'd only just recovered his senses. "Blood is a powerful agent in many kinds of magic," he said. "Especially control magic. So, the taking of the blood would have weakened him, yes. But it also strengthened the magic controlling him."

"What about a whispering voice?" Sarah asked. "It was the last thing you said. You heard a whispering voice."

"I am sorry, but I don't remember *any* voice."

"We need to know what that voice said," Sarah pressed.

"Well, what can I do if I cannot remember?"

Sarah was in info-gathering mode and pushing hard. The cold weight against the cleric's chest had probably been the snake amulet, the artifact of control. The whispered voice the controller. Whatever it had told the cleric to do would give us a major lead on what had happened to the people of Ban Mau.

"Can you go back in?" I asked him.

He cocked an eyebrow and leaned his head away. "And get my throat cut again?"

"It was a memory," I said. "And it wasn't *your* throat. You're fine, right? This is important. We need to know what the perp told him."

Yoofi rubbed his neck again, as if to double-check that he hadn't been cut, and eyed the cleric's body. Once more, he flattened his palms against the temples. But after a moment, he *tsk*ed and shook his head.

"No, I am sorry. Dabu's magic has shaken free all of the memories. They are gone now."

I swore at myself for giving the order to burn the other bodies.

"So what else do we know?" I asked Sarah, who was reading over the transcript.

"That the perp has accomplices," she replied. "And that they're large and speak in whispers."

"Prod is?" Takara asked.

"Sounds like it," she said. "I'll swab the temple."

I nodded for her to go ahead. "I want the rest of us to give this place another pass. Look for journals, logbooks, a record of visitors, that sort of thing. I want to know everyone who's been here. Cleric Dao might have known the perp."

While Sarah performed her forensics, the rest of us searched. We located a cache of visitor logbooks, but the last entry was from two years before—which meant either the temple had stopped keeping records, or someone had grabbed the most recent book. I called the team together in the sanctuary.

"I want to finish reconning the town while we still have air support."

"Hey, boss?" Rusty radioed. *"I think you guys should get back here."*

"What's going on?"

"Something triggered an alarm on the perimeter. Whatever it was took off before Olaf could draw a bead, but the drone got a brief visual."

"Can you send an image?"

"Sure, hold on a sec."

A moment later, the image arrived on my tablet. The others huddled around. The greenish image showed a spot where pasture met jungle. A pair of narrow eyes glowed from the dense foliage. I zoomed in. The fleeing creature was upright and peering back over a shoulder. But even with the drone's night vision, the rest of the body was hard to make out. It was slender and looked like it was wearing a hood.

"Did you get it?" Rusty asked.

I imagined the creature speaking in a whisper.

"Stay inside until we get back," I ordered.

10

Back at base, Takara, Yoofi, and I offloaded from the personnel carrier. Along with Olaf, we took positions alongside the vehicle as Sarah drove slowly toward the place where the creature had been sighted.

"Drones 1 and 2 are overhead," Rusty radioed.

The Centurion helos were also close enough for additional air support on short notice. My biggest concern was that the creature's appearance was a prelude to an attack.

Sarah stopped at the jungle perimeter. I signaled to Takara and we probed into the trees, using our weapons to push aside leafy branches. Within a few steps, she pointed out a small area of flattened foliage.

"It stood there," she whispered. "When it tried to come closer, it triggered the sensors. Fled that way."

My nostrils flared. A ton of scents were competing for my attention, but I narrowed in on one that was reptilian and a little oily. As I stepped into the path our visitor had left by, the scent grew stronger. I attempted to peer ahead, but my vision couldn't penetrate the dense growth. Three meters, tops. The frenzy of nocturnal sounds threw up an auditory barrier as well. As I considered splitting the team and taking Takara and Olaf on a tracking mission, Purdy's warning rose like a ghost.

This one is beyond Legion.

"We're heading back to base," I said.

"Why?" Takara demanded, blocking my path.

"Because we don't know what in the hell we're facing."

"Could be a lead."

"Or we could be walking into an ambush."

I moved around her and collected several leaves bearing the creature's scent for Sarah to analyze. Takara stalked back to the carrier with a heavy tread that voiced her disagreement.

———

I found Rusty in the room he had set up for his command-and-control station. He'd swapped his helmet for a trucker hat. The foam front—"You look like I need a beer"—bobbed above his three-panel monitor as he punched away on a keyboard.

"I've got Drone 1 overhead and Drone 2 a kilometer into the jungle scanning infrared signatures," he said.

I came around to look at the monitor. One panel showed our base and the surrounding pasture. I could see Olaf behind the portable barrier near the front doors and Takara on the rooftop, where she'd flown wordlessly upon our return. The neighboring panel showed miles and miles of dense jungle canopy.

"Anything yet?" I asked.

"That crud is hard to penetrate. Hits here and there, but they're matching to animals. Did you know there are freaking bears out there?"

"Focus, Rusty. Nothing like what you picked up earlier?"

"That's the thing, boss. When I pulled up the data on the surveillance perimeter, it wasn't the infrared that triggered the alarm, but the ground sensors. That thing wouldn't have gotten so close otherwise."

"Cold blooded," I muttered.

"What's that?"

"The intruder was cold blooded."

Rusty stared at me as if it was only now dawning on him that there were worse things out there than bears. "You think it's one of those snake people?" he whispered.

"Could be," I said, remembering the reptilian scent. "But snake person or not, it's got thick canopy for cover and is invisible to our infrared. That leaves us with little advance warning. And I doubt the creature came alone."

"Damn," Rusty muttered.

"I want more air support," I decided. "Contact the Centurion team. Have them stay in New Siam's airspace, no more than ten minutes out. They can refuel in shifts. I want them around till morning."

I caught his sidelong look even as he said, "Will do, boss."

My feelings toward the Centurion forces that accompanied our missions were no secret. I'd had enough bad experiences with them in the service to leave a permanent bitter taste in my mouth. But when faced with a large number of enemies, air support was vital. Even a team as capable as ours could be overrun. The thought brought back Purdy's warning again.

"I'm going to make a call," I told Rusty.

Leaving the command and control center, I ducked into the room where Olaf had set up the cots. I pulled out my private sat phone and dialed Purdy's direct line. The call went to his voicemail.

"It's Wolfe," I said in a low growl. "Listen, we've made contact with something out here. I don't care how you know what you know. You need to tell me what we're facing. Call me right away."

I swore as I killed the connection. I'd tried him several times following his visit to my suite, but he'd gone incommunicado. Afraid of eavesdropping? Maybe, but that raised a whole new set of questions, none of them immediately relevant to our situation.

"Got the affirmative from the Centurion team," Rusty called as I stepped from the room. "They're going to hold their flight patterns in country."

"Good," I called back. "Keep an eye on that jungle perimeter."

I checked on Sarah's progress at the far end of the main room. She'd begun work on the samples she'd collected as well as the leaves I'd given her. Machines for biological and chemical analysis whirred around her. The machines were connected to a laptop she consulted with quick rotations of her head.

"Negative on chemical agent," she said when she saw me coming.

"So whatever Yoofi and Dabu sensed didn't come from a weaponized chemical?"

"Or any chemical that would be even remotely toxic," she said. "I'm running scans on the temple swabs for biomatter."

Her eyes flicked over a screen of scrolling letter and number combinations. Occasionally, a sequence would highlight blue. "Getting a lot of mundane matches..." she said distractedly. "Wait. This is new." The scrolling had stopped on a sequence, this one highlighted red. "It's cellular matter, not the degradable residue you often find with manifested forms." Sarah entered something with a rapid tapping of keys, then frowned. "Unfortunately, it doesn't match to anything in the bio-base."

"Close matches?" I asked.

Sarah went to work unpacking the sequence, which produced additional screens of info. Portions of the sequence flashed now as the analysis software picked it apart. Sarah's gaze followed as if she were reading along.

After several moments, she said, "Both human and reptilian features."

"Can you crosscheck the temple matter against the sample from the jungle perimeter?" I asked.

"The scanner is still preparing it." Her gaze flicked to one of the humming pieces of equipment before returning to the laptop. On the surface this was typical Sarah McKinnon, but underneath I sensed a frostiness.

"It's a match," she said suddenly. "Same species."

"That means whatever was involved in controlling the cleric and acolytes was watching our base earlier."

"It appears that way."

"Nice work. Let me go out and tell Takara what you found."

And deal with whatever's going on with her, I thought.

———

I arrived on the building's rooftop from a dead jump ten feet below. Takara was standing on the far side where Olaf had mounted a heavy gun. Though I'd landed with a thud, she didn't turn, which meant she was cold-shouldering me.

"How's it going?" I asked, walking toward her.

She remained silent, her gaze fixed on the jungle.

"This has to do with the princess's visitor, doesn't it?" I said. "It's got you on edge."

I was prepared for a one-sided conversation, so Takara surprised me by speaking.

"There was no evidence of them in the town."

"That's good, right? Tells us a team probably wasn't brought in."

She went silent again, and I could see by the tension in her body she wasn't convinced.

"Listen," I said, arriving beside her. "Our evening sessions these past months have helped me. *You've* helped me. I'm not talking to you as your captain now, but as someone who's come to consider you a friend. Who did the princess meet with?"

"A *bushi*," she replied after a moment. "Samurai."

I knew from Takara's file that she had been born into a samurai family in Hiroshima. She was just a girl when her city was A-bombed in '45, an event I suspected had seeded her dragon powers. It had also left her horribly scarred. Forced from her clan, I could only assume, she ended up joining a mercenary group devoted to the practice of ninjutsu, ultimately becoming what she was today.

"The red band the prince described," I said. "Does it stand for a clan?"

"Yes."

"Do you know them?"

"I know of them," she answered cryptically.

"Are they going to be a problem?"

"Not for you."

"We're a team. Whatever this is, we'll face it together."

When Takara angled her body away, it didn't feel like a cold shoulder this time. More like she didn't want to get the rest of us involved. Once again, experience and instinct told me to give her a little room.

"Sarah found a match between material from the temple and the Prod 1 that was watching the base," I said. "Sounds like we're dealing with a reptilian humanoid, possibly the snake people Sarah mentioned in briefing. Based on the temple evidence, they're hostile. The one at the pasture edge was probably doing recon."

"So we're just going to wait for them to attack?"

"We have good visibility and air support out here. We'd lose both in there."

"What about the five thousand missing?"

"We can help them better if we're alive."

"Is this because you're close to the end of your term?"

The muscles in my shoulders bunched up. "What are you saying?"

"I don't remember you being this cautious."

"Yeah, and I don't remember having this little intel to go on," I snarled. "We're facing unknown creatures, and someone or something out there is performing powerful spell work. That's not the kind of scenario you dive into. Sarah and Yoofi are working on getting more info. Give them time."

She made a scoffing noise.

I needed to walk away, but I was still burning over her suggestion that I was holding back to spare my own skin. "What about you?" I challenged. "Is this really about recovering those five thousand missing, or are you trying to get in and out before your samurai friends know you're here?"

That touched a serious nerve.

The red crescents in her eyes flared like twin suns emerging from a total eclipse. "Don't talk about things of which you know nothing," she said in the quavering voice of her dragon. My chest swelled to meet her challenge, but I stopped and exhaled.

"Maybe that's good advice for both of us," I said.

The red crescents pulsated as Takara continued to stare at me. But I recognized the pattern of her breaths—she was calming her beast nature too, bringing it back under her will. I felt guilty now for invoking it.

When her eyes darkened again, I turned toward the jungle. In OCS training, we'd learned strategies for keeping our emotions from undermining our decision-making. That had never been a problem for me, but now I wondered if Purdy's vague warning coupled with my promise to Daniela were doing just that.

"We'll have the info we need soon," I said firmly, as much to reassure myself as Takara.

She seized my arm and gave a hard twist. I didn't realize she'd brought a leg behind mine until we were going down.

The hell?

We landed hard on the rooftop, Takara straddling my chest, her face inches from mine. I was gripping her shoulders to push her off when I heard something strike the far retaining wall. I craned my neck and spotted an arrow bouncing to a rest.

"We're under attack," Takara whispered, her hair brushing my ear.

Like the start of a hailstorm, arrows began impacting everywhere.

11

"Engagement!" I radioed as Takara rolled off me.

Staying low, I bounded for the .50 cal machine gun. By the time I'd grasped the handles, Takara was kneeling to my right, her rifle propped on the retaining wall. She began squeezing off rounds in a steady sequence. On the ground, gunfire blew from Olaf's MP88.

"Arrows incoming from the north," I radioed, as they cracked off my gun's protective shield. "At least ten shooters, maybe more. Sarah and Yoofi, take positions on the east and west sides of the bunker and watch our south. Rusty, call in air."

"Roger that," he answered. *"Didn't even see the damned things coming."*

I depressed the thumb trigger. The big gun shook as I sent bursts of heavy fire into the trees two-hundred meters away, but I couldn't tell if the mixed rounds were hitting anything besides vegetation.

"Can you see them?" I shouted at Takara.

"Just movement behind the trees. Hard to get a clear shot."

"Yoofi," I radioed, "can you cast an animation on the foliage?"

"Not without spreading tumba seed there, but it is too far away."

I made a mental note to weaponize his tumba seeds.

I depressed the trigger and pivoted the weapon on its turret. In an explosive wave, leafy branches and small trees collapsed along the jungle's perimeter. The sustained hammering rang in my ears, and I finished the belt on my fourth pass.

"Hold fire," I ordered, peering out at the bank of smoke rising from the jungle's edge.

The incoming arrows had tapered during my attack with the .50, and now they stopped altogether.

"Not seeing anything from on high," Rusty radioed.

"Was there engagement from the south?" I asked, loading a new belt.

"Negative," Sarah answered.

For several moments, I scanned the tree line for movement. Had they retreated, or had we cut them down? I glanced over a shoulder at the arrows littering the rooftop, then at one that had landed beside my boot. The projectile looked primitive: a wooden shaft ending at a narrow tip chiseled from stone. I picked it up and brought the tip to my nose. A sharpness hit my sinuses, making my eyes water.

"The arrows are poison tipped," I radioed, tossing the projectile aside. "Use caution."

"Are they gone?" Yoofi asked.

"Possibly in retreat."

I was preparing to give security orders when the tree line returned to life, and a fresh barrage of arrows lanced in. Shit.

"Keep heavy fire on them," I radioed. Instead of returning to the .50, I recovered my MP88 and sent a stream of grenade rounds into the thicket. Their detonations flashed and thudded.

"Helos are on station," Rusty radioed.

Above the firing, I could hear our air support thumping in.

"Send them the coordinates," I ordered. "Have them unload ten, thirty, and fifty meters deep along the line."

If the hostiles' strategy was to hit and run in the hopes of catching us by surprise, we would eliminate their run option. I slammed in a fresh mag of grenade rounds and resumed the attack, keeping my fire shallow.

A moment later, the missiles began roaring in. They slammed into the jungle, throwing gouts of flames above the tree tops. One by one, the helos shot their payloads and veered away.

The next time I called a hold fire, the jungle was a burning wreck, but our massive counterassault had ended the follow-up attack. I ordered the helos to remain in close airspace in case we needed their heavy guns.

I turned to Takara. "Let's go see what we're dealing with."

I leapt over the retaining wall, and she flew down, landing at a run beside me. I ordered Yoofi to our six, and Sarah and Olaf to remain at base. The harsh smells of smoke and spent munitions drifted past as we ran across the pasture.

By the time we reached the tree line, the jungle's inherent dampness had subdued most of the fires. We stalked through the smoldering wreckage, pushing in five meters, then ten.

"Where are the damned bodies?" I growled.

On a large leaf that had been trampled flat, something black glistened. I stooped low and sniffed. The foul-smelling liquid had qualities of blood, but not any blood I'd smelled before. It was similar to the oily scent I'd picked up earlier.

Signaling to Takara that we had a trail, I took lead. The blood from the wounded hostile dripped deeper into the jungle. At about twenty meters it cut around a fallen tree. Beneath the exposed root structure, a dark hole opened into the earth. I ducked back and pointed the hole out to Takara and Yoofi.

"Retreat route," I whispered—which explained the lack of bodies.

Yoofi peered at it between our shoulders and made an ominous sound.

I craned my neck for a better look. The tunnel descended at an angle for about ten feet before curving northward. From the blackness came a stink of wet earth and reptile. If the people of Ban Mau were down there, I couldn't smell them. I gauged the hole's diameter. Too narrow for my frame.

"I'll go in," Takara said.

"Could be booby trapped."

"There are few traps I haven't set myself," she said.

"Just recon," I told her. "Fifty meters, no further. Come back if it feels off."

I didn't want a repeat of Mexico, where Takara had entered a hole and ended up in another dimension she barely escaped. I stood aside as she removed her rifle by the strap, then I handed her my sidearm.

She entered the opening head first and crawled out of sight.

While Yoofi and I stood guard, I updated Sarah and Rusty on our finding.

"The commander of the local military outpost called," Sarah radioed back. *"He heard the explosions and wanted to know who we were engaging."*

"I hope you told him it was none of his business."

"Not in those words, but yes. I said we would give our report to the prince in the morning."

"Good."

The commander wasn't our client. And no matter how loyal he was to Prince Ken, I didn't want him or his forces mingling with our team. Almost as dangerous as facing a foreign military was trying to cooperate with one—especially if New Siam's military was as divided as it appeared to be.

I was about to radio Takara for an update when I heard her returning. She emerged head first and sprang to her feet. A column of smoke leaked out after her.

"Three more tunnels join in," she said. "Their openings aren't far from here. I also found a room that looked like a weapons depot. Spears and stores of arrows, which I set fire to. Beyond, the tunnel continues north. That's where the blood trail went, but I saw no other signs of the hostiles or the missing."

Nodding, I radioed the team back at base. "Sarah, I need you to take over Rusty's post. Rusty, I want to set up visual surveillance on this tunnel. Pack some explosives too."

"The C4?"

"No, claymores. Olaf, cover his approach."

Before long, Rusty was swearing his way through the foliage toward us, lugging a duffle bag. I could just make out Olaf standing guard at the jungle's edge.

With Takara's help, Rusty set up two night-vision cameras in the tunnel, one shallow, one deep. If the hostiles returned, we would know. While Takara crawled away to locate the other entrances, I planted the claymores on either side of the opening.

"Whoa," Rusty said. "That's nasty even for you."

"Hey, they're the ones firing poisoned arrows."

He turned serious as he trained his ocular into the jungle. "Any idea what they are?"

"Given that they're reptilian, deal in poison, and can tunnel underground, I'm thinking the snake people Sarah mentioned in briefing." I began scattering debris over the tops of the claymores.

"I don't like the sound of that."

"You and Yoofi both," I grunted.

"I mean, snakes I can handle," he clarified. "Growing up, we used to have a rattlesnake roundup every Labor Day weekend. Two bucks for every rattler you brought in. Just about the whole town would turn out to comb hill and holler. Sheriff Perkins had a giant cage set out and everything. You should've seen that cage at the end of the weekend—just a writhing sea of diamond backs." He shuddered. "Got my fair share of bites, too. First one was the worst. Fact, I still got the scar here on my forearm." When I looked up, I found him struggling to peel down the sleeve of his suit.

"Not now," I said.

"Oh, right." He straightened his sleeve. "All's I'm saying is that I've got no problem with the snake part. But you start mixing in people, and something's wrong. How does that even happen?" He lowered his voice. "You think someone got it on with a snake?"

"I'm at an opening," Takara radioed.

"On our way," I answered. "Rusty, back to base. Lock Drone 1 onto these coordinates."

Rusty gathered his gear and left shaking his head, clearly disturbed by his own question. I signaled for Yoofi to follow me. We found Takara about fifty meters away, standing beside another hole. I turned to our magic-user.

"Bury it as far down as you can."

With a bolt from Yoofi's staff, the earth rumbled and the tunnel collapsed.

We repeated the ceremony at the other two entrances Takara had located. That done, I headed back to the first opening and double-checked the claymores. Satisfied, I took the lead with Takara back toward base.

"We'll run security at fifty percent tonight," I said. "Olaf and I will do full shifts so the rest of you can split and get some rest."

When Takara didn't answer, I remembered our confrontation from right before the attack.

"Are we good?" I asked her.

"I still say you're being too cautious."

"I'm being *cautious*," I stressed, leaving out the *too*.

"Don't let it silence your instincts," she said. "You have some of the best I've ever seen in a leader."

I frowned, not sure whether to take that as a compliment or a criticism. I glanced up to make sure Olaf was covering our approach, but he wasn't at his post. I peered around, then keyed my radio.

"Olaf? You copy?"

The silence kicked up my heart rate.

"Hey, Rusty. Is Olaf in there with you?"

"Negatory, boss. I haven't seen him since ... Heck, I guess since he brought me down to you guys."

"He didn't escort you back?" I was already pulling up our GPS positions on the tablet.

"I should've been paying attention, but I was thinking about those snake people."

On my screen, pulsing icons came up for everyone except Olaf. I swore silently.

"Man missing," I radioed.

12

Nostrils flaring, I grabbed Olaf's scent and followed it back to the edge of the jungle. His musk traced a line along the boundary between pasture and jungle, as if our teammate had used the overhanging branches for cover.

"Olaf!" I called.

"Did someone take him?" Yoofi asked behind me.

"No. The scent's solitary."

"And I only see one set of prints," Takara said.

I picked up the pace until we were running. After a few hundred meters, the trail broke into the jungle. I shouted his name again. The dense growth and waves of insect noises seemed to muffle the sound.

"No sight of him from the air," Rusty radioed, *"but that's not saying much. The drone feed shows him moving off a minute ten after he escorted me down, so he's under deep tree cover by now. I'm rebooting his locator."*

I pulled my Bowie knife from my belt and hacked a path into the jungle. With leaves and limbs flying around me, I chastised myself. I had been so fixated on the tunnels, I'd left Olaf unmanned. But what had made him take off?

"I can fly ahead," Takara said.

"No," I grunted, slashing through a small tree. "We need to stay in visual contact."

"He has too much of a head start."

"He's also being slowed by the terrain," I said. "We'll catch him."

After a quarter mile, the trees opened onto a narrow ravine with a rushing river at the bottom. Olaf's heavy prints broke down one side of the bank and up the other. I stopped, expecting to hear him crashing through the growth ahead, but I couldn't hear anything above the water and jungle sounds.

I sniffed. No scent of snake people, either.

I cocked my head for Takara to cross first, covering her as she took flight. When she signaled that the far side was secure, I seized Yoofi around the waist and leapt the ravine. My feet crashed down on the far bank, and Yoofi began to scream.

"What is it?" I said.

"Poison, Mr. Wolfe! Poison!"

Takara pivoted with her weapon while I searched Yoofi's body, sure he'd been hit by an arrow. He clasped the back of his neck, sweat pouring from his face.

"Aiieee! Poison!" he continued.

When I didn't find anything, I shook him by the shoulders. "Where, Yoofi?"

His staff fell from his grip, and he slumped forward, passed out. I set him on his back and joined Takara in sweeping the surrounding jungle with our weapons. The trees seemed darker on this side of the river, more hostile. They held no obvious dangers, though. When I swallowed, the back of my throat stung, like the start of an illness.

Yoofi drew in a sharp breath and his eyes shot open. Only they were yellow, the pupils reptilian slits.

"Yoofi," I barked.

He hissed and lunged for his fallen staff. I stepped on it. Takara dropped behind him and wrapped him in her arms and legs, feet interlocking across his thighs. He writhed and spit, unable to break from her grasp.

"Yoofi Adjaye," I said. "Can you hear me?"

His eyes fixed on mine and narrowed, as though coming into focus.

"Who are you?" I asked.

"I am cursed Poison and blessed Medicine," he hissed. "I have the Fang that Takes and the Fang that Gives..."

"What's your *name*?" I demanded.

"I am Destroyer of Mortals and Granter of New Life..." he continued.

I pressed my rifle barrel against his chest. "Where's Olaf? Where are the people you took?"

His face twisted into a fierce expression that looked nothing like Yoofi's. "They are *mine*," he spat.

"Where are you keeping them?"

"Forget about them, intruder," he whispered. "Or you will lose *everything*."

His reptilian eyes cut to the top of my vest. Though he couldn't have seen it, he was staring at where my wedding band rested against my chest. Something warm and slippery wriggled in my head. I steeled against it while fighting an urge to cover the ring with a hand. Yoofi's lips forked into a grin.

"Where the hell are they?" I shouted.

Moaning, he squeezed his eyes closed and renewed his struggle against Takara.

"Let go ..." he managed after another moment, but in his own voice now. "Can't breathe..."

When his eyelids fluttered open, the yellow was gone and his pupils had regained their shape.

I moved my weapon away and nodded at Takara. "It's him."

She released him slowly. As I knelt to the ground beside him, Yoofi sat forward and cradled his head in his hands.

"Ooh, I did not like that at all."

"What happened to you?" Takara asked.

"Mr. Wolfe was carrying me across the river, and all at once I started to burn inside, like I had been poisoned. Then I am in a dark place, very warm, very damp. And with a bad smell. Something was wrapped around me, like a giant snake. I tried to call to Dabu, but I had no breath. I thought for sure it was the end. But then the snake let me go."

"A warning," I said, peering around.

"A warning, Mr. Wolfe?"

"While you were in that dark place, someone or something spoke through you. The entity claimed the people it had taken belonged to it now. Told us to forget about them or we'd lose everything."

Yoofi's eyes widened. "I was possessed?"

"Yeah." So as not to freak him out further, I didn't mention the part about his eyes changing. "Do you have any protections against that?"

"I will need to have a talk with Dabu."

When he tried to push himself up, I helped him. He recovered his staff from the ground and, pulling his wooden idol to his god from a coat pocket, began speaking to it. I moved off a few paces to pick up Olaf's scent. The possession had cost us precious minutes, but I couldn't detect a damned thing now.

Takara said, "I don't see a trail."

"So, what, he just disappeared?" I asked, already thinking portals.

"Or being cloaked. Did you notice that we lost communication to the outside?"

I hadn't. I consulted my tablet, but it wasn't relaying info. No satellite signal.

"Sarah, do you copy?" I radioed. "Rusty?"

No response, even though I could still radio-comm with Takara.

Yoofi shouted a Congolese word that sent energy rippling past us in a queasy wave. Sparkles, similar to those Yoofi had cast on the Oni's mist, began glittering around us. He looked at them and nodded gravely.

"There is magic here," he said. "Bad magic. It wraps the jungle like the big snake that tried to strangle poor Yoofi. See the side of the river we come from? There is no bad magic over there."

"A barrier of some kind," I said. "Probably what's hiding Olaf's trail and screwing with our signals."

"It also makes us vulnerable to possession," Takara said. "You and I have training, but the others...?" She arched an eyebrow.

Yoofi's brow furrowed. "What are you trying to say about me?"

"It's not just you," I said. "I felt something in my head too. A squirming, like when I touched the amulet at the temple."

Yoofi refocused on his idol. A moment later, he nodded.

"Dabu says I have woken him from his nap, but yes, he will give us protection."

With the next word he spoke, smoke erupted from his staff. The geyser gathered into a cloud that settled around us like smog. I expected to start coughing, but the cloud only smelled vaguely foul, like old cigar smoke. When I swallowed, I noticed that the stinging in the back of my throat was fading.

"It is trickster magic," Yoofi explained. "It will not let the bad magic get a good fix on us."

"And you can maintain this?" I asked. "Dabu can maintain this?"

"For a case of his favorite brandy, yes."

———

Under Yoofi's protective magic, we searched the area but were unable to pick up Olaf's trail again. After a failed locating spell —Yoofi had warned us they weren't his strength—we returned across the river. Our equipment came back online, and I radioed an update to Sarah and Rusty. Per Rusty, he hadn't been able to restore Olaf's GPS.

"Anything show up on the tunnel feed?" I asked.

"Nothing, boss."

"I can explore where it goes," Takara said to me.

I didn't argue this time. Right now the tunnel was our best lead to Olaf and the people of Ban Mau. By the time we arrived at the opening, the sky beyond the canopy was beginning to pale with the coming morning. Takara handed me her rifle by the strap. As she prepared to descend, Yoofi dug furiously in his coat pockets.

"Wait," he said.

He emerged with one of the snake amulets from the temple and hung it around her neck.

"What in the hell are you doing?" I demanded.

"Do not worry, Mr. Wolfe. There is no bad magic left. I made sure, and so did Dabu. The amulets remain very good objects to hold magic, and I want to send protection with her."

Before I could respond, Yoofi touched his staff to the amulet's face. The red gems in the serpent's eyes darkened, and the same smog-like cloud that hung around us began to emanate from the stone pendant.

Yoofi stepped back and smiled at us.

"Do you feel all right?" I asked Takara.

"Except for the smell, fine."

"Stay in radio contact," I said. "If your equipment loses functionality, come back."

When Takara disappeared into the tunnel, I followed her progress on my tablet. At fifty meters, the farthest she'd gone the last time, she slowed and appeared to pick her way forward. Wanting to stay even with her, I waved for Yoofi to follow me. The way was dense with growth and slow going.

"I can see why they use the tunnels," Yoofi whispered, yanking his sleeve from another in a series of branches he was getting snagged on. "So much faster."

I nodded in agreement. Even using my knife as a machete, I was having trouble keeping pace with Takara. According to the stories, the snake people had lived in communities under the jungle floor. If this connected to one of them, it might lead us to the victims. At five hundred meters, I radioed Takara.

"How's it going down there?"

"It's been a straight shot, but there's an opening ahead. About fifty meters."

"We'll meet you there," I said.

A few seconds later, she came back on. *"Wait, there's something down here."*

"What is it?"

Static broke through my earpiece. When I checked the tablet, I saw we were offline.

"Takara?" I called. "Takara, do you copy?"

Her voice broke through, but I couldn't hear what she was saying.

"The bad magic is back," Yoofi said, meaning we had hit the damned barrier again.

Hacking and slashing with my blade, I charged ahead. I wasn't going to lose another teammate.

Within moments I spotted the opening Takara had referenced—a hole at the base of a tree. I sheathed my knife and lifted my MP88. Yoofi came up behind me. I signaled for him to approach the hole from the left while I circled to the right. Something heavy scuffed underground, coming to the surface.

My finger contacted the trigger.

When a head appeared, I hoisted my barrel skyward.

"Hold fire," I called to Yoofi. "It's Takara."

He relaxed his staff, and the magic he'd been gathering dispersed.

We watched Takara's upper body emerge, her left arm straining to pull something behind her.

"It's a body," she said.

I stepped forward, already bracing for it to be Olaf's. With a final grunt, Takara heaved a cloaked figure onto the ground. Black fluid oozed from a wound on its hip, sending up an oily, reptilian stink.

Snake person.

13

Sarah leaned over the stiff body with her scalpel and tweezers.

The hairless creature I'd carried back was like nothing we'd encountered before. Measuring in at a little over five feet, it was human in shape, its muscles lean and well-defined beneath a scaly layer of pale-green skin. The face was what set it apart. Its nose and mouth protruded to a blunt point, as if punched from the inside. Yellow-green eyes with slit pupils stared at the ceiling while retracted lips revealed hooked fangs and poison sacs.

"It's a species match to the earlier samples," Sarah announced.

I nodded, not surprised. "It's also the one we clipped in the firefight. I recognize the smell from the blood trail we followed." I eyed the ragged hole above its left hip. "Must have succumbed to the injury."

"Actually, there was a second wound, covered by the cloak," she said. "Something drove a blade into its brainstem."

"The team deciding to shed its dead weight?"

"The hip injury would have slowed their escape," she agreed. For someone who'd had the "leave no soldier behind" doctrine drilled into his soul, seeing a creature, even a hostile one, not just left behind by his teammates, but executed, filled me with a sick feeling. Probably more so because Olaf was still out there and likely in the clawed hands of these same creatures.

"Still nothing from the pilots," I said, referring to the Centurion helos I'd ordered to sweep the jungle. Though I was hoping for a heat signature, a sighting, something, their equipment wasn't having any more luck penetrating the barrier than ours. And if Olaf was underground, forget about it.

That left foot patrol.

There was no back and forth in my mind now about entering the jungle. Olaf was a teammate, and delaying the search would be the equivalent of signing off on his death warrant. I'd be damned if I was going to descend to the ranks of these snake people. But we'd have a better chance geared up and informed on what we were facing. Outside Sarah's makeshift exam room, I could hear Takara prepping and Yoofi chanting as he instilled the remaining amulets with Dabu's protection.

I eyed the dead creature again. "What did you learn about its venom?"

"It contains a powerful neurotoxin." She prodded a poison sack with her tweezers. "A single drop into the bloodstream will cause paralysis, anaphylactic shock, possibly cardiac arrest. A person would die without immediate treatment."

"Same venom that was on the arrows?"

When Sarah nodded, something occurred to me.

"How would Olaf's regenerative abilities handle a toxin like that?"

"Hard to say without a test. Why, do you think he was hit?"

"Yeah, and knowing Olaf, he probably pulled out the arrow and kept fighting. Hell, he's taken bullets without comment."

Sarah bent over one of her open laptops and tapped out a query. Beyond her glowing lenses, I watched her eyes absorb the results. "Though he could conceivably heal from the venom, it's still potent enough to overcome the oxytocin that bonds him to the team. That could explain him wandering off."

And once he entered what I'd come to think of as the *poison zone*, he would have been susceptible to possession.

"Fortunately, our antivenom is effective against this particular toxin," Sarah continued. "If we find Olaf, a high dose of antivenom will destroy the toxic cells. A booster of oxytocin will restore him."

"*When* we find him," I said, checking my watch. "And we've already been here too long."

I just wished we had a damn location so we knew where we were going.

"Do we need to SITREP Director Beam?" she asked.

"Already did. He cleared the search and rescue." I suspected Beam was only interested in recovering his multi-million-dollar asset, but as long as we were all on the same page, his motive didn't matter to me. When my sat phone rang, I checked the display, hoping it was Purdy, but it was Prince Ken.

"Captain Wolfe," I answered.

"What was the commotion last night? The commander described a bombardment."

"We were attacked."

"By whom?"

I looked over at the snake person on the table. I didn't want any kingdom involvement until we'd recovered Olaf. "Didn't get a good visual. At least a dozen combatants came up through tunnels at the edge of the jungle and shot poisoned arrows at our position. They retreated under heavy fire and air support."

"Air support? I thought I asked for discretion!"

"We didn't know how many we were facing."

"You could have contacted me. I would have sent military backup."

"With all due respect, we don't work with forces we haven't trained with."

The prince, who sounded more alarmed than angry, took a deep breath and let it out. "Do you still have helicopters in our airspace?"

"No," I lied.

"Good, keep them away. The military outpost received calls last night from several mayors worried about the explosions, but one contacted the provincial base. Word reached the capital. My father has scheduled flyovers for today."

"Noted," I grunted.

Damn, gonna have to call the helos off the search.

"Tunnels and arrows?" the prince said, getting back to last night's engagement. "I've never heard of anything like that up there."

"How about the army patrols around Ban Mau? The official investigation? They never came under attack?"

"Not that I'm aware of, no. Did your search of the town turn up anything?"

For a second, I thought about holding back on that too, but as long as the army stayed in town and didn't come nosing around our base... "Five dead bodies at the temple, including the head cleric. Their throats were cut."

I left out the part about their corpses coming to life. There was no point. The prince was an admitted skeptic, and he'd already denied knowing about any supernatural activity in the area.

"Murdered?" he asked.

"Definitely. We found the bodies in a cellar under the kitchen."

"I'll see that their remains are removed."

"There's not much left. We had to burn them for security purposes."

"Burn—? Never mind, I have some information too. You asked about recent activity in the area. A source tells me that this past summer my father commissioned an expedition into the jungles north of Ban Mau."

My senses sharpened. "What kind of expedition?"

"We don't know the details, but it appears to have been a search for a lost city."

"Lost city?"

"My source obtained a set of coordinates."

"Go ahead."

The prince read the numbers off, and I entered them into my tablet. A location appeared on the topo map about twenty miles north of our present position. I zoomed in. The site appeared to be an arrangement of hills around a depression. A clearing at one end appeared large enough to land helicopters—but that wasn't an option until the king's flyover ended. I couldn't make out anything beneath the rest of the thick canopy.

"Do you know what the expedition found?"

"No," the prince said. "They never returned."

This was sounding more and more like a lead. And maybe more and more like a reason not to drop into the site on a helo.

"What about your sister?" I asked. "Any updates?"

"No one knows where she is. She's disappeared."

"Should we be worried?"

He gave a short laugh. "I'm sorry, that came out wrong. I should have said that she's left. And no, it's nothing to be worried about. She's taken off like this before when something's upset her. Probably to Japan. Think of it like an adult temper tantrum. She'll be back once she's worked it out of her system."

The prince obviously had sibling issues, but that wasn't my problem.

"All right," I said, "I'm going to take a closer look at these coordinates."

"Do you think there's a connection?"

"Given the timing, it's very possible. We've seen accounts of supernatural elements inhabiting ancient sites. I want to know more about the expedition, though. Who went, how many, its specific purpose."

"I'll see what I can find out."

"You sound doubtful."

"It's just that my father has ... well, tightened down in recent months."

The way the prince said it, I imagined the king executing suspected traitors, both real and imagined.

"Try anyway. We're all taking risks here."

"I will. But again, no helicopters ... Please."

"We'll keep them out of your airspace," I assured him.

I ended the call, prompting Sarah to look up from the body. "What was that about?"

"A possible location about a day-and-a-half trek from here. We'll brief in ten and head out in thirty."

I called out prep commands as I strode toward the room we'd set up as an armory. With air support out, we were going to need all the ordnance we could carry. I surveyed the racks of weapons and containers of rounds and explosives. With my superhuman strength, I could carry plenty.

I started loading the big pack.

14

I wiped a forearm through the soaking rug of my brow and shook it off. I was bearing five-hundred pounds on my back, easy, and the environment wasn't helping. From the lead position, Takara hacked a path through the steamy growth. The going had been slow. Three miles in a little over two hours.

"Ooh, spider!" Yoofi whispered.

I peered back just as he brushed a hairy arachnid the size of his hand from his shoulder. He had distributed the amulets, including one for himself, and the protective smoke that emanated from them covered us in a brown haze. Given that we were well into the poison zone now, they appeared to be working. No soreness in the back of my throat, either.

I looked past Yoofi to Rusty.

"Any progress?" I radioed.

"*Negatory, boss,*" he replied, still fussing with a tablet. He had packed our small nuclear generator with the idea that he could channel additional power into our signals to overcome the effect of the poison zone. But he'd been unable to contact the backup force or data satellites. All the more reason to embed him rather than station him back at base outside our current range of communication.

"Keep at it," I said. "How we doing in the back?"

"Still clear," Sarah answered by radio.

I usually assigned Takara to the six position, but I needed her stamina for path-clearing. Fortunately, the trek had been uneventful, punctuated here and there by the roar of jets—the ordered flyover the prince had mentioned.

I'd sent the Centurion helos back across the border as promised. They would reenter tomorrow and remain within range of two locations. The first was a clearing I'd spotted near the supposed lost city. The second was the only other reasonably sized opening in the trees I could find, about halfway between our base and the city. That would serve as our retreat point, if needed. The pilots knew our planned route, and they would be on the lookout for signal flares to indicate we were ready to be lifted.

"River is just ahead," Takara said between machete hacks.

With no access to GPS, we were down to old-fashioned route finding. The unnamed river was our first objective. We would follow it for the next sixteen miles. It wasn't a direct shot to the target, but it simplified navigation and would mean a lighter water carry. Where the river veered west, we would break northeast. Three more miles of jungle trekking would deliver us to the lost city—or to the prince's coordinates, anyway.

"We'll stay on this side unless the route becomes impenetrable," I said.

As I hiked the load on my back, I revisited a formula that had come from my time in Central Asia. Every twenty-four hours a friendly soldier went unrescued, the chances of recovering him alive fell by half. Judging from the lethal wound on the snake person, we were probably looking at an even steeper drop in this case.

With the river acting as guide now, I upped our pace.

———

By the time the jungle canopy started to dim and the nocturnal creatures to riot, we were entering a small clearing about two miles from the point at which we would be leaving the river. That put us less than five miles out from the lost city. If I had been alone, I would have night-trekked there, but I wasn't, and I needed support from a team that needed its rest. Besides, the reaction force wouldn't be looking for a flare until tomorrow.

"We'll stop here," I announced.

"Hallelujah," Rusty panted while Yoofi muttered his own prayer. Both had so much sweat dripping off them, they looked like they'd taken a dive in the river.

I gave security orders, then lowered my quarter-ton load to the ground and helped Takara clear out spaces for the tents. That done, I planted a ring of mines around the clearing while Rusty set up camera surveillance.

By the time we returned to the clearing, the tents were up, their chemical camouflage blending them into the surroundings. The patented material also cloaked odors and allowed a person on the inside to see out. Sarah had arranged the tents in a ring so we had a three-sixty on our surroundings as well as views of the overhanging branches.

"How's everyone doing?" I asked.

"Much better if I had a cold beer," Rusty said as he began plugging devices into the nuclear generator. "But I'll live."

An odd sound, like a horse's whinny, came from Sarah. Rusty's face creased in puzzlement as I wheeled toward her. With reddening cheeks, Sarah coughed and brushed her plastered bangs from her forehead.

Had she just giggled?

"Heat must be affecting me," she said.

Though she sounded like herself again, I watched her for another moment to be sure.

At last I turned to Yoofi. "Any updates on the hostile energy?"

"Oh, yes, the poison magic is still here. And it is getting stronger."

"Too strong for Dabu?" I asked, stealing another glance at Sarah.

"No, not too strong, Mr. Wolfe. The magic still tricks the poison very good."

When I swallowed—my litmus test—my throat felt fine. "All right, let me know if that changes. We'll split tonight and pull two-hour shifts. I'll take an extra to make sure everyone gets at least six hours sleep."

"I'll take first," Takara said.

Despite spending the day path-clearing, she showed no signs of fatigue as she cradled her rifle.

"Yoofi and I will join you," I said. "Rusty and Sarah, calorie up and hydrate, then get to sleep."

"No arguments here, boss," Rusty said.

By the time he and Sarah settled into their tents, it was full night. Takara, Yoofi, and I took up positions around the clearing. As I listened into the jungle, I could have sworn it was listening back—as if something was trying to draw a bead on our position. I studied the camera feeds on my tablet. Except for bats zipping past in pursuit of giant insects, we seemed to have the area to ourselves.

I tested my throat again. No sting.

When Rusty started to snore from his tent, I made my way over to Takara.

"You doing all right?"

"Fine," she replied.

"We should reach the site by mid-morning. When we're close, I'm going to send you ahead for recon."

She gave the barest nod, as if I'd caught her in some deep thought. Her body carried the same tension it had the day before, even though she knew the princess was AWOL, likely in Japan. It made me wonder if there was something besides the prospect of a group of samurai that was bothering her.

"Anything you want to talk about?" I tried.

"I know this place."

I followed her gaze into the jungle. "What, here?"

"No, not a location."

I exhaled. First Sarah giggling, and now this?

"Takara, I don't know what you're talking about."

"We make hundreds of choices a day. Day after day. And yet we arrive in situations we seem destined to have ended up in all along. Like we've been following a well-tread path the whole time." She turned to me. "Do you ever have that feeling?"

I thought about the path that had led me to the Blue Wolf and the sense, sometimes, that I belonged in this body.

"No," I lied. "I can't say I do."

Takara turned back toward the jungle. "Then this can't make any sense to you."

I still suspected the root of her apprehension came from the prospect of still being here when any samurai arrived.

"Look," I said, "it's going to be the same drill as always. Neutralize the hostiles, eliminate the source of magic, and recover Olaf and any survivors. Quick in and out. We'll be gone before anyone knows we've come." I squeezed her shoulder, a little surprised she accepted the gesture. "All right?"

She gave an unconvincing nod.

When our two hours were up, I awoke Sarah and Rusty. I planned to join them on the second shift, but Takara said she wasn't tired. Despite my earlier attempts to reassure her, she still carried a haunted look.

"Get some rest," I said.

"I'm fine," she insisted.

Relenting, I climbed into my tent. Not until I had reclined in full battle gear and set my MP88 beside me did I realize how tired I was. My heart beat a strong, steady rhythm that slowed my concerned thoughts.

I fell asleep immediately.

15

"You're coming back, right?"

Dani was straddling my waist, hands pressed to my chest. A teasing smile quirked her lips, but familiar concern hardened her eyes. It was two days after our wedding, and I was due back at the Legion compound that afternoon.

I laughed. "If you'll still have me."

She leaned down and gave me a firm kiss. I inhaled her clean scent, feeling secure between her solid body and the soft mattress beneath me. Morning light streamed through the white curtains, haloing her as she straightened again. I rolled her over so I was on top, her hair splaying on the pillow.

"I'm worried about this one, Jason."

"What one?"

"New Siam," she said.

My brows crushed down. How could she know about New Siam? The timing wasn't right. That had been months after our wedding, not days. My thoughts contorted into strange shapes, trying to reconcile the discrepancy.

Her muscles stiffened underneath me.

"Why haven't you told me?" she demanded.

"Told you what?"

"About this."

When I looked down, I saw she'd gathered a fistful of my chest hair. Blue chest hair. My mind jumped into a panic. I felt over my face, my taloned hand encountering a muzzle and thick hair. I was changing back already?

I expected to see fear on Dani's face, but there was anger. She yanked my hair hard enough for it to hurt.

"Why the fuck haven't you told me, Jason?"

———

I jerked awake, heart slamming.

Lenses glowed in the side entrance of my tent.

"What are you doing here?" I demanded, nerves still twanging from the nightmare.

"I just came to check on you," Sarah said, easing all the way in. "You were making noises."

I dragged a hand over my damp face and checked my watch. I'd only been in here for fifteen minutes.

"Do you want something to help you sleep?" she asked.

"Naw, I'm good. Just need to settle back down."

I was about to tell her to return to her sentry position when she spoke again.

"Why didn't you tell me about Purdy's warning?"

The words arrived like a strange echo from my dream of Dani. Sarah lowered herself onto her knees beside me. I squinted at her from the elbow I'd propped myself on. This kind of closeness wasn't like her.

"It's been bothering me," she said.

I remembered the frostiness I'd been picking up. Was that what it had been about? Me not telling her about Purdy's visit?

But I was distracted by the way she was acting. Sarah wasn't one to share her feelings like this, either.

"Are you sure you're doing all right?" I asked.

"After the Canada mission, we agreed to share everything. I took that very seriously. I imagine as seriously as you took your wedding vows." She glanced away, and when her eyes returned to mine, they glistened with moisture. She snorted and shook her head. "This happens every time. You'd think I'd learn."

"What happens every time?"

She removed her glasses and wiped her eyes with the back of a fist. "Forget it."

When she started to back out of the tent, I seized her wrist. "No, not 'forget it.' You giggled at what Rusty said earlier—something I've never heard you do. And then you come in here and start tearing up?"

"I'm not allowed to have feelings?"

"That's fine, but showing them is a big change for you."

"What?" she asked through gritted teeth. "Would everyone rather I remain a machine? I see the way the rest of you joke and carry on. Even Takara's part of the club now. Am I supposed to just stand on the outside and act like this?" She forced her face to go flat —the expression I'd become accustomed to on her. Before I could say anything, she began to punch the hand holding her wrist.

"Hey," I said sternly, even though I could barely feel the blows.

Like another switch had flipped, her face softened and she began stroking my walnut-sized knuckles.

"Sarah," I said, pulling my hand back.

She blinked several times, as if struggling to understand what was happening.

"I need you to think clinically for a second. If a man brought his wife to you and said, 'She's always been really serious, but lately she's gone into fits of laughing, crying, anger—all very suddenly.' What would you think? Quick."

"Frontal lobe involvement," Sarah answered automatically. "Orbitofrontal cortex, specifically. The area of the brain involved in emotional inhibition and decision-making. It could be caused by a number of things: closed-head injury, stroke, tumor, certain age-related diseases."

"What about possession magic?"

"Possession magic," she repeated. I could see her mind working behind her eyes.

"Earlier, Yoofi said the hostile magic in the poison zone was getting stronger," I explained. "He claimed he could hold it back, but what if some is getting through? Just enough to disrupt your decision-making and emotional—"

"Inhibition," she finished. "Crap."

"It's all right."

Her face blanched with mortification.

"Yoofi," I radioed. "I need you in my tent."

"Yes, Mr. Wolfe," he answered groggily.

By the time he arrived, I'd convinced Sarah to take my mat. There was no way I was going to send her back out on sentry. While I filled Yoofi in, she lay quietly, a crease growing between her closed eyes. I could sense her clinical mind struggling to restore her self-control. Yoofi passed his staff over her.

"Ah, yes. Some of the bad magic is in her."

"I thought you said you could keep it out," I snarled.

He gave a nervous laugh. "Well, that is what I was told. Sometimes the gods will exaggerate to make themselves seem stronger than they really are." His eyes shifted. "No, not you, Dabu. Your brothers and sisters." He listened for a moment before giggling. "Haha. Yes, she is funny like the baboon."

My jaw stiffened. "Can you purge it?"

"Yes, Mr. Wolfe. We can do that for sure."

Hoping this wasn't another exaggerated promise, I watched him reach into a coat pocket and emerge with a handful of crushed leaves. He sprinkled them around Sarah's head and across her chest. Holding the bladed end of the staff over her face, he began to chant. Within moments, the leaves curled and white smoke rose from them. As the smoke enveloped Sarah, she started to cough.

"Are you all right?" I asked her.

Her coughing became more aggravated.

I turned to Yoofi, who only chanted more loudly. He dipped the end of his staff into the smoke and gave it a sharp twist. When he raised the staff again, I saw he'd snagged a faint band of energy. It writhed like a snake. Yoofi worked quickly, twisting the staff so that the energy wrapped the length of wood. Sarah's coughing strengthened into what sounded like dry heaves. After several more twists, Yoofi reached a flicking tail.

Holding up the staff, he shouted, *"Esansu!"*

With a faint screech, the serpentine energy blew apart.

Yoofi looked at me, sweat glistening over his face. He nodded to indicate the purging had been successful. I waved a hand to clear the smoke from Sarah. She gave a few weak coughs and lay still. A constellation of purple dots covered her cheeks. It took me a moment to realize this was one of Dabu's jokes.

I glared at Yoofi, who bit back a giggle.

"Dabu promises they will be gone by morning."

"They better be."

"Anyway, it is best if she rests now."

"How do we know the magic won't re-infect her?"

"Dabu will make the protection stronger."

"And that will be enough this time?"

"I pray so, Mr. Wolfe."

Not the answer I wanted, but I couldn't fault him for being honest. "How's your capacity to channel holding up?"

"Right now, pretty good. But if the poison magic gets stronger, it will become harder."

"Then let's make maintaining the protective magic your priority. Use your firearm for any engagements from now on instead of your staff, all right?"

"Okay, I will do that."

I picked up my MP88 and looked down at Sarah. She appeared to be resting comfortably.

"I want you to scan the others," I told Yoofi. "Make sure no one else is infected, including you and me."

"Yes, Mr. Wolfe." He hesitated. "There is one more thing you should know, though."

"What's that?" I asked, not liking the way his large eyes moved from me to Sarah.

"Whoever is casting the bad magic knows we are here now."

16

I stayed up on watch while the others rotated in and out in shifts. I caught occasional eye shine on the surveillance feeds, but each time it proved to be an animal, and I relaxed my thumb from the detonator. We were vulnerable, but I doubted we would have been any safer moving than remaining in the clearing, where we at least had perimeter defenses. And I wanted rest for my teammates, especially Sarah.

At 0600, I heard her stirring. I passed off perimeter surveillance to Rusty and poked my head into the tent.

"How are you feeling?" I asked.

"Humiliated," she replied, putting her glasses on. Dabu's purple dots had mostly faded. "But if you're asking if I feel like myself again, yes."

"Good, because we need to move."

"How are the others?"

"Fine. Yoofi checked them out. You were the only one affected."

She studied me for a moment. "Captain, those things I said last night—"

"Forget it." I raised a hand. "I know that wasn't you."

"I'll keep closer tabs on my mental state from now on. I'll also brief the team so they'll recognize the early signs."

"That's a good idea. You can do it while we pack."

Within the hour, we were following the riverbank again, my gaze scanning the jungle on both sides. For me it wasn't a question of if we were going to be attacked today, but when. Where the river veered west, we broke away and began our three-mile trek toward the coordinates Prince Ken had given us.

After two-hundred meters, something caught my eye. "Hold up," I called.

Takara lowered her blade. I leaned toward a splintered hole in a tree trunk and sniffed. Beneath a knot of hardened tree sap, I picked up a scent of metal and the unmistakable bite of silver. Using a talon, I dug out a flattened rifle round. I peered around. More holes peppered the surrounding trees.

"Firefight," I said, examining the first hole again. "Looks like a couple weeks ago."

"Do you think the army came here?" Sarah asked.

"No, the round is silver-laced. Similar to ours, in fact."

Takara signaled for silence and pointed ahead. I peered past her until I saw something hanging from a tree branch. I sidled past her into the lead. Within steps, we joined up with another hacked pathway.

A group came this way.

As I neared the hanging object, I saw it was a tactical vest. I lifted it down with the barrel of my MP88. It felt light for standard military issue. I removed the breast plate. What looked like a thin piece of black foam slid free. Ridiculously light, and yet durable enough to have stopped the rounds that pocked it.

I passed the plate to Rusty for a look and checked the vest's pockets. Empty. I brought the vest to my nose. The material had no doubt been rinsed by a few hard rains, but I picked up the faint scent of blood.

"Some sort of synthetic steel," Rusty said of the breast plate. "We're talking high tech shit."

I nodded and scanned our surroundings. "It belongs to another group," I said. "I don't think we were the first one's hired."

This story has played out already, Purdy had said. *With tragic consequences.*

I looked over the vest again. Was this what he'd been talking about?

At my order, we searched the area. Within minutes, Takara found what looked like a former encampment. I kept the others back while she and I swept the patch of jungle for traps. Gouges in the earth and munitions debris showed where buried mines had detonated.

In the encampment itself, a couple of vests, like the one we'd just found, littered the ground, along with helmets, empty packs, and a high-tech camo suit. Several tent structures lay in tatters. I examined the detritus, not liking what they suggested.

"The area is clean," Takara reported. "No weapons, even."

"Taken, most likely," I said.

"I did find this." She handed me a small tablet with a cracked screen.

I examined the handheld—it looked a little like the ones we carried. I slid it into a pocket and nosed around the encampment. From beneath the toxic magic that permeated the jungle rose traces of human blood and the oily scent of snake people. I signaled for the others to join us. Rusty arrived first, jerking his M4 around the destroyed encampment.

"Anyone else getting a freaky sense of *seen this before*?" he asked.

"Ooh yes, very much." Yoofi came up behind him. "It looks like our camp from last night."

"That's because the group was special-ops trained too," I

said. "Probably a team of twelve. Intense fire fight, heavy blood loss. Several or all killed."

"By the snake people?" Sarah asked.

"Snake people were here, but I think it was to plunder the aftermath."

"No arrows or poisoned projectiles found," Takara confirmed.

"Then who killed them?" Sarah pressed.

"Judging by the ballistics on the vests and helmets," I said, "they killed each other."

Yoofi made a noise of surprise while Rusty swore under his breath. Sarah peered around the encampment with a tense expression. When her eyes returned to mine, I caught a shade of fear in them.

"So they were possessed," she concluded.

"That would be my guess." Maybe that was why nothing had attacked us yet—the magic-user was waiting for us to succumb to the effects of the poison zone. I turned to Yoofi. "How are we doing?"

"The bad magic is stronger, but Dabu is keeping it off us."

"This other team," Rusty said. "Where the heck did they come from?"

"Based on their armor technology, they'd have to be privately funded," I said. "And we're talking a lot of money. That leaves a handful of competing defense companies. Some are supposedly making moves into the monster-hunting space."

Sarah ticked off a few of the names.

"Well, who do you reckon hired them to come here?" Rusty asked.

It was a good question, one I would have liked to put to Prince Ken, but with commo to the outside down, that option was out. "No telling. Could have been the prince, his sister, someone else in the royal family. Takara did find this." I handed

Rusty the damaged handheld. "Can you see if there's any info on there?"

"Yeah, if I can crack the security protocols." He turned the device over doubtfully. "I'll take a look."

The rest of us covered the jungle while he unshouldered his pack, took out the portable generator, and jammed a cable and some secondary equipment into the tablet. He began typing on a mini keyboard. The early morning was already hot. Mosquitos buzzed around us, but Yoofi's magic seemed to keep them from drawing precise beads on our bodies. Up in the canopy, birds screeched and darted around.

"Booya!" Rusty said.

"Got something?" I asked over a shoulder.

"Yeah, lucky. They're running off the same security protocols as ours. Looks like someone ripped off someone else's tech. Anyway, I bluffed the device into giving me access, and I'm in like a tick. Now let's take a little look-see..." He resumed typing in short bursts. "Dadgummit. Like ours, it front-ends to data somewhere else. No data on the device. Not much I can do about that without a signal. Unless of course they knew they were walking into the Twilight Zone..." His voice fell to a mutter as he went back to the keyboard. "Oh, hello there, sexy. What do we have here?"

Takara sighed. "Instead of the play-by-play, why don't you just tell us when you find something?"

"Just did, T-cakes," he said. "Someone stuck an app in a test folder, probably to hide. The security is flimsier than a laminate roof in a twister, though."

"What's the app?" I asked, beginning to lose my patience too.

"A translator set to... Hm, I'm not recognizing the language."

I got Sarah's attention and cocked my head for her to go take a look.

"It's Hung," she said after a moment. "One of New Siam's tribal languages."

"Tribal?" Yoofi repeated. "The prince said there were no tribes in the jungle."

"He also said there were no snake people," I grumbled.

Sarah brought the device to her mouth. "Hello. How are you?"

"Nyob zoo," a simulated voice spoke from the device. *"Koj yog leej twg?"*

Sarah waited a moment, then repeated the Hung phrase back to the device.

"Hello," it said in clear English. *"How are you?"*

"Anything else on there?" I asked Rusty.

"I've found the easy stuff, but I can keep digging."

I wanted to learn a few things, such as what had brought their team out here and if they knew anything we didn't. But the longer we delayed, the poorer our chances would be of recovering Olaf. The twenty-four-hour rule.

"Fifteen minutes," I said. "Then we've gotta keep moving."

Rusty frowned. "That's gonna be—"

Gunfire exploded from Takara's rifle. I wheeled with my MP88 in time to see a figure dart behind a tree. I let rip with a blast of automatic fire to keep it pinned. At my signal, Takara circled its position from the left. Yoofi and Sarah covered us as I moved right. Rusty remained back to protect our rear.

I squeezed off more gunfire, hoping our target hadn't dropped into a tunnel.

"It's climbing!" Takara called. Splinters flew from the tree trunk as her bullets tracked it.

I cut around for a better angle, but the damned thing was moving too fast. The figure disappeared into the canopy. Takara and I opened up. Leaves and branches rained down from our sustained fire. After another moment, I called a hold. We moved our barrels across the canopy, searching for a shadow or movement. In the distance, a troop of monkeys hollered their disapproval of the racket.

No way that fucking thing got away...

Behind us, Rusty let out a gargled cry.

I spun to find a snake creature holding him around the neck. The yellow eyes that appeared above Rusty's helmet were full reptilian. What I first mistook for a hood was a cobra-like feature of the thing's head, while an actual coat flapped around its body. The canopy was still rustling where the creature had dropped down behind Rusty.

When its scent reached me, I recognized the smell.

"It's the hostile that was watching our compound last night," I said.

Meaning we were looking at the scout. That would explain why he was out here alone. My teammates all had their weapons trained on the creature, but I had the best shot. As I squinted down my sight at the thing's head, it shifted behind Rusty. Rusty gargled beneath the creature's cinching grip.

"Release him!" I shouted at the creature.

The handheld Rusty had been hacking remained plugged into the generator at his feet. It detected my voice and translated the order into Hung. A moment later, the snake person spoke in a hiss. Something about the texture marked the creature as male. The handheld surprised me by translating his words into English.

"Stop. I don't want to hurt anyone."

The creature was speaking Hung.

"You harm him, and we'll destroy you," Takara said.

As the tablet translated her message, she took a step forward. The creature produced a sharpened stick and held it to the side of Rusty's neck. My teammate was no more than ten meters from where I stood, but the stick's poison-damp tip was less than ten millimeters from his jugular. It wasn't a race I could win.

Takara stopped and tensed for a shot, probably to take out the creature's weapon arm, but it would be too damned close. Even Rusty was waving his hands, telling her *no*.

"Hold fire," I ordered.

Takara glanced over, lips compressed, but raised her head from the sight.

"Release him and we'll let you go," I said.

With the tablet acting as translator, he replied, *"I want to talk first."*

I remembered the part of Sarah's briefing where she said the snake people were shrewd, even manipulative. Apparently, Sarah was remembering that part too.

"Why?" she demanded.

"We can help each other."

"Help?" Sarah said. "You scouted our base last night and attacked us."

"I was there, yes. I heard you arrive and went to see who you were. But I was not involved in the attack."

"And we're to believe that was just a coincidence?" Sarah said.

I could see by her face she remained bothered by last night's possession.

While the handheld translated her response, I made eye contact with Yoofi and turned up a hand in question. He had manipulated forces over distances in the past, and I was asking if he could do so now. He returned a quick nod and angled his staff slightly. As he began speaking under his breath, the brown mist that drifted through our space gathered behind the snake person, who had resumed speaking.

"I knew they were in the area..." the handheld translated as the creature spoke.

Yoofi's force seized his weapon hand and yanked it from Rusty's neck. The snake person twisted and snatched the stick with his other hand. Shit. I fired a round, but it glanced off the shoulder of his coat.

He drove the stick forward, but not into Rusty. He was aiming at the gathering mist.

With a shouted word, Yoofi commanded the force to yank Rusty forward while knocking the snake person back. For the first time, I realized that the creature's lower half was a tail—one he was coiling underneath him to retain his balance.

I sprinted past Rusty, who had fallen to his hands and knees, and my entire four-hundred pounds landed against the snake creature. We slammed against a tree trunk, the force shaking the branches. I smashed the stick from his grip and pinned him by his throat. The flesh under my forearm was cold and pliant. I drew my knife and pressed the tip between the scaly ridges of the creature's brow.

"Not so fun being on the wrong end of a sharp object, huh?" I growled. "Get cute, and I drive it into your brain."

The handheld translated my threat. I didn't know if there was a Hung equivalent, and in that moment I didn't give a shit. Besides being involved in Olaf's disappearance, this creature had just threatened another teammate. He dropped his hands from my arms, indicating he'd gotten the message.

Takara and Sarah arrived on either side of us, barrels aimed at his head. I noticed Sarah had retrieved the handheld, which now protruded from one of her vest pockets.

The creature's yellow eyes darted between my teammates before fixating on my face. I hadn't bothered to turn my collar on, so he was seeing the Blue Wolf.

"Where's our teammate?" I snarled. "The one who disappeared last night?"

I eased off his throat enough for him to hiss out a response. *"They took him to Meong Kal."*

"Where is that?" I pointed in the direction we'd been trekking. "That way?"

"Yes, but that way is death."

Threat? Warning? The creature's reptilian face didn't give off the same emotional cues as a person's. Neither did his scent.

"Are the others there too?" I asked. "The people from the town?"

"Yes."

A bolt of hope shot through me. "Are they alive?"

"I don't know. I haven't been able to get close."

"Who's behind this?"

"Akeila, the serpent goddess."

"Is that the god of your kind?"

As the tablet translated my question, the snake person's face seemed to recoil. His hisses turned to spats.

"It is a goddess of evil."

"Who your kind happen to be working with," Takara said.

"Their minds have been warped by Akeila's return."

"Then why aren't you affected?" Sarah challenged.

"Not all of us were. We tried to hide, but Akeila sent hunters after us. We were more than ten once. Now I am the only one left. I found it safest along the edges of the jungle, where Akeila's power is weakest. When I saw you enter the jungle, I followed. You want to help your people, and I want to help mine."

I studied the creature's eyes—narrow and unblinking with vertical slits for pupils. I couldn't read them, but did I even need to? The creature had plenty of reasons to make up a story. We'd captured him, and I was holding a knife to his head.

But if he's telling the truth, his knowledge of the jungle and snake people could be invaluable.

My gaze fell to his knee-length coat. In the canopy it had

blended with the dark green leaves, but against the tree trunk, it was brown. In addition to being bulletproof, the coat was operating off the same or a similar chemical technology as our camos. There was no way his kind had manufactured something like that in the jungle. He'd plundered it from a dead soldier at the encampment.

"Not working with the other snake people, huh?" I growled, driving my forearm back against his throat. "Then explain your coat. Sticking to the edges of the jungle, my ass," I added in a grumble.

His words emerged in gargled hisses, which the tablet managed to pick up and translate.

"I was ... their guide."

17

I patted the snake person for weapons, then bound him to the tree with plastic restraints. With Rusty and Yoofi covering him, I met with Sarah and Takara a short distance away, the translator turned off.

"What do you think?" I asked.

"Execute him," Takara said. "We can't trust him."

"We're also operating with minimal information," Sarah cut in. "If he's telling the truth, he could be an asset."

"*If* he's telling the truth," Takara shot back.

I peered past them at the restrained creature. "Lots of coincidences. Spying on our base right before the attack, then showing up here not long after your possession." Sarah averted her eyes. "His explanations are reasonable, but that sounds like part of their nature. The coat story seems suspect too."

"I agree," Takara said firmly.

"But that said, I'm with Sarah," I continued. "He could fill some big intel holes."

"Or he could lead us into an ambush," Takara said.

"Agreed, but right now I just want to hear his version of what happened. Because something happened, something *changed*, for the snake people to invade Ban Mau after hundreds of years of staying hidden in the jungle."

"And we know from the temple that the snake people are working with a magic-user," Sarah put in. "One who uses possession as a tool. It's reasonable to conclude that the magic-user possessed the snake people too. There could also be some connection to the goddess that he mentioned."

"Or he made all of that up," Takara said.

"We'll evaluate the info like we do everything else," I told her.

Back at the snake person, Sarah turned the translator on again.

"What's your name?" I asked him.

Following the translation, he answered, "Leej."

"Tell us everything that happened, from the beginning."

Bound to a tree and with several weapons on him, he appeared to listen to the translation intently.

"We have always lived in the jungle," he said, continuing to talk as the handheld translated his words. *"But many generations ago, we split into two groups. One remained in the jungle we knew. The other traveled to the jungle's darkest part and built a city where they said a city had been long before. That place came to be called Kal, the dark city. They raised a temple to Akeila, an evil serpent goddess."*

"And that's in the direction we're trekking?" I asked.

"Yes," he said. *"Over time, their worship to Akeila changed them. They began raiding the other tribes and stealing children to use as slaves. My forebears could not tolerate this evil. They banded together and, following a great battle, destroyed the city and temple. The threat was ended, but the evil remained. For generations, it blackened the trees around what was once Meong Kal and turned the waters foul. It is said those who ventured there lost their minds. My people learned to avoid that place. And so it was until this rainy season past. A human group arrived in a flying machine, like yours."*

He was talking about a helo.

"*We watched them land. We watched them trek to Meong Kal. The elders wanted to warn them, but there were stories of human armies destroying settlements outside the jungle, and these humans had weapons. I led a small group, and we followed them as far as we dared. When the visitors entered the place where the city once stood, we stopped. That night, we heard screams.*"

His account was consistent with the prince's intel of an expedition for a "lost city" this past summer. When I glanced over at Sarah, she nodded back. We were on the same page. Takara continued to watch Leej with cold eyes.

"*We did not see the human group again. But near the end of the rains, something changed. You could taste it in the air.*" A forked tongue flickered out. "*Soon, the tribes closest to Meong Kal began to disappear. No one knew why. One night, our elders called a meeting. They said we should journey to Kal to learn what was happening. For strength, they wanted us to go as one—the entire tribe. The others agreed, which surprised me. There is an old saying: 'They who avoid Meong Kal go on to multiply.'*"

Something had no doubt been lost in translation, but I got the gist: you stayed the hell out of Meong Kal if you valued your life.

"*I offered to lead a search party,*" Leej went on, "*so we could learn what was happening without endangering the entire tribe. But the elders were determined we all go.*"

"How were they behaving?" Sarah asked.

"*Not themselves,*" Leej replied. "*And I wasn't the only one who thought this. Our tribe set out the following night. I could feel the poison of the evil city. It was spreading like blood through water. But it only seemed to drive everyone on. Partway there, we were met by a group of armed hunters from another tribe. They had been to Meong Kal, they said. The old city was being restored. They had come to escort us, so we could see the marvel for ourselves. But first they had to determine our worthiness."*

"Ooh, this does not sound good," Yoofi said.

"Yeah, that's when I'd be saying, 'See ya,'" Rusty put in.

Both had become engrossed in the story, but I was still keeping a critical distance.

"The hunters went down our line, looking at each member closely. My brother was standing near the front. Like me, he'd had doubts about traveling to Meong Kal. A hunter asked him a question I could not hear. When my brother answered, the hunter drove a blade through his chest. No one in our tribe reacted. Something was wrong. I got the attention of several others like me, and we slid to the back of the line. As another member of our tribe was being driven through with a blade, we stole away. The tribe continued without us. That was the last I saw them. We hid for many nights, but the hunters found us. And each time there were more of them. After a time, I was the only one left."

So far, his story was adding up, but my captain's mind was telling me to stay wary.

I waved the smoke from my chest and held the stone amulet toward him.

"Does this mean anything to you?"

His reptilian eyes moved over the image of the serpent. *"It is an idol to Akeila. They were made when Meong Kal was a city. I found one in the river when I was young. I took it to an elder, and she cleansed the amulet of its evil. When she finished, she smashed it between two stones."*

"We've cleansed these too," I said. "Do you know what they're for?"

"The elders say wicked things can still be invoked in Akeila's name, with or without the wearer's knowledge." I thought about Cleric Dao and the acolytes and how the amulets had been used on them. As Leej looked from the amulet to the five of us, I

wondered whether he was as uncertain of us now as we were of him.

"Your elders can cast magic?" Yoofi asked.

"They can dispel magic," he replied, *"but not cast it."*

It didn't sound as if an elder was the magic-user, then.

"How many of your kind live in the jungle?" I asked.

"Before this, more than four hundred."

Damn. That was going to mean a lot of hostiles.

"You told us you were staying on the edges of the jungle," Sarah said. "Did you ever see the hunters make incursions into the towns?"

"I watched them enter Ban Mau. They did not stay long. I don't think they like to be outside the influence of Meong Kal. That is why I found it safest on the outsides of the jungle. Maybe it weakens them."

Or it weakens Akeila's influence over them, I thought. That had probably been the point of the amulets—to extend the serpent goddess's influence to the temple and, ultimately, to the entire town.

"The exodus of Ban Mau began not long after," Leej said. *"The hunters met the people in the jungle and led the way to Meong Kal. I followed, trying to understand what was happening. It was much like the night my own tribe set out for the city. Most went willingly. Those who turned back were killed, but there weren't many."*

I thought of the girl whose journal we'd found. I prayed to God she wasn't among the killed.

Takara gestured to the encampment. "How did you meet this group?" she asked, suspicion still edging her voice.

"They arrived in flying machines. They stayed in the same place as you."

"The building on the edge of the jungle?" I asked.

"Yes."

It sounded like Prince Ken *had* hired a team before ours.

"I watched them for a night," he said. *"They saw me, somehow,*

and captured me before I could get away." He trained his eyes on the translator. *"They had this thing you hold, and I was able to talk to them. After asking many questions, they said they were looking for the missing people of Ban Mau. I warned them about the danger of Meong Kal, but they insisted on going. They asked me to guide them. The men moved quietly. They wore special masks they said would protect them from the evil. We arrived here at the end of the first day, but something happened at night. The men began to argue and fight one another. They used their weapons. I grabbed this and hid."* He looked down at his coat. *"The snake hunters came later and took their bodies and weapons."*

"Did the men say who they were?" I asked.

"They said little to me," Leej replied. *"They spoke of rescuing the people of Ban Mau as their* mission. *They used this word often.* Mission."

"What else can you tell us?" Sarah asked.

"That if you go straight to Meong Kal, you will end up like them."

"We have protection," she said.

"So did they."

Leej had a good point, but it sounded as if their protection had been technical instead of magical. "We have a mission too," I said. "And it's not just to rescue the people of Ban Mau. One of our teammates is out there."

"I watched the hunters take him."

Yoofi and Rusty murmured in surprise.

"They didn't kill him?" I asked. "Like the others?"

"No. He went willingly."

I released my pent-up breath.

"But the poison of Akeila is only one challenge," he said. *"The patrols around Meong Kal are heavy. I tried to get close but could not. And the ones who defend Meong Kal are not like the hunters who patrol the jungle or the ones who attacked your building. They are bigger, with more arms."*

"You mean weapons?" Rusty asked.

"No, arms. Parts of the body. With them, they can handle more weapons."

Rusty looked around. "Anyone else confused?"

"How close can you get us?" I asked Leej.

Takara shot me a dark look. She still didn't trust him.

"Overland, not very close," he replied. *"They watch from everywhere, even the trees. But there are many tunnels in the jungle. The ones to Meong Kal were buried following the great battle. Not all of them, though. When I was a boy, I found one. It was beside a river, the entrance overhung with roots. When I stepped inside, I could smell the evil. The tunnel is still there. I went back after seeing the defenses around Meong Kal, but the evil is stronger than ever now. I could not bring myself to enter."*

"Sounds like the perfect place for an ambush," Takara said.

Leej listened to the translation. *"I cannot guarantee that there are not guards within,"* he said, missing her cynicism.

"We can assess it when we get there," I said.

Takara narrowed her eyes at me. "He's not leading us anywhere."

I signaled for Sarah to turn off the translator. "You wanted me to listen to my instincts?" I asked Takara in a lowered voice. "That's what I'm doing. His account lines up with what we know. It also explains why the tablet's translator was set to Hung. If he *can* show us how to get into Meong Kal without attracting the entire snake army, we need to explore that option."

"I agree," Sarah said.

Takara scowled and stepped away.

I turned back to Leej. "Can you lead the way?"

His snake face showed no emotion as he hissed out a response.

"If you unbind me, yes."

18

I removed Leej from the tree and refastened his wrists behind his low back.

"Until we know we can trust each other," I said.

As the handheld in my vest made the Hung translation, I expected him to argue, but Leej accepted the terms with a nod. With one hand gripping the band of his cuffs, I motioned him forward and followed. He slid easily on his serpentine tail. Sarah, Yoofi, and Rusty trailed at close intervals while Takara watched our six.

Our guide quickly established his knowledge of the jungle, leading us through seams in the dense growth that allowed us to progress in relative silence. My trust only went so far, though. In addition to keeping him cuffed, I watched my compass. Our course wound like a snake, often going the wrong direction— which prompted radio calls from Takara—but Leej always got us back on track. And we were making better time than the day before.

At mid-morning, I heard flowing water. Leej hissed something and jutted his face forward.

"The tunnel is on the other side of the river," the handheld translated.

I pushed aside a branch with my weapon. Ahead, a broad river churned past.

"We should cross here," Leej said.

"Potential danger area," I radioed. "Sarah and I will take lead."

As Sarah made her way to the front of the line, Rusty and Yoofi moved out along the riverbank. I dropped down the bank with Leej and waded in. The riverbed was soft and spongy. Muddy brown water broke around the calves of my suit, but by virtue of his tail, Leej remained on the surface.

By mid-river, the dark water had climbed to my knees. Sarah came up beside me, the water to her waist. We swept the surroundings with our weapons as we moved. The jungle on the far bank was especially dark, and I searched the seams half expecting to find snake creatures, but we were alone.

When we emerged, I radioed for Rusty and Yoofi to follow. I maintained a solid grip around Leej's cuffs while noting the way his reptilian eyes scanned the trees. Was he searching for danger? Aid?

I couldn't know, and that was the essential problem.

Sarah and I covered our teammates' crossing, me one-handing my MP88. Takara watched from the opposite bank. Rusty eyed the water climbing his legs while Yoofi tried to hold up the hem of his coat to keep his spell implements dry.

Rusty stopped. "The heck was that?"

"What was what?" Yoofi asked, dropping his coat and peering down now.

"Something big just touched me. Damn—there it was again!"

"Quiet," I hissed.

Rusty ignored me and began splashing in high steps to reach

our side. Yoofi followed his lead. Aside from looking ludicrous, they were making a hell of a racket. I moved my barrels over the water anyway.

Then, as if someone had jerked a rug out from under them, Rusty's and Yoofi's legs flew up, and they crashed ass-first into the water. Brown pods the size of basketballs surfaced around their thrashing.

The fuck?

Leej said something, but I was already taking aim at the nearest pod. I lost the translation beneath the ensuing cracks of gunfire. The pod exploded in a gout of black goo. More pods popped like giant pustules as Takara and Sarah took shots. But Rusty and Yoofi remained underwater, as if something was holding them there. Leej braced against me when I tried to lunge in. He spoke quickly.

"It will ensnare you too," the translator said.

"What is that thing?" I asked, picking off another pod.

"A river feeder. They trap and absorb their victims. They cannot be defeated with force, but there is another way. Release me."

What looked like a massive flap of rubber peeled up from the far side of the river, its surface covered with more pods. It was what I'd felt underfoot when I'd stepped into the river. Our crossing must have agitated the thing.

The flap rose and doubled over, pushing a large wave out in front of it. The creature meant to envelop our teammates, sealing them inside its body.

I opened fire, ripping a line across the giant flap. More black pus exploded, but the river feeder didn't stop. Rusty surfaced long enough to let out a choked scream before the flap landed on top of him and Yoofi.

"Release me," Leej repeated.

I undid the cuffs and followed him toward the river, but he shoved me back with surprising strength. He slid into the water head first, his coat billowing out behind him until that too sank under the thrashing water.

Sarah, Takara, and I kept our weapons trained on the river.

"He led us here," Takara said. "He knew that thing was waiting."

I watched the water tensely. Suddenly, the river feeder surfaced. Its grotesque body gave several shudders and went still. The current carried it downriver like a deflated raft.

Leej emerged a moment later, dragging Rusty and Yoofi by the handles of their tactical vests. Our teammates were both awake, gagging and coughing up river water. By some miracle, they'd retained their weapons.

Sarah went to Yoofi, and I knelt beside Rusty.

"Hey, man, you all right?" I asked, sitting him up.

Rusty's face was covered in red welts, probably where the thing's digestive pods had attached to him. He coughed for several more seconds, then spit and wiped his mouth with the back of a hand.

"That frigging sucked."

I turned around and looked at Yoofi, who was sitting up now too.

"His vitals are normal," Sarah said, removing a probe from his ear.

"Ooh, I never want to see the inside of that thing again."

"But you're okay?" I asked.

"Yes, Mr. Wolfe."

"Good, because our protective magic is thinning."

Yoofi's eyes popped wide. He thrust himself to his feet with his staff and chanted until fresh smoke issued from our amulets. I waved Takara over, watching the water as she flew across. The episode made me realize just how vulnerable we were this deep in the jungle, even with established exfil points. If we had lost

Yoofi, how long would it have taken before we started using each other for target practice?

I turned to Leej. "How did you free them?"

"I bit it," he replied. *"The river feeders are susceptible to our poison."*

Before I could thank him, Takara cut in. "And you didn't know it was there when we crossed?"

"His tail never touched bottom," I answered for him, recalling the way he had glided across the water's surface. "He wouldn't have felt it."

"We were lucky," Leej said. *"It fed recently so was slower than it would have been."*

"Yeah, real lucky," Rusty muttered as he struggled to his feet.

He cleaned the muck off his sleeves, then checked his weapons. The Centurion versions of the M4 and SIG were waterproof. Ditto their mags. But we were less than a mile from Meong Kal. If it was as heavily guarded as Leej claimed, the sound of shooting had certainly reached the patrols, meaning a group would be on their way. We needed to move.

Seeming to sense my urgency, Leej pointed upriver.

"The tunnel is around that bend."

"Let's go," I said.

Sarah capped a vial of river water, no doubt hoping it contained a biological sample of the river feeder. Takara retrieved the cuffs I'd dropped on the ground and tossed them to me. But instead of putting them back on Leej, I returned them to my pack. That drew a scowl from Takara. But if he'd meant to hurt us, he could have left Yoofi and Rusty in the river, cutting our force by forty percent. And without Yoofi's protection, the rest of us would have been compromised by the poison magic.

As far as I was concerned, Leej had proven himself.

"Take lead," I told him, lifting my MP88 into both hands.

He slithered along the riverbank. As I fell in behind him, I shot Takara a look that said this was no longer up for discussion. We followed the bank until a deadfall forced us from the river and into the jungle.

"The entrance is on the other side," Leej said. *"Wait here."*

I called a halt and watched Leej slide past the deadfall and down the riverbank to scout the tunnel site. The rest of us covered the jungle in sectors. Something large and batlike flapped overhead, but it wasn't like any bat I'd ever seen. I tracked the leathery creature with my barrel until it was out of sight. As the episode at the river had taught us, it wasn't just snake people and poison magic we had to worry about.

A sharp hiss sounded from the river.

I swung my weapon around as Leej reappeared. He said something quickly.

"There's a large force coming up the tunnel," the handheld translated. *"We must leave."*

I could hear the hisses and slithering now too.

"Lead the way," I said.

He slid back around the deadfall. The rest of us followed in formation, jogging to keep up. After about a quarter mile, Leej pulled up suddenly.

"More hunters ahead," the device translated for him.

"You want me to believe he didn't plan this?" Takara said.

I ignored her and addressed Leej. "If we can't evade them, we'll need to fight. Any open areas we can draw them into?"

He waved for us to follow and took off north. Arrows began whistling past.

"Helmets secured," I radioed the team. "Masks on. Face shields down. Nothing exposed."

An arrow struck Leej's coat and caromed off. Gunfire chattered from Takara's rifle. She was running sideways, firing into the trees at our backs. Ahead, the jungle opened beside a waterfall, and tall trees rose over a floor of ferns. The waterfall crashed down a hillside ten meters high before flowing away in pools.

We can back up to the hill, use the trees as cover.

"Sarah and Takara, up front with me," I called. "Yoofi, keep behind us. Focus on the protective magic. Rusty, watch the hill for anything coming down."

"Roger that, boss."

"What happened to your friend?" Takara asked.

I glanced around, but Leej had disappeared. There was no time to worry about him. As I took my position, arrows were already thunking from my helmet and suit, sending up small sprays of venom. The protective wear did its job, though, and I raked their numbers with auto fire. Even at close range, the creatures were difficult to track, but we were dropping them now.

I paused to change mags.

"They're coming in," Takara radioed.

By the time I lifted my weapon again, five of the large, multi-armed creatures Leej had described emerged from the tree cover opposite us. Grotesque snake heads sat on cloaked human torsos with broad chests and thickly muscled arms. Below their bellies, their bodies morphed into snake tails like Leej's. In their many hands, the creatures wielded spears and an assortment of blades.

I hit the lead with a burst of gunfire that should have cut him in half. But though the exploding rounds knocked him backwards, they didn't even leave singe marks. Energy shimmered around him.

As Takara and Sarah engaged the others, I saw that they were protected too, like the Oni in Massachusetts. But unlike the Oni's protection, our sustained fire didn't seem to weaken it—meaning their protection was immune to salt, silver, and iron.

The lead snake creature heaved a spear. I ducked behind a tree, but not far enough. The stone blade nailed my shoulder, opening a deep bruise. These jokers were strong. Armored or not, my teammates were going to start feeling the effects of the impacts. With my bruise already healing, I stepped forward to draw the assault from the others and radioed Yoofi.

"They're wrapped in a magical defense," I said. "Can you take it down?"

"I will try, Mr. Wolfe."

In the meantime, if I can't hurt them...

I switched to my weapon's flamethrower and sent a jet of napalm into the face of the one who'd thrown the spear.

...I'll blind them.

Fire erupted over his snake head and dripped down his body. He released a withering hiss and wiped at the jelly, which only succeeded in spreading the fire to two of his four hands. I hit the others until their heads were engulfed too.

While Sarah kept steady gunfire on them, Takara took aim at their weapons. Spears fractured in their clawed grips, and blades broke from hilts. With arrows still zipping in, I sent a volley of grenade rounds into the trees behind them. As the concatenation of thuds went off, I radioed Yoofi again.

"How we doing?"

"They are protected by a concentrated form of the bad magic. Do you see?"

A wave of Yoofi's energy rippled past, and the clearing glittered with random sparkles. The effect gathered around the creatures, revealing what looked like scale armor. The glitter seemed to swirl from whatever secured the cloaks at their throats.

"What's at their necks?" I asked.

"Yes, Mr. Wolfe!" Yoofi exclaimed. *"That is where the magic is coming from!"*

I took aim at the snake creature closest to me, zeroing in on what turned out to be a stone brooch. Like a mini hurricane, the force around the brooch featured a small eye. I steadied on the eye and squeezed. The rifle round hit dead center but flashed off it. Damn. I sent another volley of grenade rounds into the trees to keep the shooters back, then dropped my MP88 on its sling.

Time to get my hands dirty.

"They're wearing protection," I radioed. "When I disarm them, take them down."

"Roger that," Sarah and Takara answered in unison.

I bounded toward the nearest snake creature. He had managed to hold on to one of his blades, a nasty crescent of black metal. Squinting through the flames guttering over his face, he swung the blade at me. The blow glanced off the top of my helmet as I ducked and cut behind him. Hooking my talons into the back of his cloak, I pulled. The force yanked the massive creature to the ground, but the stone held.

His tail thrashed as he tried to push himself upright, but in the next instant I was on top of him, slamming my fists into his head. The magical armor shimmered, absorbing the blows—but the concussions were getting through. With his brain rattling inside his reptilian skull, his efforts to claw me weakened.

I dug my talons beneath the stone and yanked. The damned thing still wouldn't give. But I noticed something: the magic coming off my amulet was disorganizing the hurricane-like rotation around the creature's brooch.

"Up my protection!" I shouted to Yoofi.

A moment later, more magic puffed from my amulet. When I yanked this time, the cloak tore away. The scale-like armor disappeared from around the snake creature. He clawed for the brooch, but I threw it out of his reach.

His jaw yawned wide, revealing a deadly set of fangs.

"Sorry, pal," I grunted, bringing my forearm against his throat and unsheathing my knife. "I know you're not yourself."

The creature hissed and strained against me, poison dripping from his fangs.

I plunged the blade into his ear hole and gave it a violent twist. His body spasmed once, then fell still. I drew out the blade, shoved myself off him, and went in for the next creature. This one was advancing on Sarah, a hood of flames still covering his head.

Sarah stopped firing as I eased up behind him. With Yoofi's magic billowing around me now, I tore the creature's cloak away easily. He wheeled, raking me with two sets of claws, neither one penetrating my vest.

"Engage!" I shouted, throwing myself flat.

Gunfire ripped open his back. As the creature's body thudded to the ground, I peered past him. Sarah switched her aim to the other creatures, joining Takara's field of fire. Despite my instructions to watch the hill, Rusty had joined in too, the muzzle of his weapon flashing hot. I glanced up the steep wall of foliage beside the waterfall.

Dammit, movement.

A group had worked its way above us, and they were wielding large stones. I fired a stream of grenade rounds into their midst. The explosions knocked them around. Like the shooters, they didn't seem to be wearing the same protection as the multi-armed snake creatures. They managed to hurl several stones anyway. The stones plummeted toward Rusty and Yoofi, neither one aware of the danger.

"Move!" I shouted, waving them from the hill. "Incoming!"

Rusty looked up, mouthed a four-letter word, and flung himself out of the way. A stone the size of a home vault impacted where he'd been standing. More boulders thudded around him. Ten meters away, Yoofi remained engrossed in his chanting.

"Yoofi!" I shouted, firing more grenade rounds into the trees. That softened the bombardment, but didn't stop it. Dropping my weapon onto its sling, I bounded toward my teammate, breaking through the fog issuing from his staff.

A moment before I reached him, a large stone smacked into the side of his helmet, grazed his left shoulder, and thudded to the ground. Yoofi's eyes rolled up to reveal their whites as his legs collapsed.

I caught him and lowered him to the ground.

Off to the left, Rusty gained his feet and raked the trees above us with gunfire.

"Yoofi." I gave his good shoulder a shake.

"There are more coming," Takara radioed.

I craned my neck around. Another unit must have arrived, because at least ten more of the multi-armed creatures were charging into the clearing, brandishing blades and hurling spears. One of the spears struck my back, and I winced from the blow. The creatures were wearing the same stone-fastened cloaks as the others, but I was more disturbed by the thinning smoke coming from our own stone protections.

"Yoofi," I said, giving him another shake.

He was unresponsive, out like a light. He didn't even moan. Without Yoofi's protection, we would be at the mercy of the poison zone. When I swallowed, a small barb pricked the back of my throat.

"Get behind me," I ordered my teammates. "Hit anything in the trees that moves."

I slid Yoofi's staff through his tactical belt and threw him over a shoulder. As my teammates scrambled past, I hefted my MP88 one-handed and hosed the newcomers with napalm. I looked around for Leej, hoping he'd taken refuge nearby and could lead us out, but he was nowhere to be seen.

"Takara, take lead!" I shouted.

"Where are we going?" she asked between bursts of gunfire.

We had two choices: retreat ten miles to the exfiltration

point, or press on the last mile to the city and try to hold off our attackers long enough to signal and land a helo. And the second was assuming there weren't a few hundred more hostiles in the city. Arrows whistled past and thunked into trees, while more boulders crashed down behind us.

Shit.

"Back the way we came," I called.

19

Takara moved as fast as the jungle would allow, her right blade slashing through the tangles of growth, but she didn't know the terrain like Leej. Arrows began coming in from the sides. Rusty staggered as one deflected from his hip. With the number of shots he'd already taken, I imagined his body covered in welts.

Sarah steadied him and took a couple of arrows to the ribs in the process, causing her to grit her teeth. I used the pause in our progress to switch mags and rip the trees on both sides with automatic fire.

Behind us, the large snake creatures slithered in pursuit, heads flickering like torches from my flamethrower attack. The lead one hurled a spear blindly. I timed it, bashing it aside with my weapon's barrel.

"A group's circling ahead," Takara radioed. *"They're trying to surround us."*

I swore. With Yoofi's magic fading, we were going to exhaust our ammo just keeping the hostiles off. And that wasn't taking into account the effects of the poison zone, which had already wiped out at least one spec ops team.

Need to find refuge for Yoofi to recover…

When something appeared through the foliage to my left, I swung my barrel around.

It was Leej, showing his hands. He hissed something and waved for me to follow.

"This way!" I radioed the team.

I ducked into the foliage behind Leej's shifting coat. With our line inverted, Takara fell to the rear position. Her weapon chattered as she covered our escape. With the snake creatures circling ahead, they'd left an opening on our flank. I ducked and weaved through the jungle growth, trying to keep up with Leej, who slithered ahead. Yoofi's legs flopped against my back, telling me he was still out.

Our guide rounded a hillock covered in dense growth, then seemed to disappear inside it. I slowed until I spotted his glowing yellow eyes. He had entered where a cave opened into the hillock and was holding the foliage aside.

I waved Rusty, Sarah, and Takara inside, then handed Yoofi through. Leaves and branches scraped my helmet as I ducked into the cave myself. Leej arranged the foliage so we were screened from the outside. He pushed his hands toward the ground, the universal gesture for *stay low, keep quiet.*

I hunkered in the refuge, MP88 slick in my grip. Takara and Rusty were opposite me, Rusty's wincing face dripping sweat inside his helmet. He gave me a look that said he'd rather be anywhere than here.

Deeper in the cave, Sarah knelt beside Yoofi, who was flat on his back.

Leej sank low on his tail as brush began breaking outside. Through the seams, I saw the snake creatures moving past. More units must have joined them, because they had grown to the size of a small army. They communicated back and forth in sharp hisses. I kept my barrel trained on them. Though a few of them slowed, none stopped. After several long moments, their slithering and hissing faded away.

I signaled to Takara and Rusty to keep watch while I moved to the back. I found Sarah holding Yoofi's left eyelid open and passing her flashlight over the pupil. She repeated the procedure on the right.

"How is he?" I whispered.

"He's passed the neuro field test, but he's badly concussed."

"How long will he be out?"

"Hard to say." She swapped the light for a hypodermic needle, uncapped it, and inserted the tip into a vein on the back of his hand. He didn't respond to the puncture. "Could be minutes or hours," she said, depressing the plunger. "And it will be at least another day before he'll be able to concentrate enough to cast."

I swallowed again to test my throat. The barb was sharper.

"I thought the amulets wouldn't require constant input from Yoofi."

"If he were just sleeping that would be one thing," Sarah replied. "But he's injured on top of being unconscious, and the magic he's instilled in these is returning in an effort to restore him. Magic and their casters have a symbiotic relationship."

"Well, we're on fumes." I tapped my temple. "How are you feeling?"

She replaced the needle in her bag. "Before we broke camp this morning, I tested my blood. The poison in the zone might be energetic, but it still triggered an antibody response in my system. That suggests our antivenom might be effective against it. It won't be the same as having Yoofi's magic, but it could buy us time."

I noticed she hadn't answered my question.

"Enough to get us to the exfil point?" I asked.

"I won't know until I've injected everyone."

But my captain's mind was already planning ahead. With a lift back to base, we could resupply and give Yoofi time to heal. Centurion could drop us back in tomorrow. The decision I needed to make between now and then was whether to risk a drop into the lost city itself. Every minute we delayed lessened our chances of recovering Olaf.

While Sarah began preparing our injections, I waved Leej over. "We need to reach a place where our team can pick us up in a flying machine," I said. "Can we ask you to lead us again?"

"I can get you there," the device translated for him.

"Why did you disappear earlier?" Takara demanded.

"I agreed to lead you," Leej replied. *"Not fight against my own."*

"Give him a break," Rusty said. "He got us here, didn't he?"

"He also failed to warn us about the monster in the river that nearly ate you," Takara snapped back. "Did you forget about that?"

Irritation flared hot in my head. "Guys, that's enough."

"No, I didn't *forget*," Rusty argued over me. "I also didn't forget that he saved my butt."

Takara jabbed a finger at his face. "Yes, after we'd expended gunfire that attracted the snake creatures. And if that wasn't enough, he led us right to another unit before he conveniently disappeared."

"Yeah, like you've never disappeared mid battle," Rusty said. "Isn't that how you ended up in that freaking worm hole in Mexico?"

Heat pulsed from Takara's body. I moved between her and Rusty a split second before she lunged at him. She had actually extended her blades. Rusty was slow to react, but brought up his M4 to meet her. I kept Takara off him with an elbow while knocking the weapon out of Rusty's hands.

"What in the hell's wrong with you two?"

The irritation I'd felt a moment before erupted into a rage

that wreathed my brain in flames. I seized Rusty by the throat, a savage part of me wanting to crush his windpipe. When Takara tried to struggle past my other arm, I slammed her against the wall. Her eyes flared bright red, causing Leej to slither backwards.

"Oh, your dragon wants a piece of this?" I asked Takara. "Tell her to bring it."

Something sharp pricked the side of my neck. Cold fluid streamed into my vessels, icing my rage. I turned my head to find Sarah retracting a needle. The anti-venom. "The poisonous energy is getting to us," she said.

I looked at Takara and Rusty, who were still struggling to get at one another.

Damn. The effects had come on so quickly, I'd barely noticed the change.

"Leej," I said. "Can you hold him?"

When my request translated, Leej wrapped Rusty's body with his tail and pinned his arms.

"Hey!" Rusty shouted as he struggled. "I was sticking up for you, you damned belly-crawler!"

With Rusty restrained, I pinned Takara so Sarah could get an injection into her. Takara panted and writhed, her eyes glowing inches from mine. Hot, preternatural energy crackled through her body. For a moment, I saw the specter of her dragon form. If it emerged here, we were going to be in deep shit. But slowly the fire waned from her eyes. Soon I was looking into a black pair of irises again.

She nodded. "I'm all right."

I eased my weight off her. "You sure?"

She nodded again, scooted against the wall, and went into her breathing practice.

I turned as Sarah finished injecting Rusty. When he stopped struggling, I signaled for Leej to release him. As his tail uncoiled from around Rusty's legs, my teammate craned his neck to face him.

"Hey," he said, "sorry about calling you a belly-crawler."

"I doubt it translated," I said. "You feeling yourself again?"

"Yeah but, dude…" He shook his head. "Don't know what in the hell got into me. One second I was telling Takara to back off, and the next, it was like I was in the lead-up to an MMA event. I was so amped, I couldn't see straight."

"One of the effects of the zone," I said, thinking about the spec-ops encampment. "We need to move."

"Is it safe out there?" Sarah asked.

"No, but we're not much safer in here." I nodded at her line of needles. "How many doses?"

"Three each. I won't know how long they'll last until someone has another episode," she added ominously.

I checked my watch and turned to Leej. After describing the location of the clearing, close to the river and midway between our base and our current location, I asked if he could get us there before nightfall.

"It will depend on the patrols," he answered.

Even through the translator he sounded doubtful. According to Yoofi, the entity responsible for the poison zone and possessions knew we were here. And following our battle, the snake people would be combing the jungle for us, which meant a high likelihood of another encounter. But what was the alternative?

I began pulling fresh mags from my pack and restocking my vest.

Leej spoke. *"There is another group in the jungle."*

I looked up. "What do you mean, 'another group'?"

"They are outsiders like you. Human, I believe, but they do not move like humans. They are silent. I followed them several nights ago but lost them in the deeper jungle. That has never happened. I

assumed they had perished, but when I was leading you today, I saw one of them near the river.

Takara straightened. "And you didn't say anything?"

"The human did not act in a threatening way, and he disappeared again."

Sensing why Leej was mentioning their presence now, I turned to Takara and Sarah. "Attempting to liaison with them might be a better option than a day's journey to the exfil point."

Takara shook her head. "We have no idea who they are."

"My guess is another spec-ops group," I said. "If they were hostile, they would have engaged us."

"We weren't vulnerable then like we are now," she said.

"But if they've been here for days, they probably have protection against the poison zone."

"Captain Wolfe is right," Sarah spoke up. "I don't know how long the anti-venom is going to be effective. It could be hours or minutes, and the duration will vary by team member."

"Leej saw them near the river," I said. "That's not far from here."

"How many were there?" Takara asked Leej, who appeared to be following the translated conversation.

"Eight."

"What did they look like?"

"They wore all black, like the jungle at night."

"Same as the men you guided?" I asked. "Armored suits and vests?"

"No, these were suits of cloth."

I turned to Takara. "The *bushi*?"

"Maybe," she answered.

"Will they help us?" I asked.

She looked away. "It is part of their code."

The fear from the day before was back in her voice.

"Look," I said to her, "if there's a reason we shouldn't seek their help, you need to tell us. Because it's either that or risk a journey to the extraction point, and there are no guarantees with the second."

Takara's gaze fell to Yoofi's unconscious face before glancing around at the rest of us. "Then we'll go to them."

"All right," I said firmly. "If we can't find them, we'll continue to the clearing. Calorie up and hydrate now, because it's going to be a straight march." I pulled more mags from my pack and handed them around.

One way or another, we were going to get out of this.

20

We slipped from the cave, and Leej led us along a different route back to the river we'd crossed earlier. This time I had Takara fly Sarah, Rusty, and then Yoofi across. Leej slithered over the dark water while I cleared the span between banks with a leap. The last thing we needed was an encounter with another river feeder.

On the far side we continued our trek south. We hadn't gone far when Leej stopped and hissed. I'd turned down the hand-held's volume for the sake of stealth, but my preternatural hearing picked up the translation.

"I saw the human over there."

I followed Leej's reptilian eyes to a dense thicket of growth. After switching on my holographic head, I signaled for Takara to check it out. The rest of us covered the surrounding trees while she crept around the area, studying the ground and foliage for signs.

When she returned, she shook her head.

"No traces, which isn't a surprise," she whispered. "It's how they're trained to move."

"So what do we do?" Rusty asked. "Bawl out, 'Is anyone home?'"

I scanned the jungle again. Even though I couldn't see or smell anything, my wolf's instincts told me we were being watched. By friend or foe, I couldn't say. Given our situation—Yoofi unconscious and the rest of us susceptible to the poison zone—I decided we could risk some noise.

"Can you make our introduction?" I asked Takara.

She hesitated before nodding in what appeared a kind of resignation.

She called out a phrase in Japanese, the words tight and clipped, then followed it with another.

When she finished, we listened. Mosquitos whined around our helmets in thick clouds, Yoofi's magic no longer deterring them. Rusty swore and waved a hand through his cloud only for it to grow larger.

After a minute, Takara tried again.

"If they can hear me, they're not answering," she said at last.

"All right, then we need to move." I hiked Yoofi up my shoulder.

"Captain," Sarah said. "I'm going to need to inject again."

"You're feeling the poison?"

She nodded and drew a needle from a compartment in her tactical belt. "How are the rest of you?"

I swallowed. The bite was still there, but my thoughts remained clear. Rusty and Takara grunted that they were fine. I peered closely into their eyes to be sure. The faintest color of diluted iodine was forming in Rusty's.

"He needs one too," I said.

Rusty cocked his head. "The hell I do!"

"Stop and listen to yourself," I said.

He'd puffed out his chest, but now he stopped, eyes cutting

to the side. A moment later, he dropped into a slouch. "Holy hell, that fast? Sarah shot us up just twenty minutes ago."

I exhaled through my nose in frustration. Unless Takara and I proved unusually resilient, we weren't going to have enough anti-venom to last the journey. Sarah injected Rusty, then herself, and hoisted her weapon again.

"Let's go," she said.

Leej spoke. *"When the hunters do not find us, they will guess we are trying to return to your base. They will position themselves along the most direct route. I can lead you another way to the clearing, but it will take longer."*

"Thanks for the warning," I said, "but we don't have longer."

"Then we will need to stay ahead of them. They will use the tunnels."

"Can we avoid those?"

"The tunnels are everywhere," he said.

"Talk about home field advantage," Rusty muttered.

Taking a final look around, I signaled for Leej to lead.

We'd only been moving for a few minutes when the canopy shook. I heaved my weapon up as snake creatures began dropping from the branches. Leej had been right, dammit. They'd set up an ambush along our route. And these were the cloak-wearing snake creatures, the ones protected by the power of Akeila.

They landed on coiled tails and advanced with long blades and spears. Others began firing arrows from the thick growth.

I unleashed a roaring torrent of napalm, igniting the multi-armed creatures as well as stands of trees. Rusty's and Sarah's weapons sent rounds exploding against the creature's protection while Takara fired to keep the shooters back. With another roar, my flamethrower lit up two more of the multi-armed creatures.

When I paused to adjust Yoofi's body over my shoulder, I noticed Leej beside me. He stood in a crouch, arms out to the sides, head rotating between us and the snake creatures. I could tell he wanted out of there, but there was nowhere to go. His kinsmen were coming at us from all sides through the trees.

A spear caught Rusty in the stomach. He doubled over onto his hands and knees. Another spear banged against the side of Sarah's helmet, sending her into a stagger. When she resumed shooting her aim was off.

"Keep your fire on the outer ranks!" I shouted to Takara.

If she could thin the shooters while I took down the big snake creatures, we might get out of this mess. Leej surprised me by helping Yoofi to the ground, where he covered his body with his own. I dropped my pack beside them for additional cover.

But with only Sarah's errant fire to keep the snake creatures back, they closed quickly. I charged the first one and landed a punch against his flame-wreathed head. His upper body rocked back like it was on a spring. When it came forward again, I drove a boot into his stomach. The blow launched him into the trees.

I rounded on the next snake creature only to find someone targeting him too.

Lithe and dressed in black, the newcomer slipped through the trees behind him like quicksilver. I knew immediately I was observing a samurai, a female one. She circled the snake creature's tail and withdrew just as quickly as she'd arrived. A force jerked the creature to the ground and began pulling him across the jungle floor.

She tied a wire around him.

Her partner, another samurai, tugged the creature toward a tree where he had been crouched. *Now what?* I thought. *The creatures are too well protected.*

The answer came a moment later when a giant samurai with a metal helmet and mask stepped from the trees. He drew one of two katana swords from his belt and raised the long blade overhead. Fire erupted along its length. He brought the sword down, smashing through the snake creature's protective magic, sending its head rolling from its jerking body.

I spun and grappled with another snake creature. I could see more samurai arriving in my peripheral vision. One by one, the remaining creatures, including the one I was trading blows with, crashed to the ground and were dragged to their decapitation. Takara's gunfire had forced the shooters to take cover, but if we'd learned anything at the waterfall, it was that reinforcements would be on the way.

The large samurai sheathed his katana and called to Takara in a barking voice.

"He's telling us to follow them," she said, a bitter bite in her own tone.

He ran into the trees with surprising stealth, and the other samurai slipped after him.

I donned my pack quickly. Leej rose from the ground and helped Yoofi back onto my shoulder.

I lifted Rusty by an arm. "Can you walk?" I asked him.

He winced with his first step, a hand bracing his stomach where the spear had impacted. "I can probably limp."

"Then limp fast."

We took off after the samurai. After a short distance, they passed between two trees and disappeared from sight. Takara followed and then Sarah. I didn't know what we were stepping into, but I didn't slow. I lifted Rusty and passed him between the trees before stepping through myself.

We were suddenly in a clearing populated with tents. The trees around the periphery shimmered with magic, obviously cloaking us from the outside. The air inside was clean too, no bite of poison.

The samurai stood in a semi-circle, facing us, while the masked one towered over them at their center, his long katana drawn. I leaned toward Takara, who was watching him with narrowed eyes.

"Aren't you going to explain who we are?" I asked.

Leej slithered between the trees at our back and into the camp. The big samurai's gaze shifted from Takara to him. He closed the distance in two swift steps, his katana spewing fire as it arced down. Leej crouched. I stretched an arm out to jerk our guide behind me.

Flames billowed, and the space shook as the samurai's sword collided against Takara's extended blades. She had blocked his attack.

"He is a friend, Kaito," she said.

"But you are not," the samurai snarled.

They know each other?

Their bodies trembled as they braced against their blades, flames licking from the point of contact. Expecting the other six samurai to rush in, I readied my MP88, but they remained where they were. Takara and this Kaito remained at a stalemate, even though the giant samurai hulked over my teammate's lean frame.

"Hey," I barked. "You're messing with a friend."

"This does not concern you," the samurai grunted.

I raised my MP88. "Oh, yeah?"

"Enough," a voice called from the camp.

A tall woman in a dark kimono emerged from one of the tents, her black hair pinned up over a sculpted face. She approached with a strong stride that lacked the samurai's grace. Staring at where Takara and Kaito remained locked together, she spoke sharply in Japanese, accenting the words with a cutting gesture.

A kill command?

But the large samurai scowled through the frown in his mask and shoved himself back from Takara. When the tall woman spoke again, he returned his katana to his belt. Takara waited a moment before sheathing her blades.

I lowered my MP88.

The woman appraised us with deep jade-colored eyes. "Prince Kanoa hired you."

"And Princess Halia hired you," I said. "The only thing that matters is we're on the same side."

Her lips turned up in a dangerous smile. "Are we?"

I wondered now if Takara's assessment about a samurai's obligation to help had been wrong.

"Look, we don't want trouble," I said. "I'm Captain Wolfe. We have an injured teammate and another who's been taken by the snake people. We just need somewhere to safehouse until he's recovered, then we'll head back out."

"Into the poison?" she asked.

"We have defenses against it."

The woman regarded Yoofi's slumped-over form for a moment. The large samurai, Kaito, barked something in Japanese and thrust a hand toward Takara. The woman's reply silenced him, but I could see in his eyes he wasn't placated.

"What are you prepared to give?" the woman asked.

My brow furrowed down. "What do you mean?"

"We have already taken a great risk by exposing ourselves to the *khon ngu*. Until moments ago, they had no knowledge of our presence. We arrived silently, like darkness itself. You might as well have entered on a herd of elephants for the noise you made. It is little wonder you have drawn the ire of the serpent goddess."

I bristled at her condescension.

"You know about Akeila?" Sarah asked.

"I know many things about her," she replied mysteriously. "But I ask again, what are you prepared to give for aid and shelter?"

"Look," I snarled. "Both of our teams are here to rescue the people of Ban Mau and end the threat, right? The fact you've been pinned here tells me the challenge is bigger than your team. What are we prepared to give? Collaboration. Our chances go up if we join forces."

Kaito unleashed an explosion of Japanese, but the woman's gaze remained fixed on mine.

"You have no idea what *pins* us here," she said with a snort. "And as for joining forces, what makes you think you'll be any kind of assistance? You could hardly cross that river earlier, Captain."

I had a teammate missing, another one out of commission, and the rest of us struggling with the effects of the poison zone, and this diva was trying to score snark points? Plus, her comment suggested she'd witnessed our struggle with the river feeder and done nothing to help.

I was about to smart-off back when a familiar scent hit my smell centers. The woman's face wasn't the porcelain white of the photo, and she looked different with her hair pinned up, but the scent didn't lie. It was virtually the same as her brother's.

"You're Princess Halia."

Rusty gawked and whispered, "Well, ho-lee shit."

Sarah accessed her tablet, no doubt to check the image, before remembering we were offline.

"Congratulations," the princess said. "But you still haven't given us a reason to help you."

"I gave you one, and you rejected it," I growled. "How about a counteroffer?"

"Fine." The princess's eyes shifted to Takara. "Her life."

21

I stepped between Princess Halia and Takara.

"What in the hell are you talking about?"

"That's the counteroffer," she said. "Accept it or leave our sanctuary."

Rusty came up beside my right hip, shoulders thrown back. "Takara's *life*? How is that any kind of counteroffer?"

Sarah moved in on my other side so that the three of us formed a barrier in front of our teammate.

"She's committed an unspeakable offense for which the penalty is death," Princess Halia said. "It seems she eluded her fate once, but fate spins an incomprehensible web that few see and even fewer actually escape. It was just a matter of time." She glanced over at Kaito, who was still grasping his long katana.

"What *offense?*" I demanded.

Takara stepped around us. "I accept the offer."

I grasped her arm. "Are you out of your mind?"

She shook me off and strode up to Princess Halia and Kaito. "In exchange for refuge and assistance for my teammates, I give my life."

"T-cakes!" Rusty cried.

I watched her, stunned. Had the poison zone gotten to her?

"But I have my own condition," Takara said.

"And what is that?" the princess asked.

"That I be allowed to complete the mission with my team."

The princess turned to Kaito. They went back and forth in Japanese, Kaito speaking in a harsh bark. Several times, flames licked from his katana. I steeled myself to gun him down. Takara watched the exchange between them stoically.

At last, Halia nodded. "That will be acceptable."

Kaito grunted, sheathed his katana, and strode away. As he disappeared into the largest tent, Princess Halia addressed the other samurai. I tensed when several swarmed toward us, but Takara showed me a staying hand.

"They're taking Yoofi into their care," she explained.

I watched the inscrutable eyes in the samurais' faces as they lifted Yoofi from my shoulder and carried him toward the tents. Sarah looked up at me, brow taut. I signaled for her to go with them.

"Our medic will attend to him too," I said.

Princess Halia nodded and relayed the message to the samurai. As Sarah joined them, I grasped Takara's arm again. This time she didn't shake me off. I walked her to the edge of the encampment, sensing the same resignation I'd felt yesterday.

"You want to tell me what's going on?" My lowered voice was almost a growl.

"It was the only way they would help us."

"For your life? That's a hell of a give, Takara."

"We weren't going to make it out of the jungle otherwise."

"We're not sacrificing you. No way in hell are we sacrificing you."

"I'm honor bound."

"To *what*?" I thundered.

"My clan."

I looked past her at the samurai. "That's your clan?"

"They're a branch of the Sukumis. I belonged to them once."

"Yeah, past tense. And you were what, fourteen, when you left? What offense could you have possibly committed at that age that they'd hold against you eighty years later?"

"There is a lot about me you don't know."

"Look, your past is your business," I said in a lowered voice. "Just tell me this is a bluff."

Takara's gaze slid toward the tents before locking on mine again.

"It's a bluff," she echoed.

But I could see she was only saying what I wanted to hear. She made no effort to disguise it, either. Takara usually wore her expression like a mask, but now I was picking up subtle layers: regret, surrender—sadness, even.

"While your teammate recovers," Princess Halia called, "you're welcome to rest." She strode back to the tent she'd emerged from when we arrived. The remaining samurai took positions outside her tent and around the camp on watch.

"Rusty and I will set up our shelters," Takara said.

"So that's it? You're just going to accept this bullshit offer, no discussion?"

"Your instinct was right. We'll be more effective if you can convince them to join forces."

I followed her nod to Princess Halia's tent. By the time I looked back, Takara had taken the translator and was calling orders to Rusty and Leej. We weren't done, not by a long shot, but she was right. I needed to talk with the princess.

The samurai moved in front of me as I stalked toward her tent. When I didn't slow, they grasped the leather-bound hilts of their katanas. A part of me wanted a fight.

"It's all right," Princess Halia called from inside her tent. "Allow him in."

The samurai stood aside, and I ducked between the tent flaps. The inside of the tent was roomier than it appeared from the outside and largely barren. The princess had taken a seat opposite the opening and was sitting cross-legged on a woven mat, head bowed over a piece of parchment paper. She seemed to be writing on it, but as I moved closer, I saw she was making small strokes with a slender brush, leaving tracks of dark ink. The result was a mostly finished image of a city in a jungle.

I snorted. "I didn't realize the death decree interrupted your arts and crafts time."

"That was between Takara and her clan," she replied, not looking up. "I was merely the arbitrator."

"You seemed to take a pretty active role," I growled.

"Actually, I postponed her sentencing. Kaito was prepared to kill her."

"Fine, if you're the *arbitrator*, I want to work out another deal. One that doesn't involve my teammate's execution."

"I'm afraid it's too late. Takara's word now binds her to the fate."

"Yeah, we'll see about that."

Princess Halia looked up for the first time. Her green eyes sparkled from the dimness as she gazed over my hulking form, MP88 at my side. If she was intimidated, she didn't show it, but I didn't think she was. Though she resembled her brother in many ways, she carried a poise that he'd seemed to lack.

Her gaze found the eyes of my hologram. To appear authentically human, the holographic eyes were more closely aligned than my wolf eyes. Princess Halia watched them for a moment before shifting her gaze slightly inward. A light seemed to come over her face, and the corners of her mouth turned up.

I squinted back at her. Could she see my wolf face?

She pointed with her brush to the mat opposite her. "Have a seat, Captain Wolfe."

I grunted and lowered myself down so I wouldn't have to keep crouching. I set my MP88 beside me, in easy reach. The princess resumed painting. It looked less like she was making art than caressing what she'd already created. Each brush stroke sent up a subtle whisper of energy that put me strangely at ease.

"Is there a reason you've been here for several days?" I asked.

"Are you familiar with Himitsu paintings, Captain Wolfe?"

"No," I replied, having to force brusqueness into my voice. "And I didn't come here for an art lesson."

She continued as if I hadn't spoken. "Himitsu comes from an occult religion in Japan. A powerful belief system many millennia old. So powerful that Emperor Muromachi forbade its practice, had its masters massacred. As is often the case, the most violent leaders also tend to be the most fragile." By the shake of her head, I guessed she was making commentary about her own father. "Those who survived developed a system to communicate, and so was born the Himitsu painting. What appeared as a temple or landscape on the surface concealed information and key teachings. So thorough was the deception that Muromachi himself became an admirer. His palace featured the largest collection of Himitsu paintings in Japan." She laughed and dipped her brush into a small well of ink.

"That's great," I said. "But what does it have to do with anything?"

"The Himitsu paintings are a language, Captain. Several languages, in fact, depending on the power and mastery of the painter. A master does not render a Himitsu painting so much as pose questions. Much can arise from that co-creating: Potent spell work. Lost secrets. Divinations as well as revelations of past events that mirror future ones. Your teammate was trapped in one such mirror event."

I bristled at the reference to Takara, but it made me consider what she had said the night before about destinies.

"To understand what a Himitsu painting is saying," Princess Halia continued, "for it to be *sensical*, one must first take the time to listen."

"And that's what you've been doing for the last few days? Listening?"

"You're a quick study, Captain. Yes, listening for how to proceed."

I watched her stroke the painting. "And what's it saying?"

She gave a soft laugh. "Am I to share, just like that? We're in a tricky place, your group and mine."

"How so?"

"My brother hired you, for starters."

"He said he hired us at your urging."

She snorted. "That doesn't surprise me. It's how Kanoa operates, waiting too long to make a decision, then assigning his choice to others in case it goes bad. That last group he hired, for example. I'm assuming he didn't mention them?"

"Who were they?"

"Private contractors. Big weapons, fancy tech, and no chance. Judging by the state we found you in, your team is only a slight upgrade. I give my brother credit for trying something less conventional, anyway."

Her gaze touched on my wolf eyes again before tilting her head as if to view the painting from a fresh angle.

"Can you forget the painting for a minute?" I said. "Your brother told us that your father commissioned an expedition this past summer to the lost city of Meong Kal. Our guide confirmed that a group helicoptered in, trekked to the ruins, and then disappeared. Do you know anything more about them?"

While I talked, Princess Halia seemed to make a point of continuing to paint.

"My father commissioned the expedition, yes, but at the insistence of Boonsong."

"Who's that?"

"My brother didn't tell you that either?"

"His information was thin," I admitted. "He obtained some coordinates, but that was it."

"Because he tiptoes around anything having to do with our father," she muttered.

"Sounds like he has good reason."

Princess Halia shook her head. "If he wants to live in fear, that's his choice. Boonsong is my uncle. He's also father's spiritual advisor. When I was a girl, he entertained us with little animations, dancing spoons and forks. The magic was impressive, but even then I could tell he used it to hide weakness. Some lack the capacity, Captain. They reach a limit they can never surmount. My uncle was not a bad man, but he hungered for power he couldn't manifest. That will often make a person more dangerous than if they *were* evil."

I'd seen a few examples of those types in my own work.

"Boonsong tried to sate his power hunger by ingratiating himself to my father. Eventually, he looked to other sources. When he learned about the lost city and stories of a powerful goddess, he believed he'd found an opportunity. He convinced my father to fund the expedition, but it was only a means to deliver him to Meong Kal to perform his rites."

"To conjure Akeila?"

"He believed he could channel Akeila's power. Instead, he became her slave and vessel."

Understanding clicked into place. Her uncle was the one who had enspelled the serpent amulets with animating magic. He had probably visited the Ban Mau temple in an official capacity first, to scout the temple and town for the serpent goddess. When he returned with the snake creatures to possess the cleric and acolytes, he took the logbook to hide the record of his earlier visit.

Boonsong was the magic-user at the center of this.

"Now that Akeila has control of him, what's her goal?" I asked.

"A return to the primeval."

"Primeval? How so?"

"Long before humankind, reptilian beings roamed the world. As they developed basic thought, they shrieked into the night sky, calling to superior versions of themselves. That collective worship, muddy and ill-formed though it was, manifested in other planes as sentient identities. With continued worship those identities took form and became gods. With the gods' help, ancient civilizations rose from the swamps to grow, war, prosper. But like all civilizations, they declined. Few traces of them remain today."

"But the gods remained," I said.

Sarah had lectured on theories of occult gods. We had even faced a couple.

"Yes, and without the life-giving force of worship, they could do nothing but watch what was happening in their former domain. The rise and spread of humankind. The draining and cultivation of the swamps. As they watched, they came to hate humankind. But they hated in vain for they had no means to do anything. Many melted back into the ethereal clay from which they'd taken form."

"But I'm guessing Akeila didn't, huh?"

"Those early beings built a massive stone statue to Akeila and placed a gem inside, a heart stone. The heart stone held Akeila's essence. When their civilization collapsed, the statue was buried in the briny mud and preserved. A long time later, after countless rains had fallen and the rivers had changed course many times, the statue surfaced. The heart stone called out weakly. A human tribe answered. They found the statue and came under Akeila's thrall. She twisted their thoughts into fresh worship of her, restoring her power. Over the generations that followed, they built the city around her that would become Meong Kal."

I nodded. "Leej, our guide, told us about that."

"I assume his serpentine features did not escape you?" She raised her eyes to mine briefly. "By an evil alchemy, Akeila merged her human devotees with snakes until they looked like the beings that had once worshipped her."

So Rusty hadn't been too far off, I thought grimly.

"The *khon ngu* weren't already snake people?" I asked.

"No. And to be clear, the *khon ngu* are not inherently evil. After the fall of Meong Kal, the curse that held them spellbound broke. They returned to the jungle, some mixing with the human tribes, and survived the march of millennia."

I'd wondered why some snake people had legs and others tails.

"Is that what she's doing to the people of Ban Mau?" I asked. "Merging them with snakes?"

"If not yet, soon. Most important to Akeila right now is their worship by which she grows stronger by the day."

"A process that began in Ban Mau's temple."

When Princess Halia nodded, I remembered what Takara had said about not sensing the samurai in the town.

"How do you know that?" I challenged.

"The paintings, Captain Wolfe."

Himitsu paintings made about as much sense to me as horoscopes. I was used to investigation protocols, boots on the ground. But if the paintings had the divination properties she claimed, it would explain why she and the samurai had come straight to the jungle. I wondered what else the paintings had revealed.

"How have you remained unseen?" I asked. "How are you hiding the camp?"

"If you're familiar with wards, we're using something similar," she replied vaguely. "Though ours require practice to cultivate."

As I watched her work, I found I still couldn't separate her from Takara's impending execution. Given our precarious situation, though, I had to think strategically. A large and lethal force of snake people were hunting us. Further, their commander was an animator channeling powers beyond anything we'd faced. With Princess Halia's divination, the samurais' lethal skill set, and Kaito's magic-breaching katana, her team would make a potent ally, maybe even an essential one.

That was if she accepted my proposal to combine forces. If not, she could also stop sharing information vital to our own chances of success. I was surprised she'd shared as much as she had. I'd yet to learn the source of Akeila's power, though, and we would need that information at a minimum.

"So are we to assume that the war that destroyed Meong Kal buried the statue and heart stone again?" I was thinking of Leej's account of the history, and how the area around the city had carried a stain of evil following its fall.

"Presumably so," the princess said.

I expected her to elaborate, but she fell silent. Could she sense what I was doing?

"Something had to hold Akeila's essence for all this time, right?" I pressed. "Something your uncle would have accessed?"

"Yes, but the paintings aren't clear." She paused to caress the parchment with her brush. It wasn't my imagination—the entire painting shifted. "The tides that move through a Himitsu painting are powerful, Captain, but subtle. Imposing one's logic can create dangerous distortions."

"Is that what you've been waiting for the painting to tell you?"

Before she could answer, one of the samurai entered the tent.

She crouched by Princess Halia's side and spoke softly in Japanese. The princess nodded, and the samurai departed.

"Your friend is awake now," she said.

"Yoofi? He's all right?"

I planted a hand to push myself up, but the princess touched my fingers. "He is fine, Captain." Her hand was soft, but I could feel powerful currents moving beneath the contact. "They've prepared a tea that will speed his healing. He'll be able to cast shortly."

I settled back down, ready to propose a partnership. Our priority was to recover Olaf, destroy the focus of Akeila's power, and liberate the people of Ban Mau. We'd confront Takara's execution post mission, even if it meant turning our alliance into violent opposition.

"Listen—" I started.

"I accept," the princess cut in.

"Accept what?"

"Your offer to join forces." Her eyes had fallen back to the painting. She made several small strokes and leaned back slightly. "It appears you are part of the reason the Himitsu painting counseled us to wait." I understood that she had been talking with me at length just now to see what the painting had to say about us. "The heart stone that holds Akeila's essence was split," she added.

I couldn't tell whether this was new information or something she'd been holding back. "Destroyed?" I asked.

"No, divided. One half remained with the statue. The other half was placed some distance away, in the event war revisited Meong Kal before Akeila had regained her full power. Destroying the other half will not weaken Akeila—her essence is held in both—but it will weaken her influence over the jungle."

"The poison zone," I said.

"Yes."

Removing that malevolent energy would address one of the two challenges in reaching Meong Kal. That could have been the factor that made Reginald Purdy believe this mission was beyond Legion's abilities. It would also free up Yoofi's powers so we could use him in the final assault.

"Do you have a location for the other half of the stone?"

She regarded the painting for a long moment. "It will come soon."

"I'll get my team ready, then."

"Just you and two others—Takara and the magic-user. The snake person will act as guide. I'll send Kaito."

"Kaito? The one who wants Takara dead? Forget it."

"You'll need his blade to destroy the heart stone. The stone is vulnerable to intense heat and force."

After seeing Kaito's katana in action, the way it had smashed through the snake creatures' protection, I didn't doubt we would need his blade. But he could also turn that blade on Takara.

"My whole team goes," I said.

The princess looked up. "I understand your concern, Captain, but you must also understand mine. As it is, I'm taking a risk in sending Kaito with you and two teammates. No, your remaining members will stay as collateral."

I tried a different tact. "I want them for any patrols we may encounter."

She regarded the painting with what seemed fresh understanding. "There will be no patrols where you're going. The location I'm seeing was chosen for its *native* hostilities."

22

Two hours later, Leej was leading us through the jungle. For the first mile or so, I checked over my shoulder often —I didn't trust Kaito being so close to Takara—but like during mission planning, the two barely acknowledged each other.

I moved closer to Leej. "How much farther?"

When the query translated, he replied in his hissing voice.

"We are entering the swamplands," the handheld in my vest spoke. *"You will see the changes soon."*

Though our route took us away from Meong Kal, as well as from likely ambush points, Leej had been nervous about leading us into the swamplands. As a boy, he'd heard stories about hunting parties venturing inside and never coming out. Tribal elders forbade travel there. A veteran hunter described it to Leej as a primeval world of strange creatures and acid bogs. No doubt the "native hostilities" the princess had mentioned—making it the perfect place for a goddess to stash a life-giving stone.

Back at camp, I'd given Leej my Bowie knife. He coated the blade in poison from his own fangs before sliding the knife into a coat pocket. I watched him grasp the handle tightly now.

"We're close," I radioed the others. "Remain on alert."

Smoke drifted thickly from my amulet as Yoofi upped his concealing magic. He had fully recovered under the samurai's care. Better still, he claimed Dabu would give him all the power he needed to take revenge on whomever had dropped the rock on his head. His god thought it was a cheap shot. Leej was protected by his natural immunity and coat, while Kaito bore the ward the princess had mentioned.

Before long, dense foliage gave way to a foul-smelling wetland with towering cypress-like trees. Everything was bigger here. Massive ferns clumped around trunks, while giant pods in the shape of coconuts hung from branches. I looked around, feeling as if I'd stepped a hundred million years into the past.

Leej whispered. *"Follow me, but don't touch the water."*

He slithered ahead onto a raised path of dark sawgrass that looked like the start of a maze.

I radioed the warning to the others as they approached.

"It is not actual water, Mr. Wolfe," Yoofi radioed back. *"It is a living thing. In the Congo we call it* dia-yuma.*"*

"Do I want to ask what that means?"

"Hungry water."

I eyed the water again, wondering if it was related to the river feeder we'd encountered earlier. The water appeared to be more phlegm than liquid, and here and there I could see large bones and sections of vertebrae.

"It will not come onto the land," Yoofi assured us.

As we passed it, the water lapped at the grass, as if reaching for our feet.

"Or maybe it is different than the kind we have in the Congo," he added uncertainly.

"Just focus on our protection," I told him.

"Yes, Mr. Wolfe."

Though I couldn't feel the bite in the back of my throat, I sensed the growing poison. It tinted the atmosphere a faint purple. Leej's forked tongue flicked out as if tasting for the heart stone's presence. Princess Halia's painting had given us a general search area instead of a precise location. At a three-way branch, our guide flickered his tongue in each direction before setting off to the right.

A small pool of water glugged as we passed.

"Overhead!" Takara called.

I peered up sharply. Dozens of the pods that had looked like giant coconuts were separating from the branches. Takara began shooting. I joined in with my MP88.

Wings unfurled from the plummeting pods to reveal a platoon of creatures that resembled pterodactyls but with mosquito-like heads. They spiraled down, cutting sharply around each other, clearly believing they'd found their next meal.

They were going to be disappointed.

My first assault had been a general sweep, but I zeroed in on a single creature now. The explosive rounds chewed through thick hide until dark fluid burst from its chest. The thing went slack and dropped into a free fall. Takara had similar success with another of the creatures, but there were dozens, and the first were storming in.

"Get down!" I barked at Yoofi, grabbing him by an arm. We couldn't afford to lose him again. I threw him flat as a creature knifed its javelin-like snout through the space where Yoofi had been standing.

Dropping my MP88 onto its sling, I snatched the creature's tail. Muscles squirmed beneath its hide, and the tail separated from the body. The creature whipped around, its snout slashing the shoulder of my suit.

Grunting, I dropped the flopping tail and seized its javelin. The creature mewled and batted me with its wings, a small mouth at the end of its snout opening and closing, seeking blood. I swung the creature overhead and slammed it into the pool, where it flapped futilely, the hungry water already oozing over it.

As I wheeled and grabbed another of the creatures coming in, I glanced at my group. Kaito had moved up to cover Yoofi, who remained down. The samurai's katanas sang with flames as he sliced through one of the blood-sucking pterodactyls and then another, body parts raining around him. Beyond him, Takara had gone to her blades as well. She'd found soft spots in the creatures' umbilicus areas and was plunging her weapons to their hilts before ripping them free, pulling out insides.

On my other side, Leej's sinuous body bobbed and weaved as he slashed with my knife. His attacks weren't deep, but by the staggered flight of a creature he'd just gashed, his poison was getting to them. The creature crashed into a tree a moment later. I wrenched the wing of my own creature and hurled its body into the hungry water. The phlegmy organism glugged and took that one down too.

With our relentless counterattack, the creature's numbers thinned. Piercing cries went up—a retreat call—and the dozen or so remaining creatures reared up and flew away. We watched as they flapped into the distance, my chest heaving with exertion and adrenaline. Yoofi climbed to his feet.

"Ooh, I hope that will be the only bad things we see here."

"Don't count on it," I muttered, peering around. "Is everyone all right?"

Kaito nodded once as he cleaned his blades with a cloth he produced from his kimono.

Takara had already retracted her blades and now shook the gunk from her sleeves. "I'm fine," she said, nodding past me. "But you might want to check on him."

I turned to find Leej clasping his left shoulder.

"Let's have a look," I said, stepping toward him.

He moved his hand to reveal a deep gash where one of the creature's snouts had sliced him. Beneath a film of oily blood, I could see bands of muscle shifting. Leej's face remained stoic.

"Yoofi, can you spare any healing magic?"

He came over, peered at the wound, and quickly covered his eyes. "I wish I hadn't seen that. No, Mr. Wolfe, I am sorry. To heal him, I would have to take power from our protection, and the poison is too strong here."

We couldn't risk it, then—not with the three of us susceptible to the mind-altering poison and physically, or magically, capable of killing each other. The healing would have to wait until after we'd destroyed the heart stone.

I unshouldered my pack and pulled out the medical bag. But when I removed a packet of betadine to clean the wound, Leej's slitted nostrils wrinkled, and he slithered over to a clump of ferns. After plucking several leaves, he chewed them and packed them into the gash. The blood clotted around the packing, holding it fast, and Leej nodded that we could continue.

We passed the place where I'd thrown the bloodsuckers, but the creatures were practically dissolved now. Suspensions of hide and dark blood floated around a mass of exposed bones.

"Already?" Yoofi exclaimed behind me. "Ooh, the *dia-yuma* here is much different than the kind we have in the Congo. Yes, much *hungrier*."

———

As the day became afternoon, Leej led us deeper into the swamplands. We encountered more pods, but we moved silently, careful not to awaken them. The mazelike runs of grass eventually ended at the shore of a large pond. More of the cypress-like trees grew along the water's edge, their large knees jutting from the shallows.

"Where to now?" I asked.

Leej's tongue flicked out several times before he answered in a whisper.

"The stone is there," the translator said.

I followed his pointed finger to a grassy island in the middle of the pond, about fifty meters from shore. In my wolf vision, I could see a dark purple energy radiating from the hump of land, polluting the air with poison. My gaze dropped to the water. It was the same phlegmy consistency as the pools and channels we'd been walking near, meaning it was alive too. The edge of the pond lapped onto the land with what sounded like wet gasps.

"I can fly there," Takara said.

"Not alone."

I looked over our group, deciding who should go with her. Leej was injured, and I didn't want to send Yoofi; he was too valuable. My gaze landed on Kaito. No way in hell was I going to send him with Takara.

That left me.

"Can you carry five-hundred pounds?" I asked Takara.

I hated asking, knowing it would mean her calling on her dragon nature. But she nodded without hesitation. Apparently, I was her first choice too. The only problem was that it left us with poor cover. Yoofi had his sidearm, but he was an average shot at best. And I could see the lines across his face as he struggled to maintain his magic.

"Can you handle a rifle?" I asked Kaito.

I'd learned in our pre-mission meeting that he spoke passable English.

"I am samurai," he barked from behind his mask. "I do not dirty my hands with your filthy weapons."

"You confuse the tool for the trade," Takara said. "A weapon does not make one a samurai."

"How would you know, *ronin?*"

Kaito said the word like he was speaking a profanity, and he glared darkly at Takara. Heat flashed from her eyes in response. I stepped between them while searching for evidence that either was poisoned—Sarah had prepared several needles of anti-venom as a backup, and they were packed in my vest beside my Zippo lighter for quick access—but the displays of hostility came from something else.

"That's enough," I said.

Leej spoke behind me, and I turned, awaiting the translation. *"I can use it."*

I realized he was referring to the rifle. "You've shot an automatic?"

"The other group showed me how," he said. *"In case we were ambushed or became separated."*

I cocked my head for Takara to give him hers. She complied, handing him the rifle, then adjusted his grip slightly. Whatever suspicion she'd felt toward Leej was gone now, no doubt replaced by her issues with Kaito. As Leej lowered his head to the sight, Takara took a pair of spare mags from her vest and placed them in his coat pockets.

"Do you know how to reload?" she asked.

Leej nodded, sighting on the island now.

"Keep an eye on us," I told him. "Kaito, watch everything else."

The large samurai grunted, clearly pissed at having to follow my orders, but those had been the princess's final instructions to him.

"And, Yoofi," I said. "Just focus on our protection."

"Yes, Mr. Wolfe. But it is getting hard."

Magic billowed from our amulets like smoke from a steam locomotive.

"This should be over soon," I said. "Takara?"

She went into her deep breathing—not to control her dragon nature this time, but to invoke it. Fiery crescents flashed around her irises in time to the hot pulses radiating from her body. I noticed the blade of Kaito's katana responding, flames licking along its long edge. The samurai backed away from Takara.

"I'm ready," she said, her voice quavering with power and pain.

She lifted me beneath my arms, and we rose from the shore. Though my suit was heat resistant, I could feel the powerful energy from her hands. I was more concerned with the water passing beneath my feet, though. The bones at its bottom could have filled an industrial-sized dumpster. Sensing our proximity, the water bubbled up.

Takara made a pass over the island before circling back. Except for a hole at its center, the knoll of grass appeared solid. Takara set me down carefully—it supported my weight—then landed behind me. Back at shore, Leej covered us with the rifle while Kaito watched the rest of the wetland. Yoofi, who was clutching his smoking staff, motioned for us to hurry. I climbed the knoll and peered into the hole.

"Damn," I muttered.

Takara arrived beside me. "Is it down there?"

Like a well, the hole was about five feet across. At the bottom, a dark purple stone pulsed. The problem was the stone was under a good thirty feet of hungry water. Takara saw the problem and started looking around.

"If Yoofi wasn't playing defense," I said, "I'd have him retrieve it with a spell." But his magic was really cooking from our amulets, pushing back against the toxic energy from the heart stone.

"Those trees appear immune to the water," Takara said, pointing to a stand of the cypress-like trees. "We could cut a long branch and wire a couple smaller branches to the end, use it like a scoop."

"Good idea, but it'll take too long, and Yoofi's struggling. How about a long branch to pull me out if I get into trouble?"

I opened the neck of my suit to remove my holographic collar and swap my wedding band for the amulet, which I'd been wearing on the outside. After checking that my helmet was locked down, I tugged at my cuffs to make sure they were all sealed tight with my gloves and boots. When Takara saw what I was doing, she seized my arm.

"Jason, no."

"I'll regenerate."

"Faster than that thing can dissolve you?"

"It has to get through my protection first."

"That's a big risk."

"Like agreeing to your own execution?"

She started to answer, then pressed her lips together.

"Can you safekeep this for me?" I asked, holding out the chain with my wedding band.

Takara hesitated before accepting it. I removed the strap to my MP88 from around my body, then shucked my pack, vest, and tactical belt. While I did that, Takara took off and returned with a fifteen-foot branch. I nodded my approval, handed her my sidearm, and stepped to the edge of the well.

"Cover me the best you can," I said.

She peered over the rim at the hungry water. "And what am I supposed to shoot at?"

"Anything that looks alive."

I stepped off the edge.

23

I plunged in, surprised at how easily my legs cleaved the water. I had been expecting something similar to what we'd encountered in the Chagrath's realm in Mexico, a thick medium, hard to move through. But as the water rushed past my visor and closed over my head, it turned to the consistency of warm tar and squeezed me like a giant muscle.

My entry must have triggered a feeding response, because I was now in the clutches of a very strong, very hungry organism.

I fought back, instincts driving me upward, toward the surface. The organism turned heavier, arresting my clawing strokes. Muffled shots sounded. Rounds dove past, but the organism held fast. Takara, whose armed silhouette wavered above me, had been right: there was nothing to shoot at.

Tiny bubbles formed across my visor's material.

It wants to digest me, and I want the heart stone.

For the moment, our objectives aligned. I stopped struggling. The organism wrapped my body and drew me down. Seconds later, my boots touched bottom. Through my dissolving visor, I could just make out the purple mass that was the other half of the heart stone. I thrust an arm down and grasped the throbbing stone. It was unexpectedly heavy, as if time had compressed Akeila's evil essence into a dense core.

Now it's time to destroy you.

I flexed against the bottom of the hole and thrust upwards. I must have caught the organism by surprise because I made it a good ten feet before it reacted. The water squeezed me hard enough to choke off my breath. Digging my fingers and toes into the sides of the well, I inched myself up against its weight. My visor continued to dissolve in a sizzle, reducing my visibility to nil. Pain erupted over my left wrist.

Damn, a leak.

The liquid organism breaking through felt like millions of tiny fangs tearing into my flesh. My regenerative abilities went to work restoring the tissue, but how long would it keep pace with the damage?

Especially as more of the hungry water seeped inside.

My muscles burned with the upward struggle, but I kept the heart stone pinned to my chest. Even with the amulet inside my suit still active with Yoofi's magic, I was too close to the source. I could feel the poison urging me to drop the stone, to allow it to tumble back to the well bottom so I'd have two arms to climb free.

So I'd have a future.

Block it out, man, I told myself.

Pleasant images of Daniela swam through my thoughts. Her smiling face, her fresh scent, her touch. I saw our finished house. Bathed in sunlight, it looked perfect. There were specters of children too, our little monsters. They climbed over me in a riot of small bodies and happy laughter. I clutched the stone more tightly.

It's not real.

Something prodded my shoulder. Takara's branch.

I grasped it, and she pulled. A moment later, my helmet broke the surface. The organism dug in with every fingerhold it had on me, but I managed to get an arm over the rim. Between Takara's pulling and my clawing, I cleared the hole and removed my damaged helmet. As I crawled to safety, Takara tossed the branch aside and dug into my pack.

"The stone," I panted, dropping it onto the grass. "Destroy the stone."

"Get your suit off," she ordered.

For the first time, I noticed burning in other places besides my wrist. I shucked the failing suit like a banana peel, until I was down to nothing but my stone amulet. Weeping patches showed where the organism had gotten to me. Takara returned with my water bag. As she hosed the organism away, my healing took over, restoring the tissue.

I turned to the opposite shore, already jabbing up a thumb for Yoofi to increase the magic, but I stopped mid gesture. The growths that I'd likened to cypress knees were opening into tall, knotted creatures that looked like trolls. They stalked toward Yoofi, Leej, and Kaito. Several others began wading toward our island.

Takara finished rinsing my wounds and tossed away the water bag. In the sawgrass, the heart stone was pulsing faster now. I sensed the serpent goddess pushing power into it, determined to overwhelm Yoofi's magic and our minds.

"Kaito!" Takara called toward shore. "Your sword!"

But the first root trolls had reached the rest of the team, and both of Kaito's swords were in action. Fire flashed as the blades crashed against a creature's thick hide. Leej opened fire with the rifle, sending rounds exploding into the other trolls. Yoofi remained behind them, sidearm in hand, but with all his effort going into sustaining the magic that issued from our amulets, the weapon remained at his side.

Kaito dropped his foe and looked up.

"Your sword!" Takara called again.

When the words registered, the samurai seemed to clutch the katana closer to him. Even from this distance, I could read his body language. Should the executioner relinquish his weapon to the condemned?

The shadow of a giant serpent sprang from the heart stone.

Just when I thought Kaito had decided *no*, he whipped the katana around and released it underhanded. Trailing smoke, the blade flew across the pond in a line drive. Flames billowed up as Takara caught the metal hilt. In a single motion, she brought it overhead and grasped it with her other hand.

The serpent shadow reared to strike her.

Grunting, Takara brought the katana down. The heart stone shattered beneath a flash of fire. In a dark blast, the serpent shadow came apart and stormed across the pond in all directions, making the trees sway. Even the root trolls hesitated in their assault.

When the smoke from the impact cleared, the stone was in pieces.

I pushed myself to my feet, the final layers of skin cells spreading over my wounds and sprouting fresh growths of blue hair. I donned vest, belt, and pack and hefted my MP88. The root trolls that had been coming at us resumed their march. Sighting on the lead one, I took off his head. The troll's body staggered blindly before toppling into the water.

On the opposite shore, Leej followed my example and did the same to another troll. Yoofi, no longer having to focus on defense, gathered energy around his staff's blade and released a bolt into a third troll, dissolving it on the spot.

Kaito, who was down to his short blade, slashed furiously as three trolls closed in on him. One raked a hand across the large samurai's chest. He staggered back, lines of blood darkening his kimono.

"Takara!" he shouted, not taking his eyes from his opponents.

He was asking for his blade. I was tempted to tell Takara to stand down. The trolls looked capable of dismembering him. Maybe that would take care of the execution business. But who knew what the princess's Himitsu painting would tell her? I didn't want consequences for Sarah and Rusty.

Takara didn't hesitate, though. She slung the blade across the water, and Kaito caught it deftly. With it, he cleaved off the grasping arm of the troll who'd raked him, then brought the blade around and decapitated him. Using my sidearm, Takara squeezed off shots at the other trolls. With all five of us on the attack, the lumbering creatures succumbed until only twitching bodies and severed limbs remained.

I scanned our surroundings for more attackers before lowering my MP88.

Takara slotted the sidearm back into my holster. "Good look for you," she remarked.

"Thanks," I grunted. If not for the thick sweep of hair between my legs, she'd be getting even more of an eyeful. "And thanks for your help fishing me out of that hole." I peered back at the glugging well.

"How do you feel?" she asked.

"A lot better, especially with the heart stone destroyed." The atmosphere was no longer tinged purple, and I could already feel my senses sharpening. No sore throat, either. " How about you?"

She still looked weary from having to invoke, and control, her dragon.

"I'm fine," she said.

"Why did you return his sword? Because of your *bond* to the clan?"

"Because we have a mission to complete."

"I really can't understand you, Takara."

"Then stop trying."

She handed me the chain with my wedding band. I had barely gotten it back around my neck when she lifted me under the arms and flew us back across the pond to the others. Debris from the woody creatures littered the shore. While Leej handed Takara her rifle, Yoofi clasped my hand and gave me a bro hug.

"That was almost too much," he said.

"But it wasn't," I said. "You did great."

I turned to Kaito, who was holding his chest where the troll had raked him.

"Do you need healing?" I asked stiffly.

The samurai looked me up and down. My suit was gone, and I'd yet to replace my collar. He was seeing my Blue Wolf form for the first time.

"I need nothing from you, *tengu*," he snapped.

"He's not a demon," Takara said. "He risked his life to retrieve the heart stone."

He rounded on her. "And I risked mine when I allowed your hands to dirty my sword."

"You did the honorable thing," she said. "Was that so hard?"

"What do you know of *honor*?"

"You were right," I said, directing myself to Takara. "We have a mission to complete, and destroying the stone just gave us a big leg up." I cut my eyes to Kaito, not bothering to hide their menace. "We'll deal with everything else post mission."

The big samurai narrowed his eyes back and turned away.

After Yoofi had applied healing magic to Leej, I motioned for our guide to lead. The rest of us assumed our positions, even

Kaito, who remained under the princess's orders. Though Takara was doing her best to hide it, I'd just seen the fight in her. She didn't want to die. My job post mission, then, would be to stoke that fight.

Even if it meant invoking her dragon.

24

"Well done," Princess Halia said as we filed into the camp. "And everyone made it back."

"Your intel was good," I said, dropping my pack and leaning my MP88 against it. I hadn't reactivated my hologram—if Kaito knew, everyone might as well—but Halia didn't react to my Blue Wolf form. Neither did the other samurai, who watched silently from around the encampment. "Any developments back here?" I asked.

She watched Kaito as he marched wordlessly to his tent.

"Akeila has pulled her forces back to Meong Kal," she said, returning her gaze to me.

I'd figured as much when no snake creatures attempted to intercept us on the return trip. "We should move tonight, then," I said, "while she's backpedaling."

I was getting more and more concerned about Olaf. With dusk creeping over the jungle, we were nearing the 48-hour mark since his disappearance.

"Agreed," Takara said from beside me. Yoofi and Leej came up on my other side.

"Soon," the princess said. "I believe the painting has more to tell us."

"How soon is *soon*?" I pressed.

"Remember, Captain. A Himitsu painting cannot be rushed."

"Yeah, well, I don't want to pass up an advantage. Akeila knows we're coming for her, and she's seen what we're capable of. The more time we give her, the better she can prepare. Let's mission plan with the info we have. If the painting has anything more to say, great, we use it. If not, we head out."

I was about to call for Sarah and Rusty when they emerged from their tents. I'd given them assignments to work on while the rest of us were away. Sarah's was to analyze a sample of Leej's blood to try to identify and isolate his resistance to the poisonous energy. Though we'd destroyed half the heart stone and limited Akeila's influence over the jungle, the stone's other half was presumably in Meong Kal, where'd we be heading next.

Rusty's job had to do with communication to the outside. He licked his lips, eyes flicking between me and Princess Halia.

"Even after leading you to the heart stone," the princess said, "you dismiss the power of Himitsu? The painting may yet show us weaknesses in Meong Kal's defenses as well as the location of the remaining heart stone. Surely you can appreciate the tactical value of that knowledge."

"Not if it takes a month to get here."

"But go ahead and prepare your armaments," she continued as if she hadn't heard me. "I'll see what I can elicit from the painting."

I wanted to force my position, but I had too little bargaining power. We were going to need whatever intel Princess Halia already had as well as Kaito's sword to destroy the other half of the heart stone. I grunted, which the princess must have taken as consent. She returned to her tent, passing Sarah and Rusty who were coming toward us.

Sarah examined my suit-less body before touching a spot on my shoulder. My regenerative power had restored the tissue there, but it was still breaking down the scarring that showed through my hair. Her probing touch was firm, clinical.

"Were you injured?"

"Yeah, but I healed. How did it go here?"

She withdrew her hand and shook her head. "No discernible difference between Leej's blood and the sample from the deceased snake person at base. His and the others' resistance must be mental."

"Well, we've mitigated the strength of Akeila's poison anyway," I said. "That'll help with our assault on Meong Kal."

"Yes," Yoofi put in. "It took much less magic to protect us coming back." He lowered his voice. "So are we going to wait like the princess said?"

I stiffened at the suggestion she was in control. But she was —for now.

"We'll start prepping. How much tumba seed do you have?" I asked him.

"A bag full, Mr. Wolfe. It is in my tent."

"Bring it out here along with your other spell implements. Everyone else, grab your spare ammo. We're going to make some modifications. Leej, why don't you rest. Let Yoofi's magic finish healing your shoulder. You can take my tent." As he and the rest of the team moved off, I turned to Rusty. "How did your commo assignment go."

Even though the poison zone had diminished with the destruction of the heart stone, it was still scrambling our communication. I hadn't been able to reach Rusty on our trek back, and our connection to the Centurion satellites remained out. I envisioned the poison zone as an energy field over the jungle, something a projectile shot straight up would penetrate and escape. So that's what I had asked Rusty to do: create a transponder small enough to fit inside a grenade round.

"Piece of cake, boss," he said now, reaching into a vest pocket and holding up a small square of silicon. "Commo chip to the satellite. Salvaged it off Yoofi's tablet, then rigged it so I could input a message off my own tablet. But I had to wire it to a micro battery for power. Is that gonna be too big?"

I looked the contraption over. "Should fit inside the round."

"Anything in particular you want it to say?" Rusty asked.

"Not yet. Hold onto it for now."

He nearly fumbled the chip as he returned it to the same pocket. He'd been speaking quickly, licking his lips often, and I noticed a sting of nervousness coming off his sweat. He glanced back toward the tents before lowering his voice to a whisper. "Hey, uh, boss? There's something else I need to tell you."

"What's up?"

"A message came for you."

I felt my brows crush down. "Message?"

He moved his backpack around to his front as he walked toward a corner of the camp away from the tents. "I didn't tell Sarah. I wanted you to hear it first." He opened the pack and pulled out my sat phone. "I considered using the chip from in here, but it's too big. Anyway, I had the phone next to me while I was working. When you destroyed the stone, the field must have flickered or something 'cause your phone lit up. Scared the tar out of me. It'd grabbed a message. I hope you don't mind, but I listened."

"Who's it from?"

"No name, and the voice was digitally altered."

My heart rate kicked up. "What did it say?"

"You can listen for yourself. I locked it into the phone's memory before it got wiped. Here." He punched a combination of keys on the phone and handed it to me. I took the phone and pressed it to an ear.

"Well, it appears we've advanced beyond the investigation phase," an electronic voice said. It was Reginald Purdy's. Nothing about the sound or cadence gave him away—the digital cloaking disguised both—but he was referring to our conversation in my suite, specifically the part where I'd said we would only go to New Siam to investigate. *"Perhaps now you understand. Perhaps now you've seen for yourself. Given your resourcefulness, you may penetrate into the hostile area. You may even believe you have a chance. You don't. The main threat is challenge enough, but a secondary threat is in play. One that rivals you in lethality and that you won't see until it's too late. Leave now, Captain, even if you must cut losses. Princess Halia is—"*

The electronic voice fell to garbles, and the recording ended.

"The rest of the message got corrupted," Rusty said, "probably when the poison field was restored."

The other half of the heart stone must have taken up for the sudden absence of the first, if less powerfully.

"You can't retrieve the message?" I asked.

"Believe me, I've been tinkering with the danged thing for the last hour. Was that the same official who warned you before we left?"

I nodded distractedly, already dialing Purdy. But the signal couldn't get out.

"What do you think he meant by a second threat?" Rusty whispered. "He mentioned..." Positioning his body so only I could see, he pointed toward Princess Halia's tent. "Do we need to be worried?"

"I don't know yet."

And I didn't. With Purdy's message cutting out where it did, there was no way to know whether he was about to identify the princess as the secondary threat, or if his mention of her was about something else.

"Can I hear it again?" I asked.

Rusty punched in the keypad combo and handed the phone back. He shifted from foot to foot as the message started from the beginning. I strained to listen beyond the words this time, especially as Purdy transitioned from the "secondary threat" to the princess, but the digital cloaking disguised all nuances.

I lowered the phone to my side and paced the corner of the encampment.

"Either way," Rusty whispered nervously, "he sounds pretty damned sure we're in over our heads."

I looked up as Takara and Sarah emerged from their tents, packs clinking with ammo. Yoofi, carrying a bag of spell implements, hustled to catch up to them. The samurai around the camp seemed to be watching us closely.

"Give me a little time with this," I said.

Rusty got the message. "I won't say anything, boss."

————

An hour later, Takara, Yoofi, Rusty, and I sat around a ground cloth heaped with ammo in a corner of the camp. We were dipping bullet tips into a smoking paste that Yoofi had concocted, a way to weaponize the magic that had proven effective against the snake people's protection that morning.

When we completed several stacks of cartridges, I moved to my grenade rounds.

"The tumba seeds go into these," I told Yoofi, breaking apart a round. "You'll be able to animate at distances now."

He giggled nervously as he watched me drop a pinch of seed into the open round and seal it again. I placed it beside the empty round where Rusty's transponder would go if and when we needed it.

"I also want to swap these out," I said, lifting my stone amulet from my chest.

"Why?" he asked. "They were designed to hold magic, and they hold it very good."

"Designed in Meong Kal by Akeila's slaves," I said. "Look, I trust that you and Dabu cleaned them, but I'm uneasy about wearing them into the city. My other concern is that they can be removed, even shot off." We had established that with the hostiles' brooches. "You once said copper was a good conduit for magic, right?"

"Yes, can keep magic going for a long time. But do you have something copper to wear?"

"To swallow," I said, holding up an empty brass casing. "A little copper might leech out, but not enough to be dangerous. If it's no problem having your magic inside us, we can pack the casings with your paste, seal them, and then choke them down."

"Yes, but they will only last until, you know..." He hooked a thumb at his backside. "...they're passed."

"Then I'll suggest everyone takes care of that before we set out."

Yoofi burst into giggles and nodded. "Okay, Mr. Wolfe. I will work on them."

I glanced across the cloth at Takara. She'd said almost nothing since our return, and she appeared strangely calm now as she worked on her bullets. Whatever fight I'd seen in her in the swamplands was gone. Rusty looked from her to me and tossed his round onto a pile of them, where it landed with a clink.

"Permission to address the 800-pound gorilla in the jungle?" he asked.

"Go ahead," I said, warning him with a look not to bring up Purdy's message.

He removed his helmet and dragged a hand through his shaggy hair. I had replaced the destroyed visor on my own helmet and donned a backup suit. "Are we just going to sit here and act like Takara didn't agree to the death penalty?" he asked. "Why the heck isn't anyone saying anything?"

I looked at Takara, but she remained silent.

"We agreed not to address that until after the mission," I answered for her.

"After the mission?" Rusty echoed, incredulous. "What, before or after she's dead?"

"I appreciate your concern," Takara said. "But this doesn't involve you. Or Legion."

"No more ducking the question, then," I said. "Explain yourself."

"Yeah, explain yourself," Rusty said. "'Cause if it weren't for the boss man's order here, I would've cut those sons of bitches already."

Takara finished coating her bullet and dropped it into her own pile.

"I was praying in the temple when the atomic bomb detonated," she said.

Rusty looked at me, eyebrows raised as if to say, *Damn, she's actually going to tell us.*

"I'd had premonitions of the attack for days," she continued. "Rather, Senshika had."

"Who's Senshika?" I asked.

"She was a voice that spoke to me. Senshika would tell me things, and they would come true. I never told the clan. I didn't want them to think I was possessed by a *tengu*, a demon."

"Don't know that I would've admitted to voices in my head either," Rusty muttered.

"All week Senshika spoke of fire and destruction. She urged me to inform the clan, to get them to safety. I finally spoke with my grandfather. He was our leader, the wisest person I'd ever known. He looked into my eyes and sensed the truth of my words. On the morning of the attack, he ordered the clan to a bunker deep under the city. He tried to impress upon our patron the coming danger, but she would not listen. And so we went to the bunker ourselves and waited."

"Ooh, I don't like stories where you know the bad thing that will happen," Yoofi said.

"Senshika spoke to me again. She said she could protect the city, but that I must go to the temple and pray. And I must go alone. I could not tell anyone. I was the stealthiest of our clan, so I had no trouble slipping away. Our temple sat on a small hill in north Hiroshima. I arrived, cleared my mind, as had been taught to me, and prepared to pray. But Senshika said, 'No. You must not clear your mind. You must think of me as intensely as you can. You must feel my fire, my violence, my power.'"

"Oh, no," Yoofi whispered.

"I resisted. Her instructions went against the way of the samurai. But when she asked if I wanted to see my city again, my family, I answered yes. 'Then you must not question what I tell you,' she said."

Yoofi clutched his staff.

"So I focused on Senshika to the exclusion of all else. I filled my mind with her violent attributes. When my clan noticed I was missing, they sent my brother in search of me. He arrived at the temple right before the bomb hit."

Yoofi shrank back as Takara's eyes shimmered with fire.

"There was a deafening roar. The air was pulled from my lungs, my being. It felt as if all the cells in my body were bursting into white-hot flames. Agony, pleasure, fear ... I can't describe it. The next thing I remember was my brother carrying me. Blood poured from his ears, and the flesh of his face clung to the bones."

"Geez," Rusty muttered.

"See? I knew I would not like this," Yoofi said.

"He carried me through the fiery ruins of Hiroshima, back to the bunker," Takara continued. "The clan placed us in separate rooms to treat us. I was naked, my clothes burned away, my entire body a weeping wound. My grandfather knelt beside my head and whispered to me. He was counseling me to breathe, to clear my thoughts. But I was too afraid. The fear overwhelmed me and turned to fire."

"Your dragon," I said in understanding.

"My dragon," Takara echoed gravely. "The atomic explosion fused me to Senshika. I reared up, wreathed in flames. Wings grew from my arms until I was the full expression of her—a being larger and more terrifying than anything I could have imagined. And a part of me gloried in that. All the time, my grandfather spoke in his soft voice, his words like swaddling cloth, calming me, dampening the flames."

Yoofi clutched his staff more tightly, whispering, "Yes, grandfather. Please calm her down."

"But Senshika shrieked in my ear, 'He is smothering you! He is killing you! Don't let him!' And I couldn't breathe. I reacted, lashed out, seizing my grandfather in a massive clawed foot. His robes burst into flames, but still he spoke, still he tried to reach me. And I ... I crushed the life from him."

"*Senshika* crushed the life from him," I stressed.

"Yes, Senshika," Yoofi added.

"The rest of my clan didn't stand a chance." I could see the fiery massacre playing out behind Takara's eyes, but she didn't share the details. "I fled then, soaring from the ruins of Hiroshima, from the toxic mushroom that continued to spread over the city. Senshika carried me far to the north, where I flamed out and fell."

All this time, I had wrongly assumed Takara had been driven from her clan because of the horrible scarring left by the explosion, that she'd been forced to find a new family among the ninja. But Senshika had carried her there, probably knowing it was her best chance to keep Takara, her host, alive.

"Kaito is right," Takara said. "I sinned against my clan, and for that, the penalty is death."

"*Senshika* sinned against your clan," I said.

But this time, Takara shook her head. "I could have refused her in the temple. I knew what she was asking of me was wrong."

"You were fourteen, for Pete's sake!" Rusty cried.

"And a trained samurai," Takara said. "I had mastery over my mind, but I opened the door to selfish fear, and through that opening came Senshika. I delivered her into the world, into the clan. I was the vessel for her evil."

"Well, who are these yahoos?" Rusty demanded, throwing an arm toward the camp. "The clan's grandkids? Why don't you just tell them what happened? Anyone with half a working noggin would understand."

"*You're* not understanding," Takara snapped. "The order cannot be overruled. I am bonded to my clan at a soul level—and that includes the penalties. Senshika convinced me that if I stayed far away I would be safe. I tried, and look where I ended up." She snorted softly. "I see now that it couldn't have been otherwise. I've accepted this. So should you."

"I don't have to accept jack squat!" Rusty yelled.

This time, Takara didn't answer. When Rusty looked at me in exasperation, I pointed to the container of Yoofi's paste to tell him to continue working. I did the same. But even after hearing

Takara's story, my plan hadn't changed. If I couldn't rally her, I would get her dragon, Senshika, to fight in her place.

Across the camp, Princess Halia emerged from her tent.

"The painting has spoken," she called. "It's time to meet."

Before hearing Purdy's message, I would have jumped up, but now I hesitated. For the last hour, I'd been trying to decipher Purdy's warning. What further threat, if any, did the princess and samurai pose?

I'd begun by questioning the princess's motives. To save the people of Ban Mau and protect her country from the spread of Akeila's influence? Or were her ambitions more self-serving? She had said her uncle was too weak to channel Akeila's power. Did she believe she could succeed where he had failed? That kind of power would give her a huge advantage in a succession struggle with her brother.

Over the piles of ammo, Rusty watched me with worried eyes.

"Let's go," I said to the team. "Keep your weapons on you."

I seized my MP88 and slotted home a fresh mag.

25

The Himitsu painting Princess Halia had been working on —the one depicting ruins in a jungle setting—sat on the floor of her tent, mostly completed now. A second painting was beside it. This one looked more like a map. The princess knelt before both, making little touches to them with her brush. Kaito stood beside her. His frown steepened beyond his mask as we gathered opposite her.

"Have a seat, Captain," the princess said without raising her gaze.

Mistrust smoldered through me, setting my muscles on edge. Though the princess wasn't armed, I was wary of Kaito's swords, even sheathed in his belt. I'd seen the speed with which he could draw them. The other samurai hadn't entered, and my ears were cocked, monitoring their shifting positions in the camp.

"I'll stand, thanks."

"Is something the matter?" she asked.

I assumed she had picked up my edginess, but her eyes cut past me. I turned to find Takara hanging back, covering the tent door. We'd worked together long enough that Takara had read my behavioral cues.

"We're just anxious to begin the mission," I said.

The princess's gaze lingered on Takara for another moment before shifting to Leej. "I don't want him involved in the planning."

I turned off the device before it could translate her words into Hung. "He's our guide."

"He's also a *khon ngu*," she said. "It's not that I don't trust him—he led us to the heart stone—but his tribe is under Akeila's control now. Captured, he could become a liability. He can help guide our trek, but he'll turn back well outside of Meong Kal. And he can't be involved in the planning."

Grunting, I activated the device and addressed Leej. "Can you keep watch outside?"

He nodded and slithered out through the opening. After all he'd done, I felt bad bouncing him from the meeting. But though my instincts toward the princess remained conflicted, she had a point. There was no telling how long Leej would hold out under interrogation, especially with his family in Akeila's grip. And if the hostiles got a jump on our mission plan, things could go sideways in a hurry.

Killing the device, I returned my attention to the princess. "You said the painting had spoken?"

"Yes, it revealed several key pieces of information, some more clearly than others. First, we have a tunnel route to Meong Kal."

"One Akeila isn't aware of?" I asked, remembering our last experience with a possible tunnel route.

"This one was not built by the snake people under her thrall, but by the human tribes during the last war that destroyed Meong Kal. Both ends are long buried, but the integrity of the tunnel has endured. And we have the means to reopen it." She looked over at Yoofi.

"Is that something you can handle?" I asked him.

"Yes, a *kembo* should do the job," he replied with a giggle.

"The opening we will access is here," she said, touching the tip of her brush to a point on the map. If I understood the map, the location wasn't too far from our camp. "It will deliver us to the basin from which Meong Kal rises." I followed her brush to the city complex a short distance away. "Better, we will emerge here, behind a mound that has yet to be excavated. It will provide us concealment and cover."

So far, so good, I thought. *Or so it seems.*

"What else did the painting show you?" I asked.

"That my uncle is here." She aimed her brush at a pyramidal complex in the center of the city. "He watches the rebuilding of Meong Kal from the top level, but he is completely in Akeila's grip. She casts through him, directing her enthralled slaves whose worship she depends on for her power. By this arrangement, my uncle's animating magic has increased manifold. He is well beyond dancing spoons and forks now, I assure you."

When Yoofi made an ominous sound, she smiled at him without humor. She referred back to the place where we would emerge from the tunnel. "From this position you and your team will engage the snake creatures."

"They'll all have returned to Meong Kal," Sarah said. "The city's defenses will be hundreds strong."

"Yes," the princess agreed. "The attack is designed to draw their attention, something you're quite adept at." I ignored the not-so-subtle dig. "Meanwhile, Kaito and the samurai will access the temple and eliminate my uncle."

"Eliminate him?" I said. "But he's only the vessel."

"He's also the organizing force for Akeila's power right now. Without him, the serpent goddess's focus will scatter enough that we can free her prisoners: the *khon ngu*, the people of Ban Mau, your teammate."

My mind tensed with fresh suspicion. Was this part of a design to replace her uncle?

"What about the other half of the heart stone?" I asked. "Why not target that and spare your uncle too."

"That might work in theory, yes, but I still don't have a location for the stone. I'm only receiving impressions. It's somewhere underground—"

"Yes!" Yoofi cut in, looking around in excitement. "Somewhere warm and damp where it is very hard to breathe. Where the awful smell of snake is everywhere. That is where I was when the goddess possessed me."

"That does little to narrow it down," Princess Halia said, her voice tense with the annoyance of having been interrupted. "Collectively, the tunnel systems beneath Meong Kal extend for tens of miles. We'll need to search them, but only after Akeila's power has been disrupted. She currently holds too many weapons in her thrall."

"I know the stone's smell now," I said. "You get me down there, and I can track the other half."

In fact, it wouldn't be that easy. Similar to how the ambient magic in the camp was confounding my ability to pick up scent cues from the princess, the concentration of poisonous energy would frustrate my tracking abilities in Meong Kal. But I was testing the princess now more than anything, watching for her reaction.

Her dark jade eyes held mine. "Why are you doing this?"

"Doing what?"

"Proposing something you know isn't feasible."

"I'm laying out all options to make sure we're going with the best one."

"I assure you, Captain. The painting will present the best one."

"There's no space for logic in your system?" Sarah challenged.

"Himitsu is a layered, living system thousands of years old. *Logic*," she said with a snort, "is to the wisdom of Himitsu as a basin of tap water is to an ancient sea. Would you really trade one for the other?"

"Logic is the basis for science," Sarah shot back. "When was the last time Himitsu built a microprocessor or eliminated polio?"

"You sound just like my brother," the princess said dismissively.

"Hey, let's get back to the mission," I said. There was enough going on in my head without having to referee a debate on the relative merits of science versus magic. Aiming a talon at the map, I said, "So we arrive by this tunnel, position here, and engage the snake creatures while the samurai access the temple. When Akeila's power scatters, we free her slaves and then locate and destroy the other half of the stone."

"Do you have any objections?" the princess asked.

As my gaze moved across the map, I considered each step.

"How long will it take Kaito and the samurai to reach your uncle?" I asked.

"Not long," she replied.

"If you do your job," the large samurai added sharply.

I ignored him. "What about your uncle? If he's as powerful as you claim, how will the samurai take him down?"

"He will be focused on you," the princess replied.

"Well, fan-flipping-tastic," Rusty muttered.

The princess leaned toward the paintings. "With your combined forces, including your magic-user's powers, the

Himitsu is suggesting you can hold them off long enough for Kaito and the samurai to complete their assignment."

"Where will you be?" I asked.

"Since I am not trained for combat, I will remain in the tunnel consulting the paintings. Should circumstances change, the paintings may have more to say. I trust you can arrange communication for me?"

When I turned to Rusty, he nodded. "Yeah, we can rig you up something," he said.

I reviewed the plan again, but this time from the perspective of someone with power ambitions. Even with her uncle out of the way, she would need the heart stone. Did she already know where the statue to Akeila was?

"When your uncle falls, who's going to be responsible for the slaves, and who's going to search for the stone?" I asked.

"If you believe you can track the heart stone," she replied, "you and Kaito can take a team down. You'll need his blade to destroy it. The rest of us will see to the freed slaves. Sarah can use her *science* to aid the critical."

Sarah shot her a look that, for our detached teammate, was surprisingly withering.

The princess's plan sounded reasonable—unless of course she knew the stone was somewhere other than underground. Kaito unleashed a burst of Japanese, to which the princess responded calmly. Though I picked up Takara's name in the exchange, I was mulling the secondary threat Purdy had mentioned, the one we wouldn't see coming. When the princess and Kaito finished going back and forth, I spoke again.

"Threat-wise, there's Akeila, your uncle, and the beings under their thrall," I said. "Is the painting picking up anything else? Anything we might not have anticipated?"

"There are threats inherent in the jungle, of course," she answered, looking the paintings over. "The river feeder you encountered, for example. Those we can avoid. As far as specific threats to our mission? No. Not at this time."

"What do you mean 'not at this time'?" I asked.

"I mean that they could exist, but the painting has not identified them."

"I thought you said that the painting had spoken," Rusty challenged.

"It has," she said evenly. "But your Captain is correct in suggesting that if we waited for the painting to reveal *everything*, we would be too late to act. We're going on what the officers in my father's intelligence service call *minimal viable information*. The least information needed for a successful outcome."

We were looking at two possibilities: Either Princess Halia was telling the truth, and the painting hadn't had time to pick up the secondary threat. Or she *was* the secondary threat, and that's what Purdy had been trying to tell me. Taking action against the princess now would either spare us or shatter an important alliance, not to mention forfeit our access to the princess's Himitsu-divining, when both could be badly needed.

I looked around at my teammates. Rusty's troubled eyes underscored the weight of my decision. I would be making the call for all of them.

There's a third choice, I reminded myself. *Take Purdy's warning and get the hell out of here.*

Exhaling, I returned my gaze to Princess Halia. "When do we move?"

"There's a window," she said. "Ten till midnight tonight."

"All right. Anyone have any questions?"

When no one did, I said, "We'll be ready," and waved my teammates out.

In the midst of so much uncertainty and with so much at stake, one rule held for me: leave no soldier behind. If we couldn't destroy Akeila and rescue the slaves, we'd at least recover Olaf and then reassess. Purdy's message, though incomplete, had given me some minimal viable information too—enough to know to be watchful. And with a few hours before we were to set out, I had time to put safeguards in place.

Still, it wouldn't change the fact that our error margin was razor thin.

26

The moon showed through chinks in the jungle canopy as we trekked in a snaking line, the Legion team armed and bearing Yoofi's magic on the inside now. Princess Halia and the samurai followed. Leej, who had been navigating the route indicated by the Himitsu painting, stopped and pointed to an embankment just ahead.

I pulled up beside him. "Looks like we're here," I radioed.

Princess Halia joined us moments later. She had rolled the paintings into scrolls, and now she unrolled the map partway. She looked from it to the embankment and nodded. "This is it," she whispered.

I signaled for Yoofi, and he hustled forward.

"The opening has collapsed," the princess said, "but you can see the old archway."

Nodding, Yoofi raised his staff and waved everyone back. As cold energy circled his blade, I glanced over at the princess. Following our meeting, I'd told my teammates about Purdy's second warning and shared my theories. Takara didn't believe the samurai had power ambitions, especially underhanded ones; they were too honor-bound. But Princess Halia remained the X factor. I gave the team instructions for when we arrived at the city. Whatever the princess's plans, I believed that she needed us at least as far as getting her team into the temple.

I hoped to hell I was right.

Yoofi released the energy with a word. It drove into the embankment, sending up a blast of leaves, limbs, and earth, the sounds muffled by Yoofi's concealing magic. When everything settled, a hole appeared.

I moved in to investigate. The blast had driven the collapsed opening into the tunnel itself, spreading debris along its length. Farther back, old beams still supported the original tunnel's ceiling. I sniffed into the darkness. Stale, but no signs of snake creatures. Dropping my MP88 onto its sling, I hefted the stone archway back in place and strutted it with sturdy lengths of timber.

"It's good," I said.

The princess shifted her gaze to Leej. "This is where he departs our company."

I moved off several paces to where he was standing. "Listen, we really appreciate your help." I waited for the device to translate before continuing. "We wouldn't have gotten this far without you. But this is our mission now. We'll destroy the evil enslaving your people. Return to the camp and wait it out."

Leej absorbed the translation and extended a four-fingered hand. I took it.

"Thanks again, Leej." I looked at him meaningfully as the device translated my words.

He nodded, then slithered off through the trees. The princess waited until he had disappeared from sight before signaling for us to proceed. I took the lead now, ducking beneath the archway and snapping on my MP88's infrared light. As the rest of the team filed in behind me, I replayed my farewell with

Leej, hoping I'd sold it. In fact, he wasn't going back to the camp. He had an assignment to carry out.

———

The tunnel was well preserved. A few cave-ins here and there, but nothing that blocked our progress. We passed the occasional alcove in the tunnel walls, some holding small idols to ancient gods. Good reminders that the same primitive tribe that had built the tunnel had also taken down Akeila.

But did they face a secondary threat? my captain's voice asked.

I peered over a shoulder. Beyond Takara, the last in the line of my teammates, the princess's eyes glinted back at me darkly.

After another hour of steady walking, we reached the tunnel's far end. Yoofi shone light from his staff over the collapse of stone and earth.

"Is this it?" he whispered.

The princess came forward with her map. "Yes, the city is just beyond."

Yoofi began to reach his staff toward the collapse, but I stopped him. Even with his concealing magic, the blast could send debris raining over the city, which would damn sure draw attention.

"We're going to dig this one out," I said. "Keep an eye on the integrity of the ceiling. Everyone back except for Yoofi," I called.

As they pulled back, I began lifting large stones from the collapse. The work went quickly, and soon I was scooping aside piles of earth with my hands. At the top of the collapse, my talons punched through roots and into empty space. The smell of the jungle rushed in, carrying with it Akeila's poisonous energy. I checked to make sure Dabu's magic was still working inside me before widening the opening and peering out.

True to the princess's word, a concealing mound of jungle rose outside the opening. Beyond, I could hear the unmistakable sounds of labor: distant grunts, calls, and dozens and dozens of iterations of stone clinking against stone. A dispersion of smoke moved across my view like mist. I turned and gave the group a thumbs-up.

We were inside Meong Kal.

The next twenty minutes was a delicate process of opening the hole enough for us to fit through. I emerged first and covered the tunnel. Yoofi and Rusty came out next. They peered around like wide-eyed children, excited by the sounds of nearby Meong Kal. When Takara climbed through, she checked her weapon. She appeared unconcerned by our location or the fact that Kaito had emerged beside her.

When we were all out, Princess Halia waved a brush over the tunnel opening. A moment later, the leaves and branches seemed to swallow the dark hole, but it was an illusion. I peered around, marking the location in my memory, and told my teammates to do the same. This was our rally point if things went sideways.

The princess held open her map, and the rest of us gathered around. The Himitsu painting had already identified positions higher up the bowl that would give us lines of sight on each other and Meong Kal.

She pointed to the first one.

That was Takara and Rusty's. They nodded and moved off, Rusty giving me a final, anxious look. The next position was Sarah and Yoofi's. Adjusting her grip on her M4, Sarah took lead, and she and Yoofi disappeared into the trees. A thin contrail from Yoofi's staff lingered behind them.

The princess pointed to the final position, which was practically straight up. Since the Legion team was odd-numbered without Olaf, I would be heading there solo. But before setting off, I searched her eyes a final time. They remained dark and intense. Underneath, I picked up what might have been anticipation.

But for what?

It took me a moment to realize she was trying to read my eyes too. The samurai around her, even big Kaito, seemed to melt into the dense growth as they moved under the guise of their wards to get closer to the temple.

Princess Halia clasped my wrist. "Wait on my word," she whispered.

I nodded, wishing I could know for sure that we were on the same side.

She stepped back into the hidden opening with her Himitsu paintings until the illusion covered her.

Nestling the butt end of my MP88 into a shoulder, I began my climb.

———

I arrived at a rock outcropping and eased into position. Between the trees, a view of Meong Kal opened below me.

The city was the size of several football fields set side by side. Hundreds, if not thousands, of figures moved among the buildings, trees, and ancient roads like worker ants. Some piled onto rudimentary scaffolding, smoothing walls and setting new stones. Others carted earth from deep excavation pits. There were children among them, and the sight of their dirt-smeared faces drew my gut into a hard knot.

The *khon ngu* populated the work force too. I half expected them to be hissing and cracking whips, but there was no need. Though emaciated, everyone worked diligently. In the light of scattered pyres their large eyes and sweat-drenched bodies seemed to burn with the same single-minded goal of restoring the evil city.

Most of the activity centered around a tiered pyramid at the city's center. It rose as if reaching for the canopy formed by an arrangement of tall trees with broad, intersecting branches. I recognized the pyramid as the temple to Akeila. Its pillars were massive serpents carved from stone. Multi-armed snake creatures patrolled its many levels. Part of our objective was to shift the guards from the temple.

On the temple's topmost tier stood the crow's nest the princess had described. But if her uncle was inside the stone room, I couldn't see him through the two openings I had an angle on.

Back across the span of Meong Kal, I searched for Olaf, but came up empty.

Could mean any number of things, I reminded myself. *Not necessarily that he's dead.*

Now I trained my gaze along the jungle rim. On the saddles and hilltops, I picked out several of the multi-armed snake guards, but their attentions were fixed outward. Akeila was expecting us to arrive from the jungle.

So far, the Himitsu painting, and Princess Halia, had led us true. But of course that was how every good hustle started.

"Wolf 1 in position," I reported.

"Wolf 2 in position," Takara answered a moment later.

I searched until I found her and Rusty's location. I could just make the two of them out through the trees. That I could see them at all was only because I knew where to look.

"Wolf 3 in position," Sarah said.

I spotted her and Yoofi a moment later, also well concealed by foliage and magic.

"Keep an eye above you," I whispered. "Hostiles along the rim."

"I see them," Takara answered.

"Yoofi, how's your power holding up?"

He had looked fresh when we'd split, but I wanted to make sure Dabu was still feeding him.

"Very good, Mr. Wolfe. Dabu is acting like my father, still very upset that someone hit Yoofi on the head." He was referring to the boulder that had been dropped on him the day before. *"He is telling Yoofi, 'You go out there and hit them back.' For this, he will give me all the power I require."*

I nodded, thinking Dabu would probably get his wish and then some.

At that moment, the princess's voice came on my radio. *"Everyone is in position."*

"Window to move?" I asked.

"Now," she replied firmly.

"Hear that, everyone?" I asked. "Yoofi, be ready."

I scoped the city with my MP88. From the temple, I followed a serpentine road to an empty area that had once served as an ancient game court. It was the clearing I'd identified as a potential landing point. We were now calling it the distraction point, though "point of no return" was just as apt. I adjusted my aim and squeezed.

The MP88 shook with the discharge of grenade rounds.

27

M y grenade assault reached the court, kicking up explosions of earth and stone. As the reports echoed across the complex, the work stopped. The slave laborers scrambled down from scaffolding and out of excavation pits. As if controlled by a hive mind, they filed into buildings throughout the city. I imagined tunnels leading to underground bunkers.

Akeila was trying to preserve her worshipers—which worked for us too. I'd feared engagement with the people of Ban Mau, especially with children among them. We'd be dealing with snake people, though, and lots of them. A force began converging toward the game court, some with protective cloaks.

"Now," I radioed Yoofi.

Far below, the tumba seeds I'd packed into the grenade rounds began to grow and writhe, amassing into a dozen shambling creatures like the ones we'd faced in training. The snake people armed with bows stopped to fire, but the poisoned projectiles were ineffective against Yoofi's creations.

The larger snake creatures in their protective brooches sped forward on thick tails, multiple blades drawn. With their first slashes at the grasping arms of the animations, the battle for Meong Kal was on.

Let's just hope it's short-lived.

As the chaos unfolded below, I switched my gaze to the temple. The snake guards were holding their positions, dammit. The samurai couldn't move until they did, and how long would it take before the hostiles pinpointed our positions? Back at the game court, two of Yoofi's animations collapsed into heaps.

"Takara," I radioed.

Across the rim, a muffled shot coughed in answer. A stone brooch shattered at one of the creature's throats, dissolving his protection. The plant animation he'd been slashing seized him by the tail and slammed him against the ground before swinging him into two of the other snake creatures. The impact felled the two while the one who'd been weaponized slithered off in a crippled lurch.

More coughs sounded from Takara's position, and more protective stones exploded into fragments. Suddenly vulnerable, the snake creatures backed from the advancing animations. With the fight tilting in our favor, the temple guards began to move, half of them slithering down the steps to join the action.

That's right, I thought. *Come one, come all.*

I watched for the samurai's warded forms before noticing that several snake people around the court had begun to zero in on Takara's shots. They pivoted their bows toward her position, and arrows flew.

"Full engagement," I radioed.

Gunfire sounded from Sarah's position now. Rusty opened up a moment later. Not even Yoofi's magic could conceal the noise—exactly why I'd had them hold back.

I squeezed off a series of shots, sending up bursts of blood and scales, mostly from nonvital appendages. In deference to Leej, I was trying to maim, not kill. We just needed to buy the

samurai enough time to reach the princess's uncle. With the
sorcerer out of commission, the snake people would shake
Akeila's thrall.

But the samurai needed to hurry.

Takara continued to target the protective brooches, allowing
Yoofi's animations to pummel the creatures. Rusty and Sarah,
lacking our precision, riddled the fresh arrivals with semiauto
fire. But there were more than a hundred snake people now, and
they were overwhelming Yoofi's animations through sheer
numbers, hacking them into mulch.

I sent down another stream of grenade rounds armed with
tumba seed, then switched my aim to the rim around the city,
picking off several snake creatures that had begun moving
toward my teammates.

They were onto us.

I began to suspect Princess Halia had sent the samurai, not
to the temple, but to retrieve the heart stone. Fortunately, it was
one of the contingencies I'd planned for. At that moment, Leej
was making his way up the tunnel to where the princess was
positioned. He would radio me if the samurai returned to her
with the stone. But the next communication came from the
princess herself.

"My team is inside."

I cut my gaze back to the temple in time to catch blurring
where a staircase led to one of the temple's pillared openings. I
released my breath. The warded samurai were indeed inside,
and climbing fast.

Halle-frigging-lujah.

As I slotted home a fresh mag, my shoulders remained tense
—and not just from outer guards continuing to appear over the
rim. The more events went according to the princess's spoken
plan, the more likely it looked that the secondary threat was

something else entirely, an unknown entity we hadn't accounted for.

Probably why I caught a part of myself hoping it *was* the princess.

Between rounds of gunfire, I stole a look at the court. The snake creatures were destroying Yoofi's new creations as fast as he could grow them. The rest of the *khon ngu* had moved to better cover and begun climbing toward our positions. I sent grenade rounds into the paths of the ones I could see. The ensuing concatenation of thuds blew them around. Takara's rifle continued to crack at steady intervals, changing pitch as she took aim at the snake creatures approaching my position. I looked back at the temple.

Kaito and the others should have reached the crow's nest by now, but I couldn't see a damned thing happening up there.

I estimated we had less than five minutes before the first snake creatures reached us. After that, all bets were off, including being able to escape back to the tunnel. This was one of those moments when I appreciated just how valuable air support had been during my time in military special ops.

"Do you have an update?" I radioed the princess.

"Something's changed," she replied.

For the first time, I heard uncertainty in her voice.

"What do you mean?"

"The painting is fragmenting. Something unforeseen has disrupted the divination matrix."

With Purdy's warning jagging through my head, I sighted on a group of snake people climbing toward Sarah and Yoofi's position. I squeezed off another burst, not worrying about precision now.

"...need to see if the painting will reconstitute itself," I heard Princess Halia saying when I stopped shooting.

"How long will that take?"

"I don't know," she admitted.

"Do you still have contact with Kaito?"

Rusty had rigged up a radio for him too, but hadn't had enough components for the other samurai.

"No," she replied, *"he went silent when he entered the temple."*

I peered toward the pyramidal complex. On an upper tier, lights flashed through a window. The reports reached me a split-second later, accompanied by a sick wave of foreboding. The samurai hadn't been carrying firearms.

"Shots at the temple," I radioed. "Takara, help the others to the rally point."

"Where are you going?" she asked.

"To check it out."

I was already moving from the stone outcropping and making my way down the basin. One benefit of having drawn the snake people toward us was that it had thinned their numbers in the city. But my instincts were telling me that whatever was happening in the temple was the bigger threat right now.

"I'll meet you there," she said.

I had wanted Takara to keep an eye on the princess and was about to tell her to remain at the rally point, but my instincts were also telling me I would need backup. Especially if this was Purdy's secondary threat.

"Get the others to the tunnel first," I said, "then come in high."

I clipped my MP88 to my pack and fell to all fours, my long arms giving me improved maneuverability and extra speed. Trees flashed past. Vines and thickets of growth broke around my helmet. The gunfire from the temple continued to chatter. Were these the weapons the snake creatures had looted from the black ops team? Who the hell was shooting them? My ears picked up a high-pitched wavering, probably outside of human hearing.

Cutting around a hillock, I surprised three snake creatures climbing toward me. They reared back with hisses, spears in their grasps. No protective brooches, though.

Before they could organize themselves, I lowered a shoulder into the first. The impact flattened him. I arced my talons around, catching a second snake person in the throat. Scales and sinew tore away. The third snake person leapt out of my reach and then lunged in with his spear. I seized the hilt below the blade, yanked him toward me, and punched him in the snout hard enough to crush something and make his eyes roll up. Before his body hit the ground, I was barreling downhill again.

"How you doing?" I radioed my teammates.

"Moving," Sarah answered. *"We're ahead of them."*

"Good. Keep it that way. More are coming up."

With my teammates secure, we would have a backup force for whenever the princess's painting reorganized itself. I didn't trust her yet, but I was warming to the idea she wasn't the secondary threat.

I broke from the jungle and found myself on a road at the edge of Meong Kal's excavation zone. Taking my MP88 back into my hands, I pressed myself to the nearest wall to get my bearings. Ancient stone buildings rose ahead of me while the temple to Akeila loomed over the city. The restoration was impressive, I would give the serpent goddess that. Amazing what evil magic and slave labor could accomplish.

From my earlier vantage point, I'd seen that all roads led to the temple, though in winding paths. That was to my advantage as it limited lines of sight on me, especially now that the temple was clear of sentry.

Staying low, I followed the road's edge. The bullet cartridge I'd swallowed continued to act as magical concealment and protection. Like in the swampland, though, the poisonous energy was stronger down here, clouding my senses. The beating source seemed to be beneath my feet—"underground," the princess had said.

Maybe another reason to trust her.

I approached the first intersection and peered around the corner. To the west, several of the multi-armed snake creatures were on the move. As I raised my weapon, Yoofi's magic drifted from my loaded rifle mag. Squinting down the sight at the backs of the creatures' cloaks, I side-stepped into the open. Their backs remained to me, though, and I cleared the intersection without having to engage.

Beyond the next intersection, I followed the curve of the road until I was facing a broad flight of steps that climbed to the temple complex. Gunfire and the high-pitched wavering continued to sound from the top tiers. I climbed the stairs several at a time and arrived on the first level between a pair of serpent pillars. A room opened ahead, two narrower sets of steps flanking the entrance.

Leading with my weapon, I went in to ensure the room was clear. Large murals adorned the walls of the impressive space, each one featuring a different image of the serpent goddess. I imagined the enslaved people of Ban Mau packing inside to moan chants of praise to Akeila, starved bodies pressed to the stone floor. The smell of blood drifted from the joints in the stones, suggesting unspeakable rituals.

As the left side of the room waxed into view, I found someone staring up at a mural. Sighting on him, I stepped all the way into the room. He was looking at a depiction of Akeila's serpent body and sharp feminine face rising over a battlefield.

"Such a beautiful naga," he said.

"Who are you?" I demanded.

The man who turned was short and lean. His slicked-back

hair had gone an aggressive silver while his thick eyebrows remained black. Charges went off in my head. He fit the princess's description of her uncle to a T. This was Boonsong.

A dark robe with colorful ornamentation on the cuffs draped his body. It whispered as he began to stride toward me, apparently unconcerned by my size and weapon.

His mistake.

The MP88's muzzle exploded with rifle fire, and a storm of magic-enhanced rounds blew into—and through—him. He stopped and peered over a shoulder. The wall behind him should have been bullet-pocked and billowing dust, but both wall and mural were unscathed. When his eyes returned to mine, they glowed yellow.

"As I was telling you, the form you were admiring is known as a naga," he said in accented English. "When Akeila becomes flesh in our world, that is what she will look like."

He chuckled as if enjoying a private joke. I responded by leaping toward him and slashing my talons through his neck. The blow met something, but not flesh. More like a thickening in the air. I slashed twice more, but Boonsong didn't react. Instead, he gazed past me at a mural on another wall.

"Magnificent, yes?"

I was obviously dealing with an illusion, no doubt to keep me from the action upstairs. And, dammit, it had delayed me. I took off toward the entrance I'd come in by, but it was like running on a treadmill. The entrance remained out ahead of me, always the same distance away. Grunting, I upped my speed, but I couldn't get any closer. I veered toward another entranceway but with the same result.

What the hell?

Coming to a sudden stop, I checked for Yoofi's magic. Had he been taken out again? But I could feel it working inside me, continuing to protect me from Akeila's poison. I tested my throat. Fine.

"Oh, your protection is working as it should," Boonsong said. "But it's no defense against the circle you stepped into."

Circle? I looked down, but the floor was unmarked.

When Boonsong chuckled, I followed his raised eyes. On the inside of the triangular ceiling was a large casting circle rendered in the blood I'd smelled earlier, and I was standing inside its circumference.

I'd walked into a damn trap.

28

Sarah had lectured our team on circle traps. I'd also experienced one when I'd encountered Prof Croft in New York and he thought I was a demon. The traps held powerful binding energy. Though a cylinder of hardened air wasn't holding me as it had in New York, this one felt just as claustrophobic.

I ripped rifle fire at the symbol on the ceiling, but it was no more effective than my attack on Boonsong a few moments before. It was as if the circle was sucking the rounds into another dimension. I also understood that Boonsong *was* here, but he'd been careful to remain outside the circle the whole time. Had the samurai run into casting circles too? The shooting and high-pitched sounds seemed to have stopped.

I keyed my radio. Static.

"Let me out," I growled above my tightening chest.

"Why?" Boonsong asked, fingering an ornate stone necklace. "So you can kill me?"

"Tell us where the heart stone is and we won't have to."

"And why would I do that?"

Though he had become a vessel for Akeila, he wasn't

speaking in the hissing voice that had come through Yoofi. If anything, he sounded patient, almost professorial. I would take my stabs at reaching whatever mortality remained in him. That would also buy me time until Takara arrived.

"Because Akeila is using you," I said. "And when she's done, she'll toss out your bag of flesh like yesterday's garbage."

Boonsong chuckled. "Akeila's vision for the world frightens you, but only because you don't understand it."

"Her vision of the world is a nightmare."

"See? It's natural you would take that view."

"It's called the *sane* view."

"Then let me explain it in a way that will sound less insane." He began to stroll around the circle, hands clasped behind his back. "I studied Akeila for years before arranging the expedition to Meong Kal. I had my doubts, believe me. As both a creator and destroyer, Akeila is a complex goddess. It's easy to focus on the destroyer part, because it is terrible. But is it any more terrible than the devastations nature wreaks on a daily basis? Monsoons, earthquakes, massive mudslides. You must have heard about the tsunami last year in the Gulf of Thailand? Twenty thousand lives ended like that." He snapped his fingers.

"And that's nothing compared to manmade disasters," he continued. "Did you know the second World War claimed thirty million in the Pacific Theater alone? Yes, rebuilding follows such events—*creation*, you could call it—but it's disorganized and haphazard. Is it any wonder the human race has reached such a chaotic state? Look at any political map of the world, Captain. Boundaries inside of boundaries to keep us *civilized*." He leaned toward me and lowered his voice to a whisper. "Which is to say, to keep us from killing each other."

"It might not be perfect, but it works," I grunted.

He stopped and widened his eyes. "I find that surprising

coming from a soldier who has engaged in wars in, what is it now, four countries?"

I clenched my thoughts—*how could he know that?*—before remembering Akeila had been in my head twice now. Because of the way Boonsong presented, I had to remind myself that I was talking to both him and the serpent goddess.

"With the country's consent in three of those cases," I replied.

While Boonsong talked, I positioned myself so I was facing the two entrances to the room, forcing his back to them. Takara and my teammates should have been close to the rally point by now, meaning I could expect her at the temple soon. I fixed my eyes on his while monitoring the entranceways in my peripheral vision.

"Since you bring up World War Two," I said, "we've had nothing approaching a conflict that size in the eighty years since. Your slippery-slope argument doesn't work." I stepped around a little more.

"But conflicts have proliferated regardless, yes? Even inside those political boundaries? You've seen the horrors, Captain. You came to New Siam believing you were investigating an army massacre of civilians, and you had good reason. My brother has murdered civilians before. It was the last attack that convinced me to help Akeila."

"Why, so you could commit horrors of your own?"

"What do you mean?" he asked in what seemed honest surprise. "The people of Ban Mau are alive and thriving here. You saw them."

"They're *alive*," I allowed. "But what about the ones Akeila couldn't control? What about the temple servants?"

Boonsong nodded in accession. "That is the destructive part of her nature. But we're talking about a very small percentage,

Captain. And isn't it just as likely they would have succumbed to accident or illness?"

"Justified homicide based on an actuarial table? Give me a fucking break."

Boonsong showed his hands. "Allow me to finish. You're not saying anything I didn't once feel myself. But here again, you're trying to see Akeila as a person. She's not. She's a force beyond human comprehension. Would you judge nature so harshly?"

"Nature has no ulterior motives," I said. "No power ambitions."

"Yes!" He stopped and thrust up a finger as if we'd reached some point of agreement. "And that is the difference. That is what separates Akeila from both nature and humankind. She has a creative vision."

"Turning us into snakes?"

"Into gods, Captain. The beings that once worshipped her were simple but evolving. Their mastery of the physical world, or their corner of it, was unparalleled in its day. That mastery would have soon reached the astral dimensions—constructing realities by mere thought. Imagine that, Captain! Actually, you don't need to. The *poison zone* you've been complaining of was one of Akeila's astral forms coiling around her children. It was never meant to harm you, but to safeguard them."

"A little ironic that the one making god-promises is a fat serpent."

He chuckled again. "Well, you're not entirely wrong. Like her children, Akeila is not yet fully realized either. The goddess evolves along with her believers. That said, Akeila is the highest form of serpent deity. Did you know that nagas are revered in Eastern religions? Indeed, they are protectors of the enlightened. The Buddha himself was said to have been sheltered by a naga during a storm. After helping her children master the astral realms, Akeila will see that they attain spiritual dimensions. And at that point, she will break from her naga form and become a transcendent being herself."

Light shone from Boonsong's eyes, bathing his face in sickly yellow light. "Now tell me honestly, Captain, would such a race —one that transcends body and mind, space and time—have any need for political boundaries and incessant warring? Would such a race attack its own people? Bury their bodies in mass graves?"

He was referring to his brother's campaign again. His eyes dimmed, and for the first time, I caught something human. The civilian massacre had left an imprint he couldn't shake, even under Akeila's thrall.

"Listen to me," I growled. "Akeila is telling you what you want to hear. Her highest ambition isn't *enlightenment*. It's to bring as many people as she can under her control so she can mutate them and grow her own power. Have you taken a close look at the people of Ban Mau? They're not *thriving*. They're mindless drones."

"It is a necessary first step."

"To her domination!" I roared.

He shook his head. "The beings who originally worshipped Akeila were the mindless ones, and yet look what they built." I stiffened as he turned toward the entranceways, his arms open to indicate the city.

"Yeah, built for *her*."

"Imagine what we'll accomplish as we advance." He strolled toward the main entrance.

Takara would be heading this way any moment, and I needed to preserve the element of surprise.

"Well, history seemed to have other ideas," I said. "It buried Akeila in a swamp full of shit."

My effort to goad him worked. He spun back toward me, cords of muscle straining from his neck even as his voice remained calm. "Ah, but she did not stay buried, did she? Her will was too strong. She returned and—"

"Was taken down again," I interrupted. "This time by a tribe of primitive humans."

At the mention of humans, anger flashed in his eyes. "And she returned a th-th-third time," he managed, lips sputtering with hisses. "Because *I* raised her. Someone she's waited thousands of years for. Someone whose powers fit perfectly inside hers, like a hand inside a glove." He thrust his palms out to the sides. Dark, squirming energy slammed into two walls, making them roll like waves. Expecting stones to come down, I crouched back, but Boonsong folded his hands in a sudden clasp, and the walls stopped moving.

He grinned. "Do you see?"

"Yeah, and she'll use your powers until she doesn't need them or you anymore."

"You keep saying this, Captain, but you don't fully understand our relationship. I am not her servant."

"So she tells you."

"I am her husband. Her *lover*."

I stared as his smile spread from his teeth, each one filed to a sharp point. Maybe this guy was too far gone to bring back.

"I know her much more intimately than you understand," he said. "And like a good husband, I take her harshest qualities and soften them. You can imagine my pain when you destroyed part of Akeila's heart. And yet I'm willing to forgive you. You didn't know what I've since shared. You didn't feel it in your own heart."

Still smiling, he pounded his chest hard enough to leave a bruise.

"You still think you're going to convince me of your fantasy?"

"I had hoped so, Captain. But failing that I just need time."

"Time for what?" I pivoted to either side with my weapon.

"My magic can hold you inside the circle, but Akeila can't convert you. Not as long as you have protection." His yellow eyes dropped to my stomach, where Yoofi's magic continued to work.

"Then come and do something about it," I growled.

Outside the circle, he was safe from me. Inside was another story.

"That won't be necessary."

I winced as the high-pitched sound I'd heard on the top levels of the temple began to quaver across the city. My hackles stiffened. The sound was coming from the area of the hidden tunnel.

Boonsong chuckled. "You see, my niece told me of your plan."

"Princess Halia?" Had she been the secondary threat after all?

The magic inside me sputtered, meaning Yoofi was down, maybe the others too.

"Now," Boonsong said, his eyes going bright yellow again. "To *truly* bring you into our fold."

I tried to squint away, but a pair of invisible hooks snagged my eye sockets.

"Yesss," he hissed. "You have an important role with us. You will help spread Akeila's influence."

I squeezed the MP88's trigger, but like before, the circle swallowed the burst of gunfire. The hooks from Boonsong's eyes tugged, drawing my head down to his smiling face. I ignored the pain, straining back until a growl grew from my heaving chest.

"Oh, you're a powerful one," he said hungrily.

Can't let this wacko and his serpent bitch inside my head.

For the last eight months, I'd been training my wolf nature to remain in equilibrium with my human side. Now I stuck him with a sharp stick.

The anger began in the pit of my stomach, hot and feral.

With my next hard stick, the anger erupted, roaring from my throat with temple-rattling force. Boonsong staggered back from the circle, the hooks in my eye sockets buckling. I reared my head, trying to break from them entirely, but Boonsong reset his feet and leaned in again. Sweat glistened around his glowing eyes. He was no longer smiling.

"Akeila can help you too," he whispered desperately, "restore you to your human form."

Images wriggled through my head of a life with Daniela, but Akeila was drawing those wishes from Jason Wolfe, and he wasn't the one in control.

The Blue Wolf roared again and pulled back.

Boonsong's slippered feet slid toward the edge of the circle as he strained to hold me.

"Why do you fight Akeila?" he seethed. "Can't you see her godlike beauty, her *vision*?"

I felt him struggle now to release me, to retract the psychic hooks from my eyes, but my mind clamped down. I had the son of a bitch. He wasn't going anywhere until he was inside the blood circle with me.

Until he was *mine*.

Boonsong skidded forward another inch, his toes almost touching the outside of the circle now. His body trembled with the effort of leaning away. In the yellow of his eyes, small spots of blood began to appear.

"P-please," he begged. "Akeila! Help me!"

Dark astral energy streamed above him and gathered into the shape of a serpent. It circled the room, but the trap that held me also seemed to be keeping the energy out. A flaw in the design. Pink tears dribbled from the corners of Boonsong's eyes.

"No!" he wailed.

The toe of his right shoe broke through the circle.

I thrust a hand down to pull him in the rest of the way. At the same time, I picked up movement in the main entranceway. Takara?

A wall of force slammed into the side of my head, and the world went topsy-turvy. It wasn't until I felt hard stone against my shoulder and hip that I realized I'd gone down. I struggled to gain a knee, but my muscles kicked in every direction and I fell again.

A ringing pain spiked into my brain—the aftereffect of whatever had hit me.

I squinted up at Boonsong's wavering form. He had backed from the edge of the circle and was dabbing his eyes with the sleeve of his robe. Several dark figures moved in around him. I couldn't see them clearly, but I recognized the stance, the way they held their weapons. They weren't snake creatures. These were soldiers, probably the mercs whose camp we'd found. They'd hit me with an ultrasonic attack, something I didn't know had been engineered into effective handheld weapons until now.

But what in the hell were the mercs doing alive?

I struggled some more, just trying to get myself upright.

"It was my agreement with Akeila," Boonsong said, lowering the sleeve of his robe from his eyes. "After seeing the aftermath of my brother's massacre, I couldn't stomach any more deaths. Not even from Akeila, force of nature or not. She finally consented."

As the mercs sharpened into focus, so did my understanding. They peered back at me with dead gray eyes. One's jaw had been blown off. Rotting strings of flesh dangled around his upper teeth.

"Akeila allowed me to restore them," he continued. "To give them new life."

"New life?" I managed. "You turned them into fucking zombies."

"I would dispute that word, Captain. But haven't you done the same?"

He raised his eyes past me. I craned my neck around to see a large figure stepping through the other entrance, weapon propped against his shoulder. I would have recognized the figure and weapon anywhere.

"Olaf!" I called.

"The *zombie* is no longer yours to command," Boonsong said.

Olaf brought his MP88 down and leveled it at me.

I fixed my eyes on his. "Olaf, it's Captain Wolfe."

Sarah had said the snake people's venom was potent enough to break down the oxytocin in his system, the hormone that helped bond him to his teammates, to me. But if even a little of that imprinting remained...

"It's your Captain," I said.

"Put him down," Boonsong ordered.

Olaf lowered his head to the weapon and aimed with a yellow eye.

I tried to throw up an arm, but my muscles were still too herky-jerky from the ultrasonic attack. Gunfire erupted from the barrel of the MP88, swallowing my helmet in a deafening wall of explosive impacts.

29

I sat up and drew a frothing breath. The space around me was coal black, too dark for my wolf vision. A faint ring resonated in my ears while my temples throbbed with the ghost of Olaf's attack. The concussive impacts had knocked me right out.

I brought a hand to my forehead. My helmet was gone, replaced by a thick stone band that circled my head like a form-fitting halo. I dug my talons underneath it and tried to pull it off. The halo crushed down.

The hell?

I pulled harder. This time, sharp points bit into my skull. Through the teeth-grinding flashes of pain, I pictured spikes growing from the halo's inside. Swearing, I dropped my hand. The spikes retracted. Blood ran warm through the hair down the sides of my face as healing tissue filled the punctures.

I felt over the rest of my body. Stripped bare.

I patted around where I was sitting. Stone floor, thick pillar at my back. Using the pillar, I pulled myself to my feet. The effort left me dizzy. How long had I been out? I wiped my muzzle and tried to listen.

A chorus of breathing rose and fell around me.

I lifted my nose. Thick smells of stone formed the room's scent base. It was covered by a coppery layer of blood. I picked up currents of magic too. Bad magic. Beyond, a tangle of familiar odors drifted past.

My heart hammered hard.

My teammates were here, and they were alive.

When I'd heard the ultrasonic attack on their position, when I'd felt Yoofi's magic sputter, I'd feared the worst. But Akeila hadn't wanted us dead for some reason. Maybe Boonsong, the man who couldn't stand killing, had appealed on our behalf. Regardless, my immediate job was to get everyone to safety.

Sensing Sarah to my left, I whispered her name. I took an unsteady step toward her, my four-hundred-pound frame teetering in the darkness. My next step was surer. By the acoustics of my voice and footfalls, I could tell our chamber was smallish. I pawed ahead of me as I continued in her direction.

"*Sarah,*" I repeated, louder.

She didn't answer, and I didn't seem to be getting any closer to her. When I reached behind me, I felt the stone pillar again, still warm where I'd leaned against it. Dammit. Another one of Boonsong's circle traps. I moved in different directions but couldn't get more than a couple feet from the pillar.

I propped against the support, not as tired as I'd been a moment ago. As I breathed, my brain parsed through the scents of my teammates and the samurai. Princess Halia's scent was notably absent.

"Anyone awake?" I called.

Off to my right, someone's breath caught on a snort. Thick murmuring followed.

"That you, Rusty?"

"Boss?" he asked groggily.

"You all right?"

He coughed to clear his throat. "I think so. Where are we?"

The absolute darkness coupled with the stuffiness suggested underground, and that was the one-word answer I gave Rusty.

"What's this thing on my head?"

"Don't try to—"

"Ow!" he cried.

"—remove it," I finished.

"It about crushed my skull."

"It'll do worse than that. Boonsong's animating magic must be powering it." Remembering how he had made the walls move earlier, I guessed that he'd designed the halos as a backup to the circle traps.

"I thought the samurai were gonna take him out."

"That was the plan," I said thinly. "What happened on your end?"

"Well, we made it back to the rally point fine, but the princess wasn't there. Takara went airborne for a better view. Next thing I know, she's falling like a shot pheasant. Yoofi raised his staff to cast a spell, but he went down too. And then I'm getting walloped by something. Some sort of invisible force. Knocked me clear from my feet. That's the last thing I remember."

"An ultrasonic attack," I said.

"Ultrasonic?" He scuffed to his feet. "The spear-chuckers have that kind of tech?"

"No, the merc team whose camp we found. Boonsong reanimated the ones he could salvage, turned them into zombies."

And a surprisingly effective guard, I thought.

"But how did they know where we were?"

"You said Princess Halia wasn't at the rally point?"

"Sure wasn't." He hesitated. "Oh, shit. She ratted us out?"

"It's what her uncle's claiming."

She must never have intended for us to take him down. She

had used Boonsong as a dummy objective, sending the samurai to a temple mined with circle traps and zombie mercs. With the rest of us split up, she had slipped from the rally point. It was then just a matter of Boonsong positioning the remaining mercs around the tunnel entrance before we returned. As spec ops-trained soldiers with high-tech gear, they could have accomplished that without Takara sensing them, especially in thick jungle. I wondered why Leej hadn't alerted me, but they could have found him too.

"Backstabbing floozy," Rusty grumbled.

"Do you have anything on you?" I asked.

"Naw, I'm stripped to the skivvies. You?"

"Nothing. Try walking toward me."

He took several shuffling steps, but I could tell he wasn't getting any closer.

"You can stop," I said. "We're being held by circle traps."

I heard him sit heavily. "Did an ultrasonic weapon drop you too?"

I saw Olaf staring at me down the barrel of his MP88. "Sort of."

"Man, I'm really dizzy."

Boonsong had probably bled Rusty like he'd done the cleric and acolytes, but I didn't want to scare him. My regenerative abilities would have frustrated any attempt Boonsong had made on my own neck.

"So..." The acoustics of Rusty's breathing changed as he peered around. "What's the plan?"

"First, to get the rest of the team up. See what we have to work with."

"They're here too?" Rusty didn't wait for me to answer before hissing, "*Takara! Yoofi!*"

I worked on Sarah again. It took several minutes, but one by one, we got through to the rest of our teammates. Even Kaito grunted, and I heard his breaths go from sleeping to waking.

After warning them against trying to remove their halos, I called for status updates. Kaito reported four samurai killed during their encounter with the mercs. There had been no other deaths or serious injuries.

I told everyone about the circle traps holding us. As I'd done with Rusty, I had them test theirs. If even one had an imperfection in its blood ring, the person inside could escape and break the circles around the rest of us. The thought of being freed got my wolf heart racing. Every circle was intact, though.

"How's your connection to Dabu?" I asked Yoofi.

"I feel nothing right now," he replied in a wincing voice. He'd tested his halo despite my warning. "It is like someone has built a wall between us."

"Do you have anything to attempt to cast through?"

"No, Mr. Wolfe. No staff, no coat. All I have is this robe."

"They gave you a robe?" Rusty asked. "How come I didn't get one?"

"Forget the robe," I barked. "How about your swords, Kaito?"

If they could cleave through Akeila's heart stone, they had a good chance of breaking through Boonsong's magic.

"No swords," he grunted.

"Sarah?"

"Nothing," she said.

I attuned my senses to the energy around me. I had super strength and speed, but they were powerless against the forces binding us. There was nothing physical to attack except the blood circle itself, and that couldn't be done from inside the trap. We needed a power source that could overwhelm the magic holding the circles together. Takara was off to my right, but she had said little since awakening. I could barely hear her breaths. From where I was standing, she felt like a void in the darkness.

"Takara," I called. "Can you summon your dragon?"

She remained silent for so long, I thought she wasn't going to answer. Everyone else quieted down except for Kaito, whose breaths cycled harshly. I was asking her to invoke the being that had destroyed his clan.

"I can try," she said at last.

"You will not summon that demon," Kaito threatened.

"Shut it," I told him.

"Takara," he barked through the darkness.

"Jesus, dude," Rusty said. "Some of us want to get out of here alive."

"I would rather stay here and *die* than be aided by a demon."

Rusty snorted. "I'm sure that can be arranged."

"Let her focus," I ordered everyone.

Red flashed from Takara's eyes. With that bit of light, I could see the entire room. The chamber was a little larger than I'd estimated. Pillars lined the side of the room where we were being held, the circle traps around us painted on the floor this time. Against the opposite wall stood an empty dais with a doorway beside it. Except for Rusty, who was wearing a sagging pair of underwear, everyone was clad in dingy robes. Blood-spotted bandages covered throats, confirming my suspicion about the blood-letting.

The blood encircling them is probably their own.

I looked back at Kaito, who was between the two other surviving samurai. He was without his helmet and mask, and dark hair plastered his head. I keyed in on his face. It was badly scarred, the skin having oozed and hardened, not unlike over Takara's body. I remembered her account of the bomb strike on Hiroshima, how her brother had carried her from the temple. I assumed he died in the dragon's attack, but he hadn't.

The scarring coupled with his scent told me Kaito was Takara's brother.

Astral flames broke around Takara's body, and she began to rise from the floor. With the next billow of fire, wings spread from her arms and a pair of fierce eyes rose above her head. I felt the magic in the room buckle.

Kaito cringed away.

C'mon, Takara, I urged.

The dragon's fire shimmered over my teammates' sweat-sheened faces. The fire was also throwing shadows around the room. An especially large shadow occupied the dais. Like a coiled snake letting out, it slid down and weaved between the pillars. Only when it reached Takara did its tail end finally slip from the dais steps. No one else seemed to notice. It rose above my teammate and undulated, watching.

Akeila's astral form.

"Push, Takara," I called. "Push!"

The magic confining us buckled again. Then Takara doubled over with a cry and clutched the halo around her head. Her fiery dragon form collapsed back into her, and the room returned to darkness.

"Takara," I called.

Hissing laughter echoed throughout the chamber. Akeila had been toying with us, giving us false hope before killing it again.

"What the hell do you want?" I demanded.

Light glowed in the doorway beside the dais, and Boonsong descended into view. He was accompanied by several multi-armed snake creatures bearing torches and glistening spears. Princess Halia entered with them. As she took her place beside her uncle, head erect, my muzzle wrinkled from my teeth.

Half a dozen zombie mercs filed in behind her. Four carried what looked like automatic rifle/grenade-launcher combos and

the other two large box-shaped weapons that must have been
the ultrasonic guns. They arrayed themselves to either side of
the princess and her uncle, barrels trained on us.

Olaf took up the rear, his thick fists clutching his MP88.

I looked over at Takara. She lay on her side in a dispersion of
smoke, blood welling from under the stone halo. She was
conscious, though. I could hear her breaths hissing between her
clenched teeth.

"She'll be fine," Boonsong said. "I could easily have crushed
her skull."

"Yeah, you're a real saint," I muttered.

"It's called self-preservation, Captain." He reached his hands
back, and one of the snake people placed Kaito's long and short
katanas in them. "Or did you forget how she used one of these to
shatter part of my wife's heart."

"Wife?" Rusty said. "Gross."

Boonsong raised the swords, and green animating magic
swirled around their lengths. The once-lethal blades began to
soften and twist. Kaito stiffened in my peripheral vision. When
Boonsong finished, the swords looked like melted pretzels.

"There," he said, tossing them aside.

They landed with damp thuds. I looked from the swords—
allegedly the only weapons that could destroy the heart stone—
to the princess. She stared back at me with dispassionate eyes.
Backstabber was right, but I still couldn't understand why she'd
bothered to assemble her own team of samurai, unless it was to
"recruit" them into Akeila's guard. In which case the Legion
team had been a fortunate bonus.

Boonsong smiled broadly. "Hello, everyone, and welcome to
our side."

"No one here's on your side," I growled.

"Soon, Captain."

"Let my teammates go."

"That's noble of you, but Akeila has made it clear she'd like the whole set."

The snake people, who had inserted their torches into brackets in the walls, returned and stood behind Boonsong. From the dais, the shadow of Akeila's astral form rose and undulated in a slow dance behind them. I didn't know if my teammates could see her, but I had never wanted to destroy anything more.

I lowered my gaze to the princess. "So you fell for the sales pitch, huh? I thought you were smarter than that."

"I know what you cannot," she replied simply.

"My niece has a gift." Boonsong beamed at her. "She can divine the future, and she's seen exactly what I was trying to tell you. I don't fault you for lacking her abilities, Captain, but your stubborn stance in the face of powerful counterevidence leaves us little choice. What we're about to do here won't be pleasant—for me nor for you. It will be like forcing bitter medicine down a child's throat, but it will ultimately benefit everyone here. We're about to enter a phase of rapid growth. My brother's health is failing, you see. When Princess Halia takes power, New Siam and its vast wealth will be ours."

So that was why she was collaborating with her uncle.

"With the military defending our borders," he continued, "your team will have a special role. Infiltrating neighboring countries, helping to spread Akeila's influence and vision. One by one, those countries will enter our sphere of influence: Thailand, Laos, the rest of Southeast Asia. And then China."

Hunger shook his voice, and for good reason. With China, they would control over half the world's population, not to mention a formidable military and a dangerous nuclear arsenal.

"And while you're swallowing the Eastern Hemisphere," I said, "do you really think the West is just going to sit back and watch?"

Akeila's massive shadow continued to dance above them.

"There's a plan for everything, Captain," Boonsong said.

"Including nuclear war?" I pressed. "If King Savang's massacre bugged you, how are you going to feel about those deaths multiplied by a factor of thousands. You need to think long and hard about this."

Though Boonsong continued to smile, something shook in his gaze. Akeila's shadow lowered its head and whispered near his ear.

"That's enough now, Captain," Boonsong said in a tight voice. "Even Akeila's beneficence has its limits."

"She's serving *herself*," I pressed, my gaze cutting between him and the princess.

"There are three ways to do this," he said. "The first—reasoning with you—has failed. We're now offering the second, to place you under Akeila's thrall so you can see and understand her plan for yourself."

"Yeah?" I growled. "And what's the third?"

"To end your lives and reanimate you. It's not my preferred choice, but if it's the one you leave me..."

I looked at the half-rotted mercs, then over at my teammates. Takara, our best chance to escape the circle traps, remained down. Yoofi and Rusty looked back at me miserably, halos clamped around their heads. Sarah, meanwhile, was touching the bloody bandage at her neck and studying the room. I could see her brain working behind her eyes, pulling in every data point, processing our odds of escape.

Bleak, I could have told her.

"Shall we begin?" Boonsong asked.

The astral shadow of Akeila dipped her head and came up underneath Boonsong, infusing his form with her poisonous essence. His eyes turned bright yellow as he walked up to Sarah's blood circle.

She stepped back.

"Leave her alone," I warned.

Boonsong ignored me, bringing his face to the edge of her trap. From my vantage, I could see the hook-like energy twisting from his eyes to hers. She jerked as the hooks latched onto her sockets and drew her forward.

With a roar, I tried to leap toward them. The zombie mercs aimed their weapons at me, but I remained confined in the circle trap. I could only watch as Sarah struggled against Akeila's possession. My teammate's face began to twist and contort around eyes that hardened before trying to shrink back.

Her pain and helplessness were horrible to witness.

Soon, Sarah's eyes took on a yellow tint. Boonsong released her, and she staggered back, hair in disarray, robe fallen open at the neck. Even with her glasses, she looked like a completely different person from just moments before.

Boonsong dropped his gaze to the blood circle and spoke a word. A wave of animating magic shifted one of the stones in the floor enough to break the circle. In a copper-scented gust, the binding magic dispersed.

"Come," Boonsong said, holding his hand toward Sarah.

She took it and stepped from the circle on her bare feet.

"Now, is this so bad?" he asked, dipping his face to hers.

"No," she said. "It's ... nice."

Boonsong chuckled and nuzzled his nose against her hair like an affectionate father. "Perhaps you can convince your Captain that the change isn't so horrific." He turned her so she was facing me. "Go on."

On cue, she walked toward me until she was passing through my circle.

I gripped her shoulders and lowered my voice. "Sarah, can you hear me?"

"I can hear you fine."

"You're possessed again."

She smiled dreamily, as if she'd just taken a hit of morphine. "I know, but it's not forever. It's just until..."

Her smile faltered. Once more, I could see her brain working, which was encouraging. She hadn't been cored out like I'd feared. But maybe that was what Boonsong had wanted me to see. As screwed up as he was, I believed the king's massacre had truly shaken him. I believed that he thought Akeila would bring peace and spiritual transformation to New Siam and the rest of the world. And I believed that he wanted to make this as painless for us as possible. But Akeila was the one running the show, not him.

"Until..." Sarah tried again.

"Until you can see Akeila's creative vision for yourselves," Boonsong finished gently.

"Yes." Sarah's eyes turned dreamlike again, and she caressed my cheek. "Do it for the team, Jason," she whispered. "Do it for us."

Us?

In the next moment, her lips were pressed to mine and she was clutching the hair behind my ears in her fists. The aggressiveness of her kiss caught me off guard, and it took me a moment to pull her away.

"Is this your idea of fun?" I growled at Boonsong.

"Oh, that's not coming from us. It appears Akeila's influence has relaxed your teammate's inhibitions, releasing her true feelings. But stand to one side now, dear," he said to Sarah. "It's time to speed things along. Akeila has work for you and your team."

Sarah stared up at me hungrily before stepping out of the way.

I squeezed my eyes closed as Boonsong strode toward me. My halo clenched immediately, sending starbursts through my vision.

"Don't make this hard on yourself, Captain."

The halo's spikes bit into me next, sending fresh rivulets of warm blood down my face.

"I'll hate to use the third option with you," he said from inches away. "But I will."

Skull bone began to crunch. Beyond that mantle was brain.

"All right," I gasped, eyes shooting back open.

Boonsong's yellow stare was right there to snag me again, and I couldn't resist this time. Not with the halo on me.

As the psychic hooks gouged into my sockets, I managed to shift my gaze over just enough to see the princess. I expected her to be looking back dispassionately, but she was staring at her uncle's back, brow creased in resolve. In the folds of her robe, she held a dagger.

At the same moment, a shadow appeared in the doorway beside the dais.

"Now!" the princess shouted.

30

The gunfire that flashed from the doorway lit up Leej's face. With a shout, Boonsong tried to release me. I clamped down with my mind again.

"You're not going anywhere," I growled.

The stone halo squeezed my head like a vice, but as shots flashed off Boonsong's protection, the halo's grip faltered. The next shot found its mark. He screamed as his necklace shattered in a burst of stone fragments.

The zombie mercs and snake people turned their weapons toward Leej. He swung his protective coat over himself as automatic fire chattered and spears lanced in. That gave the princess her opening.

Pulling the dagger from the fold in her robe, she lunged.

"Watch out!" Sarah screamed at Boonsong from beside me.

He tried to look over, but I had him. Princess Halia's blade crunched through her uncle's right side. He arched back in a silent scream, eyes wide.

The stone halo relaxed its grip, and I pulled it off.

"Halos off, everyone!" I roared, smashing mine against the floor.

Distracted by the action in front of us, Sarah didn't resist as I removed hers too.

I felt Yoofi's magic kick back to life inside me. Meanwhile, the princess was trying to twist the blade free for another attack, but it was wedged between her uncle's ribs. With a wrench, Boonsong pulled his gaze from mine and swung his fist around. The backhand caught the princess in the temple, dropping her to the floor.

I lashed a taloned hand at Boonsong's head, but the circle remained intact, and I couldn't reach him. He staggered past me toward the back wall, one hand clutching the hilt of the dagger still buried inside him. With a flailing gesture, he animated two columns of stone in the wall and compelled them apart.

"Olaf!" he cried, staggering through the opening.

Olaf broke from the hostiles at the front of the room and lumbered toward the downed princess. I braced for him to hit her with gunfire, but his dull yellow gaze remained fixed ahead, boots plodding over Boonsong's blood trail.

A moment later, he disappeared through the opening too.

The princess pushed herself to her feet as the stone columns closed behind Olaf.

At the front of the room, Leej had withdrawn through the doorway under the cover of his protective coat. He was using the stairs to shoot down at the hostiles. Focused on Leej, they hadn't seen the princess's attack.

She approached me now and dug at my blood circle with a shoe until I felt the magic release. Stepping out of my confinement, I lowered my muzzle to her ear.

"Free the others. Use the columns for cover."

She was clearly on our side, but now wasn't the time to discuss what had happened. Nodding, she hurried off. I looked back at Sarah, who had dropped to the base of our column and was staring over her hugged-in knees. Her body remained locked in that position as I carried her to a safer position at the column's rear.

I peered out from our cover. Rounds sparked off the stone, sending dust and stone fragments into my eyes.

Damn.

In that glance, I saw that half the zombie mercs had split from the attack on Leej and were spreading toward us. One wielded an ultrasonic blaster.

I clamped my hands over my wolf ears as the blast split around the column, shaking the stone. The sound alone was like drill bits boring into my skull. With the attack ending, I uncovered my ears and heard the weapon's battery power ramping back up.

This must have been Purdy's secondary threat: zombie mercs with deadly tech. But we were no longer in the jungle. We were in a confined space with cover on our end.

I glanced over. Freed from their circles, my teammates and the samurai had stacked behind the remaining columns. Something like confidence broke through me. Other than our lack of weapons, we were in decent shape.

And we could fix the lack of weapons part.

I waved to get Takara's attention. Dried blood ringed her forehead where the halo had clamped down. I signaled and pointed to her brother and the two remaining samurai. She turned to them and relayed my message.

I showed them all a palm to say, *On my signal.*

Peeking out again, I registered the mercs' positions. I ducked back as they unleashed another attack. The ultrasonic blast was no less excruciating this time, but it was shorter. When the sound of recharging kicked in again, I signaled to Takara.

Now.

I rounded my column on the other side and sprinted in low at the ultrasonic-toting merc. The other two opened up, rounds ripping into my shoulders and the arm I was using to shield my head. I was torn up and gasping by the time I reached my target. He stepped back and squeezed his weapon's trigger.

The blaster responded with a series of clicks: low charge.

I grabbed the merc and swung him around to my front. Bullets thudded into his protective wear as the other two continued to fire. They never saw the samurai slip up behind them. Looping the mercs' necks with robe belts, the samurai pulled them onto their backs. Helmets came off, and Kaito stomped their skulls with a heel.

Takara flashed in and scooped up their rifles. She tossed one to Rusty and opened fire on the remaining hostiles. Rusty tugged up his sagging underwear and joined her.

I ripped the head off my undead merc and snatched the ultrasonic blaster from his falling body. In my healing arms, the weapon wasn't as heavy as it had looked. A digital display on the top indicated the time to the next full charge.

Less than ten seconds.

I backed toward my column as it counted down. While the snake creatures engaged Leej, the remaining three mercs turned toward us. Rounds broke over their battle suits from Rusty's indiscriminate firing. Takara focused on the other ultrasonic blaster, recognizing it as the main threat.

The room shook with the blaster's next attack. I doubled over, shoulders hunched to my ears. Takara's lips drew from her teeth, but she stood her ground behind the column. Her next shots shattered something inside the weapon. The sound of the blaster fell to a deep buzz, and smoke began pouring from its barrel.

A green light lit up on my own blaster's display: full charge.

Grinning, I squeezed the trigger.

Aimed away from me, the sound registered like a struck tuning fork. The blast pummeled the closest merc, slamming him into a wall. I swept the weapon back and forth now, hosing the remaining hostiles with the potent sound waves. The effect was like a power blower on leaves. Bodies flew around, some of them going halfway up walls. Weapons and pieces of armor rained down.

"Hot damn!" Rusty shouted.

By the time the blast finished, the hostiles were broken and scattered. We swarmed in, claimed their weapons, and finished the mercs with decapitations and shots to the head. The snake people our earlier attack hadn't killed were too battered to be a threat. They writhed or lay unconscious on the floor.

Leej descended the steps cautiously.

I gave him a thumbs-up. "Really well done."

The handheld translated from one of his coat pockets. He nodded and looked past me. I turned to find Princess Halia walking up to us.

"Glad to know we're still on the same team," I said. "A little warning would've been nice, though."

"I'm sorry. I had to work quickly." She nodded at the downed mercs. "The painting hadn't anticipated the presence of the undead. That's what made the divination come apart. When they ambushed the samurai I had to start again. Fortunately, the painting had me prepare a message for my uncle before I left."

"A message," I repeated.

"Yes, one telling him of the plot and to propose an alliance. I didn't understand its purpose, and I didn't tell anyone. I think for obvious reasons. Under the painting's new guidance, I surrendered to the *khon ngu*, compelling one of them to run my message ahead. The others took me to the temple by way of a tunnel. Leej followed. It seems he was under orders to track me." She arched an eyebrow. "But it was all as it should have been, for the painting said I was to use Leej. Though his coat hid him, I added a ward so he would blend with the guard. Our moment would come here, the painting said. It took all of my skill and training to convince my uncle, and Akeila, of my story. But it worked."

Yoofi giggled nervously. "And not a moment too soon."

My eyes tracked the blood trail, past where Sarah still sat hunched under Akeila's thrall, to the far wall Olaf and Boonsong had disappeared through.

"Where are we?" I asked.

"Below the temple," the princess replied. She pulled a painting from her robe and unfurled it. "Your weapons and gear are nearby."

"My staff too?" Yoofi asked hopefully.

"They're in the room we passed coming down," she said to Leej. "Can you show them?"

As the message translated, I took a sidearm from one of the mercs and handed it to Yoofi. Addressing him and Rusty, I said. "Help Leej. I'm going to check on Sarah. Takara, cover the doorway."

The princess sent the samurai with the weapon-retrieving team, then joined me as I went to Sarah's side. My teammate was still staring past her hugged-in knees, eyes a jaundiced yellow, pupils compressed into vertical slits.

"Sarah," I said, kneeling beside her. "Can you hear me?"

I gripped the back of her neck gently. She shuddered, her skin cold to the touch.

"Through Boonsong, she bears Akeila's curse," the princess said from behind me. "But I wounded him before he could direct her."

"What does that mean?"

"She will stay like this until the curse is removed or my uncle recovers."

"Recovers? You buried that blade to the hilt."

"Yes, but he's fled to the heart stone to be healed."

"And where's that?"

She studied the scroll again. "The location has yet to be revealed. I had to start over, remember? It will take time."

"Not sure we have time." I peered toward the doorway. "The mercs are neutralized, but more hostiles will be on the way. When our guys return with the weapons, we'll secure the entrance and get the back wall open. We can track the blood trail."

"I'd prefer more information," she said. "Especially with Kaito's blades destroyed."

"We did it your way the last time," I said, and left it at that.

The team returned shortly. They'd placed the weapons and gear on prayer rugs they'd found. With someone on each end, they carried the loads into the room. Our equipment appeared to be all there. As soon as they'd set the loads down, Yoofi picked up his staff. He clutched it to his chest and spun several times.

"Sarah needs you," I told him.

He oriented himself to me, grabbed his pack, and scampered over.

I gave Sarah's shoulder a squeeze and stood. "And no purple freckles this time."

"No, Mr. Wolfe," Yoofi replied in a way that suggested he couldn't guarantee anything.

While he worked on purging her, I geared up with the others. I checked my pack. Everything was inside, including the blocks of C4. The samurai recovered their swords. Kaito's remained on the floor in a soft tangle where Boonsong had tossed them. Back in his helmet and mask, he stared down at them forlornly.

Beside me, Rusty finished lacing his boots and stood in his full kit. One of the places where the neck of his suit was supposed to attach to his helmet had been damaged, probably when the hostiles stripped him down. A bristly section of pale flesh showed on the side of his neck.

"Can you do anything about that?" I asked.

"Already tried. Durn thing's busted."

I held the ultrasonic blaster toward him. "Take charge of the staircase with Takara and Leej. Hit anything that tries to come down."

"Whoa. You got it, boss." He took the weapon and inspected every inch of it with a tech geek's fascination. "Where are you headed?" he asked distractedly.

I hiked my pack up a shoulder. "To blow the back wall."

I stopped where Yoofi was kneeling beside Sarah. In a repeat of the night before, he was drawing Akeila's essence from her as Sarah writhed on the ground, her coughs punching through smoke issuing from a scatter of crushed leaves. The shadow serpent Yoofi wrapped around his staff was thicker this time—and meaner. Yoofi ducked from one side to the other to keep its tail from striking his head.

"*Esansu!*" he shouted, dispersing the serpentine energy.

I reached into the smoke to help Sarah sit up. "How are you?"

"Have to hurry," she said hoarsely between coughs. "Akeila is replicating."

"Replicating?" I said.

A second fit of coughing buried her attempt to answer.

"Akeila is splitting in two?" I pressed.

Sarah shook her head emphatically.

Through the smoke, the whites of Yoofi's eyes flicked between us in question.

At last Sarah got control of her coughing, and she peered up at me.

"Into hundreds," she managed.

"How do you know this?" Princess Halia asked, coming up beside us.

"While under Akeila's possession, I was in a place much like Yoofi described," Sarah said. "There are thousands of others there, the people of Ban Mau presumably, but the damp, dark place is not a physical space. It's the plane Akeila comes from. It's where she stores the minds of those she enthralls."

"Ahh," Yoofi said in revelation.

"The overwhelming urge one feels is to escape—hell, to *breathe*—but I decided that some part of Akeila's mind had to inhabit that space too. I put all of my concentration into accessing it."

I nodded for her to continue, thinking how lucky we'd been that the serpent goddess possessed our most rational member first.

"After some effort, I was able to see her thoughts. They're twisted and alien, but she's determined not to be defeated this time. Her solution is to replicate herself. To create not just one focal point of power and influence, but hundreds that can spread and operate independently of her and each other."

"Like with the splitting of the heart stone?" I asked.

Sarah squinted as though trying to see something through a fog. "The heart stone must still be destroyed, but this other thing she's doing is happening now. Once it's complete, it will make destroying her infinitely harder. Where's my kit?" she asked, gathering her loose hair from her face. "We need to move."

31

"Everyone back!"

I lined the detonation cord out along the wall, away from the primed charges pressed deep between the stones Boonsong and Olaf had disappeared through. Yoofi's magic might have worked just as well, but I wanted to preserve his power for the final assault. He and the others remained low on blood despite his healing efforts, and based on Sarah's intel, there was no telling what we were going to be walking into.

At the corner of the room I checked to ensure everyone was behind cover, then squeezed the detonator. The charges exploded in booming plumes of dust.

My teammates covered me as I returned to the site and began pulling away the cracked and pulverized stone. An opening appeared shortly. Ahead, a spattering trail and Olaf's boot prints proceeded down a narrow corridor, the scent of blood strong and fresh. Even with the poisonous energy, I'd have no trouble tracking it.

"Let's go," I called, lifting my MP88.

I was first through the opening. Princess Halia followed, still consulting her painting. She was determined to glean new information. So far, though, it hadn't given her anything besides a safe route by which Leej could leave the temple and return to the jungle. I sent him out despite his protest. When the curse broke, I wanted Leej to take charge of the snake people in Meong Kal. He would also be our above-ground contact, assuming our commo held.

Takara, Yoofi, and Sarah filed through the wall next, Kaito and the samurai behind them, carrying torches. Rusty, whom I'd ordered to cover our six, took the rear with his new toy.

"Hey, boss?" he said as he stepped into the secret corridor. "We've got party crashers."

Beyond him, I could hear the thumping of large snake bodies descending the stairwell into the temple room.

"You know what to do," I said.

He sent out an ultrasonic blast that I imagined funneling up the stairway and into the hostiles. When the blast ended, so did the sound of their arrival. I caught a few slithering back the way they'd come.

"Yep, that took care of 'em," Rusty said, bringing the blaster back to his shoulder with a look of satisfaction.

We moved quickly along the blood trail, down stone corridors as well as staircases that dropped five and ten meters at a time. Around every turn, I expected to find Olaf with his MP88 trained on my head. Boonsong had no doubt brought him as a rear guard to allow enough time for the heart stone to heal his dagger wound.

But as I eyed the growing amount of blood, I wondered whether Olaf had ended up carrying him.

When the samurais' torches began to sputter in the thickening air, I had the two low-level samurai drop off to guard against arriving hostiles. Each one set his torch in a bracket, then slipped into the shadows, blades drawn. Kaito remained with us, bearing the mundane blades of a slain clanmate.

At the bottom of an especially long stairwell, I signaled for the team to stop. The air had turned warm and humid. It carried the thick scent of reptile and beneath that, something sharper, more acidic.

I peered out. The blood trail led to the right where, after several meters, the stone corridor eroded and turned to cavern. The darkness in the far back was suffused with purple light: the other half of the heart stone.

I gave a signal. My teammates snapped on infrared lights for their night vision oculars. Takara's preternatural eyes glinted red. Whether Kaito's irises were catching their reflection, red slivered them too. The team filed past Princess Halia, who would remain back with a torch and her painting. If she could glean anything more through Himitsu, she would tell us, but my gut was suggesting we were on our own.

By her tense expression, I guessed that her gut was telling her the same.

"Be careful," she whispered just loud enough for me to hear, then receded up the stairs.

I took lead down the corridor, and the six of us stacked on the opening to the cavern. I peered inside. Boonsong was in a raised alcove at the far end, his hunched-over body enveloped in purple light. Armed snake creatures stood in concentric semi-circles of protection. Boonsong's whimpering voice echoed from the cavern walls, creating a small sound barrier for us.

I pulled back and shared what I'd seen.

"You have a clear shot at Boonsong," I whispered to Takara, then addressed the rest of the team. "When he goes down, that should disorganize Akeila's influence over the snake creatures. Rusty, scatter them anyway. Low-level blast. The rest of you cover me while I go for the heart stone."

"Do you want me to come too, Mr. Wolfe?" Yoofi asked.

"No, hang back." I wanted his magic in reserve in case shit hit the fan.

"What about Olaf?" Sarah asked.

"I didn't see him inside." But I knew what she was saying— Olaf's skills and tactical knowledge made him extremely dangerous. Even so, I wasn't going to give a kill order against a teammate. "Shoot to disarm, then to disable. Do you still have the antivenom and oxytocin?" When she nodded, I said, "Prepare me a couple syringes."

While she did that, I shifted so Takara could get into position. Using a rocky protrusion for cover, Takara sighted on the princess's uncle.

"I have him," she whispered.

Sarah handed me the capped syringes, and I put them in my tactical vest.

Crouching behind Takara, MP88 in my grip, I whispered, "Take your shot."

Her rifle coughed.

"Chest shot," she reported. "He's down."

I peered past her shoulder. In the alcove, the light from the heart stone pulsed over Boonsong's supine body. He wasn't breathing. But if his death had a disorganizing effect on Akeila's control, the snake creatures weren't showing it.

In a storm of hisses, they rushed toward the sound of Takara's shot, spears drawn. Rusty stepped in from the other side of the opening. Holding the large ultrasonic blaster at his hip, he released a sound assault. The wave plowed into the snake creatures, sending them airborne. They crashed into walls and one another.

"Yippee ki yay!" Rusty belted, sweeping the cavern again.

Not only was he having too much fun, he was going to max out the damned charge.

"That's enough," I called, seizing his arm.

Before I could pull him behind cover, a spear shot in and clattered off behind us, its poison trail stinging my nostrils. Rusty's hand flew to the side of his neck—the one exposed area of his body—and he staggered back.

Oh, don't tell me that thing got him.

Takara's rifle coughed twice, taking down Rusty's attacker.

Rusty landed hard on the seat of his pants, his face already paling as he turned toward me.

"Boss?" he said in a thin voice. "I think I just fucked up."

Blood welled between his fingers.

"Shit," I spat.

"I've got him," Sarah said. "Go."

I looked into Rusty's frightened eyes, maybe for the final time. "You die, and you're off the team."

His lips cracked into a dry smile. "Can I keep the blaster?"

"Go," Sarah repeated, her eyes compelling me to move.

She was the one who had seen into Akeila's mind, into the nightmare that would mushroom if we didn't end the threat now. I squeezed Rusty's wiry shoulder and bounded into the cavern. Downed snake creatures hissed and writhed on the floor. Takara's rifle sounded, dropping the ones that managed to waver upright. I made a line for the heart stone, my eyes searching the openings that honeycombed the cavern's walls.

No sign of Olaf, but I could feel him.

About ten meters from the heart stone, the cavern's ceiling suddenly became higher. Realizing I'd been running under a shelf, I braked and shoved myself into a retreat. Rifle rounds smacked the floor in front of me.

Olaf was overlooking the heart stone. If I'd reacted a second later, he would have dropped me with a head shot. Pulling a pair of frag grenades from my vest, I rotated them in my hand.

Would he survive the blast?

Can't reach the heart stone with him up there, I decided. His position was too solid. Swearing silently, I armed the grenades and inched to where the shelf ended. *Have to hope his regenerative abilities are up to frags at close range.*

Shooting out my arm, I hurled the grenades underhanded. The motion set off a burst of automatic fire. Pain tore through my forearm before I could draw it back. Above me, the grenades clattered onto the stone shelf and detonated. In the ringing aftermath, something heavy thudded down.

From a dead jump, I gripped the edge of the shelf, forearm screaming, and pulled myself over. The space was low and deep. Olaf had landed against a wall to my left, his suit and helmet appearing to have protected him from the shrapnel. When he saw me, he struggled to raise his MP88, but the concussions in the small space had rattled his head. The barrel wavered all over the place.

"Good to see you too," I said, knocking the weapon from his grip.

I forced him facedown and jammed a knee into the center of his back. He struggled as I unfastened the neck of his suit from his helmet. The syringe full of antivenom went in first. I followed with the oxytocin, depressing the plunger. I waited for him to stop fighting before rolling him onto his back.

"It's Jason Wolfe," I told him. "Your captain."

Olaf's eyes were no longer yellow. They regarded me dully.

I repeated variations of the phrase, trying to get him to imprint on me.

"Who do you take orders from?" I asked at last.

"Captain Wolfe," he replied in his thick voice.

I helped him sit up. "Do you know where you are?"

He looked around, then shook his head. I gave him a quick summary of what had happened, not sure how much was actually sinking in. Between the grenade blasts and coming out of his trance, he couldn't have been very clear-headed. Either way, I didn't want him armed until Yoofi had checked him for any lingering possession.

I took his knife and sidearm and patted him down to make sure he hadn't acquired any more weapons. Retrieving his MP88 from where it had landed, I removed the mags and chambered rounds, as well as the fuel tank. He watched as I loaded the ammo into my pack. I wanted to get him to the rest of the team, but the clock was ticking.

"Will you be all right up here until I get back?"

"He's not dead," he said.

"Huh?"

Olaf's eyes stared past me. I turned to find Boonsong pushing himself up from the floor. I could see the bloody spot where Takara's bullet had hit him—right through the heart— but there he was, gaining his feet.

"You've gotta be kidding me," I muttered.

"He's like me now," Olaf said.

Undead?

I lifted my MP88, sighted on his head, and fired.

The magically-enhanced round sparked off the purple light surrounding him.

When Boonsong raised his face, I recognized the dull gray of his eyes. He'd succumbed to the princess's dagger attack, but through some combination of Akeila's power and his own animating magic, he'd resurrected himself.

I fired twice more, but my rounds couldn't reach him. He'd fashioned the heart stone's energy into protection for himself. More sparks flashed from the purple light as Takara took up the attack.

His eyes still fixed on mine, Boonsong grinned and raised an arm.

The shelf beneath me rocked and stones rained down before I realized what he was doing. His magic was slamming our shelf closed like a giant mouth. I threw my arms up in time to catch the roof of the shelf.

"Get out!" I shouted at Olaf.

My arms and legs trembled from the strain of holding our space open. Olaf crawled from where he'd been sitting, grabbed his weapon, and jumped from the lip of the shelf. As he thudded into the cavern below, I tried to inch myself forward, but Boonsong was upping the force. My elbows buckled, then my knees.

The sicko's going to crush me.

With a deep crack, the floor underfoot fractured first. I plummeted into the cavern along with several tons of stone. The instant I impacted, I heaved myself to the side and went into a roll, debris crashing down behind me. I ended up near Olaf, who had also gotten clear. But his MP88 was empty, and mine was now buried.

Thankfully, I still had my pack.

"A shame we couldn't come to terms," Boonsong called, his voice raw and taunting. Whatever sympathy he'd once held for the living was gone. As an undead, he was a different creature— one who enjoyed killing.

Smiling, he looked over the snake creatures crushed by the fallen stone, then swirled his right hand. The opening I'd entered by, and where my teammates were concealed, slammed closed.

"Takara," I radioed.

No answer through the static. Had Boonsong crushed them?

"You've left me no choice but to exercise the third option," he said. "Reanimation."

He eyed the cavern walls, then the floor. Coming to some decision, he grinned and swept both hands up in front of him. The chunks of fallen stone around us began gathering into giant golems.

"Your weapon," I said to Olaf.

He handed me the MP88 without hesitation. I quickly reloaded it with the mags and tank and swung the weapon around. Three golems were fully formed now and coming toward us, their fists the size of wrecking balls.

"Stay back," I told Olaf, and fired a stream of grenade rounds.

They detonated on impact, blowing off arms and legs—but the magic quickly restored them. I directed my next assault at Boonsong and his protective dome, but he only smiled through the explosions.

"You'll not leave here alive," he promised.

The golems moved in from our right. With my speed, I could evade them. Even Olaf could probably stay ahead of the plodding animations. But I understood Boonsong's strategy. He couldn't bring the cavern down without destroying himself, so he'd deployed the golems to defend his position while herding us into one of several recesses.

He planned to crush us there.

"Keep behind me," I told Olaf in a low voice.

I backed from the golems, then shifted around to the right so they had to reorganize themselves. Boonsong laughed from the alcove, apparently enjoying the game. I scanned his position and the wall around him.

Have to get to the damned heart stone somehow.

I spotted an opening five meters above Boonsong. In my head, I cycled through going up there, planting the rest of my explosives, and bringing that tonnage of stone down on his head. Overwhelming physical force could often break powerful magic. But in a space that small, I'd be playing into Boonsong's plan.

I shifted again, forcing the golems to reposition themselves once more.

Boonsong continued to laugh as though he had all the time

in the world. And maybe he did. If Sarah's read was right, he and Akeila only had to delay us until whatever replication the serpent goddess was planning took place.

When a golem came too close, I seized its groping arm, yanked the animation toward me, and hooked an elbow beneath its crotch. It groaned in what sounded like surprise. With a grunt and heave, I slammed the giant onto its back.

Boonsong's laughter broke off, but not from that.

A new magic had entered the cavern.

32

The new magic rippled around me, gathering strength and purpose. In the next moment, it felt like the room had switched polarities.

The golems turned from me and Olaf and began plodding back toward Boonsong.

He gestured wildly, as though trying to compel them to wheel back around, but his creations ignored him. He cut his hands through the air in an X-shaped motion. His animating magic blew from the golems in squirming waves, but another magic was there to take its place—a magic I recognized.

Yoofi's.

Using each other as mounts, the golems began climbing up to Boonsong's alcove. He screamed at them in Siamese. Shimmering with Yoofi's magic, the first arrivals pounded his protection with their fists. The purple dome shuddered. Boonsong looked from his creations to me.

"I'll let you go!" he cried. "Just make them stop!"

I raised Olaf's MP88, aimed between the stone bodies, and sighted on his head.

With the next round of blows, the dome failed. Boonsong's

protection ruptured in a curtain of squiggly sparks that dimmed fast. The golems would probably finish him, but I wasn't going to take any chances.

"Please!" Boonsong screamed, stretching an arm toward me.

I squeezed three times. His undead head came apart like a ripe pumpkin. His body collapsed to its knees. It remained there, jerking, until a shadow erupted from the top of his neck in a geyser: Akeila's essence.

The golems shuffled back as the shadow took serpent form. It rose toward the cavern ceiling high overhead. Then, with a venomous hiss, it dove toward us. I met the apparition with a jet of napalm.

I hadn't expected the attack to do anything—hitting the trigger had been mostly reflex—so I was surprised at the shriek of pain. The serpent's head broke through the fire, but it was losing its form, becoming blurry at the edges. Without Boonsong, this second manifestation of Akeila couldn't sustain itself out here.

The shadow veered back around and funneled into the heart stone.

Boonsong's body collapsed onto its stomach, and one of the golems seized it up. The others grabbed at it, pulling off arms and legs in the process.

"I didn't like him," Olaf said in his dull monotone.

I grunted in agreement. He'd been starting to get on my nerves too.

But the job wasn't done. I eyed the glowing heart stone.

Behind us, the cavern rumbled. I turned to find the entrance Boonsong had closed disintegrating in a cascade of sand and stone. When it settled, Yoofi stepped through, leaning on his staff.

"Is everyone okay?" he asked.

"Fine." I knew there was a reason I'd held him in reserve.

"Remind me to put in a pay raise request for you when we get back."

Yoofi giggled weakly. "I would like that, Mr. Wolfe."

"That must have taken a ton of magic," I said, striding toward him.

"Yes, Dabu was determined to punish the ones who knocked me on the head." He sounded as exhausted as he looked, part of it certainly a result of the blood loss. "It helped that their magic doesn't like our magic. Made it easier to overcome."

"How does Olaf look to you?" I asked in a lowered voice.

Yoofi squinted toward him. "Very good, brother. I do not see the poison."

Yoofi staggered with his next step. Closing the final feet at a run, I managed to catch him before he fell to the ground. I heard the rumble of the golems collapsing into piles of debris behind me.

"Hey, man," I said. "Are you gonna be all right?"

He smiled wearily. "Yes ... after a long sleep."

His eyelids sagged closed just as Takara and her brother entered the cavern. Takara's eyes cut from the heart stone and Boonsong's dismembered body to Olaf, then finally to me. I filled her in on what had happened.

"We thought you'd been crushed," she said.

"Yeah, I thought the same about you guys. How's Rusty?"

"Not well." Takara's eyes darkened. "Sarah's still working on him."

Great, I thought bitterly. *Recover one teammate only to lose another.* And Rusty's loss would hurt badly—for us, his kids...

I couldn't think about that right now, though.

"There's still the heart stone," I said. "I was hoping Yoofi could take a crack at it, but he's going to be a while recovering."

I handed our magic-user's dozing body off to Olaf, grateful

the copper casings would keep his magic active inside us for a good while longer. Olaf accepted him stiffly but gently.

"Akeila seems to have an aversion to fire," I said. "Probably why Kaito's blades were effective."

"I can attempt it," Takara said.

I turned to Olaf, who was still cradling Yoofi. "Wait here," I told him.

He nodded, and Takara and I headed toward the heart stone. I was surprised when Kaito joined us. Now that I knew he and Takara were siblings, he struck me as a younger brother tagging along. An enormous younger brother.

"I could have smashed that evil with my katanas," he boasted.

"Your katanas aren't here," Takara pointed out.

Once more, it was good to hear her pushing back. And was that a warning I picked up in her voice?

Kaito might have heard it too, because he fell quiet.

We stepped over the debris left by the golems and past Boonsong's various parts. I leapt up to the alcove, while Takara flew and Kaito scaled the climb nimbly. A stone formation set back in the alcove created a natural altar. The heart stone rested in a depression on its top, and we gathered around the glowing stone.

Beyond its purple faces, a shadow seemed to shift and a faint voice to whisper from its depth, trying to knead our minds to its will. But I could feel how much weaker it was following Boonsong's death.

Takara took a deep breath and let it out slowly. When she opened her eyes, her irises were wreathed in flames.

"Okay," she said. "Back away."

Kaito and I withdrew to one side of the alcove.

Flames began licking over Takara's body.

"*Tengu,*" Kaito muttered under his breath.

I glared at him, but I didn't think Takara heard the insult. Her face tensed as she fought for control of her dragon. The flames gathered around her body, then migrated down her right arm as if she was pushing them there. The blade in her right sleeve extended out. As the fire took hold of her weapon, the metal began to glow.

I caught Akeila's shadow shrinking from the stone's face.

With a snort, Takara swung the blade overhead and brought it down on the heart stone.

Fire flashed with the ringing contact, and Takara's blade shattered. She stood there a moment, a plume of smoke rising around her. She stared from the intact stone to the broken stump of blade that remained above her wrist.

"Are you all right?" I asked.

"Yes," she replied distantly. "Just can't manifest enough power."

I took that to mean *enough power without becoming my dragon* —a being that might not have any interest in the heart stone nor in destroying it.

"It's what happens when you turn to the devil," Kaito said.

I was stepping between them when Takara came to fiery life.

"And you didn't?" she shot back, flames bursting back into her eyes.

"What are you talking about?" he growled.

"You tell everyone that you're channeling your innate power into your blades, but you know damned well it's Senshika. The same *devil* that's in me. You've just learned how to channel her into the inanimate."

"How dare you," he roared, drawing a hand back.

I seized the front of his kimono and slammed him against the wall.

"Don't even think about it, bud," I growled, my nose inches from his mask.

Takara snatched the blades from his belt and held them toward him.

Kaito's gaze flicked between us. His eyes were hard to interpret, like his sister's, but he must have read the situation. He'd lost the bulk of his clanmates, and the two remaining samurai were young, low level, and not here. If we ended him, there would be no one to condemn Takara. Meaning we had every incentive to do just that.

"Maybe now's a good time to rethink Takara's sentence," I said.

Kaito tried to retain a stern, haughty look, but I caught the click of a dry swallow. We had the son of a bitch where we wanted him—or so I'd thought.

Takara stepped forward. "You and I can destroy the heart stone together."

I looked over at her. She still wielded the blades, but her expression had softened.

"How?" her brother snarled.

"Your blades contained magnesium to increase their capacity to hold heat. It's an old ninja trick."

Kaito tensed beneath me, but he didn't deny the charge.

"Steel blades can hold intense heat too, but it requires more power," she continued. "You or I can't summon that power alone, not without succumbing to Senshika. But together, each of us channeling a share, I believe we can."

Kaito looked past her at the heart stone.

His hatred for evil was real, part of it probably coming from the knowledge that he harbored some himself. When the bomb struck, the enormous release of atomic energy must have bonded him to the dragon Senshika too.

"Look, man," I said, using my dominant voice on him. "It's not what we carry that defines us. It's what we do with it. You're a samurai because you abide by honor, a code. You contracted with Princess Halia because you knew you could help those five thousand people. Takara's here for the same reason. Now's your chance."

He remained staring at the stone for several more seconds before turning to his sister.

"It will change nothing between us," he said.

"That's not what this is about," she replied.

She nodded for me to release him. I still felt an urge to throttle him, but I stepped back. Takara tossed the short katana aside and kept the long one. Gripping the steel in both hands, she turned so she was facing the heart stone.

She spoke her brother's name like a summons: "Kaito."

He walked up behind her. Stooping, he brought his arms around her body and clasped the handle above her grip. Given their animosity, the embrace looked strangely intimate.

Without speaking, their backs began to rise and fall in unison, their breaths becoming synchronous. The heat that swelled from them was different than the heat Takara had generated alone moments before. This felt more contained. Flames broke over the blade now—a deep, autumnal red.

Their breaths deepened until the flames turned orange. Soon, an intense white band grew along the length of steel. It suggested the beauty and horror of Senshika's form, only now it was isolated to the blade.

Takara's and her brother's voice rose together, and the sword arced overhead.

With a shout, they brought it down. In a searing flash, the blade crashed through the heart stone like it was made of glass. I threw a forearm to my eyes as Akeila's evil energy blasted past. It raced around the cavern, but I could sense it coming apart.

The walls shook before settling again beneath a fading hiss.

I lowered my arm to a pitch-black darkness. By the time I activated the infrared light on Olaf's weapon, Kaito had stepped back from Takara. I regarded the shards of shattered heart stone at their feet.

"Solid job, Takara. Kaito," I added.

Though their irises were ringed in the same red light, Takara's lingered, while her brother's shrank quickly, as if being suppressed.

"Is it done?" Takara asked.

"Yeah, I think so."

I brought my pack around and dug out my spare tablet. When the screen came on, I noted the positive indicator for the satellite connection. I looked over the display to be sure. One corner showed our present GPS coordinates.

"We're online again," I said.

Sarah radioed me. *"Our connection is back."*

"Where are you?" I asked, trying to see them from my vantage point.

"We pulled back to the stairs," she said. *"Rusty's still breathing, but I had to intubate him to keep his airway open."*

"All right, hang tight. We're headed your way."

Waving for Takara and Kaito to follow, I leapt from the alcove and radioed Leej.

"It's Wolfe," I said.

He responded in his hissing voice to indicate he'd received the transmission. I waited for him to get the translator in position before continuing.

"How is it looking up there?"

"Everything just changed," the device translated. *"My people are standing around in confusion. Your people are starting to come out from the buildings."*

I gave Takara a thumbs-up to tell her the curse had been lifted.

"Go ahead and make contact with your people," I said. "We'll be up shortly."

"Okay," he replied.

When we reached Olaf near the cavern's entrance, he was still holding Yoofi. Our magic-user had apparently slept through the final act. I clapped Olaf's shoulder and motioned for him to come with us.

As we left the cavern for the stone corridor, I hit the button on my tablet for the quick reaction force. We would need to airlift Rusty and triage the thousands of survivors. I trusted Princess Halia had contacts in country who could help. With the curse lifted, we could safely land helos in Meong Kal's clearing. Unlike past missions, I planned to stay this time to help with the aftermath. I smiled at the thought of getting the little girl home to her journal.

The signal to the QRF didn't go through, though. I checked the display.

"Satellite's out again," I called to Sarah, who was just coming into view. "How's your connection?"

"Down," she called back.

I heard the strain in that one word. She was sitting beside Rusty's head, her bag open, medical implements and packaging scattered around. Rusty looked as bad as he sounded. Above the plastic tube that channeled his rasping breaths, his eyes had swollen closed. Without commo to the outside, we weren't going to get him help in time. I tried to shake Yoofi awake, but he was down for the count, his magic exhausted.

Sarah's night vision ocular glinted up at me. "Maybe we're too deep underground."

"The satellite signal should be effective to two-hundred meters. I think it's something else."

"Like what?" she asked in a strained voice. I could see in her eyes that she was thinking of the hundreds of iterations of Akeila.

"When Takara and Kaito destroyed the heart stone, I felt the,

I don't know, the *matrix* that held Akeila's energy come apart," I said. "But it's forming again."

"How do you know?" Takara asked.

"The loss of connection for one. But there's also a sharpness in my throat, a prickling in my ears."

"Forming from where, though?" she pressed.

"You saw the heart stones before they were destroyed," I said. "I don't know about you, but they didn't look to me like they would have fit together. It was like there was a piece missing."

Takara's face went still as though she were searching her memory. She began to nod. "A center piece."

"Exactly."

"There's a third heart stone," a woman's voice said.

The glow of torch light appeared on the staircase, and Princess Halia descended into view.

"The information just appeared on the painting," she said, "but this heart stone is not like the others."

"How's it different?" I asked.

"I'm waiting for the painting to tell me."

Great. "The original heart stone was placed in a statue to Akeila, right?" I said, thinking out loud. "I haven't seen any statues down here."

"Boonsong talked about a statue room," Olaf said.

I rounded on him. "Did you ever go there?"

"No, but he sent others." He hiked Yoofi up in his arms and stared past me. "That way."

I peered over a shoulder to where the corridor that turned left from the stairs fell away. It was where the reptilian and acidic scents I'd detected earlier were coming from.

"They never returned," he added.

When I turned back to the team, I sensed them awaiting my command.

I knelt and dug into Rusty's vest pockets until I had the

commo chip he'd hacked for me. Inside his pack, I found a mess of connectors. I used one to attach the chip's dangling wire to my tablet. I might not have been at Rusty's level with this stuff, but my commo sarge on Team 5, Hotwire, had shown me a few tricks.

Takara and Kaito moved closer, no one speaking as I accessed my tablet's command screen. Looking from our last recorded coordinates to the dark corridor, I performed a little mental math. Fortunately, it wouldn't have to be exact. I entered two short messages and set them to repeat at quarter-second intervals. With a Send command, a tiny red light on the chip began to pulse. I disconnected the chip from my tablet, pulled the empty grenade round from my vest, and placed the chip inside.

Perfect fit.

"I had Rusty design a commo chip for me back at camp," I said, closing the round again. "It's sending messages right now—one with coordinates for Rusty's medevac. If you still don't have a sat connection by the time you surface, I want Olaf to fire this straight up. It should punch through what's left of the poison barrier."

I unstrapped the MP88 with its grenade launcher from my body. Olaf adjusted Yoofi while I threaded his meaty arm through the strap and secured the weapon over his shoulder. I then slid the round into his vest pocket.

"Can I count on you?" I asked.

"Yes," Olaf replied without hesitation.

I turned to Kaito. "I need you to carry Rusty up."

When he hesitated, Princess Halia repeated the command in Japanese. He stooped and lifted Rusty behind the back and legs. Rusty's breathing hitched through the tube once before resuming its gasping cycle.

"Move," I said. "Sarah and Princess Halia, go with them. I'm going to investigate the statue room. Takara, I want you to join up with the other samurai and clear the temple. Get everyone out. Take the blaster."

"If there's a third heart stone," she said, "won't you need Kaito and me to break it?"

"If there's a third heart stone, I'll call you."

But what Sarah had said about the hundreds of iterations was still going through my head.

As the team filed up the staircase, Sarah turned back to me.

"You don't have a weapon," she observed.

I had my sidearm, but I knew what she meant. "I'll recover my MP88."

She hesitated. "You said messages plural. What's the other one."

"Standby orders for a thermobaric strike."

Understanding sunk into her eyes.

"It's just a backup," I assured her.

33

I found my weapon under a slab of stone. Luckily, it had landed such that it was trapped more than crushed. Still banged up, though.

I inspected the scratched outer casing, then the ammo ports. The rifle magazine was bent, and the fuel tank oozed napalm. A replacement mag wiggled after I slotted it home, but it responded to the charging handle and my test shots.

Removing the fuel tank, I found a broken seal around the port. Dammit. No spares in my pack either. I pulled out a tube of polymer that was supposed to patch anything, squeezed a generous amount of black goo around the seal, and screwed in a fresh tank.

Not pretty, I thought as I brought the weapon back into position, *but as long as it works.*

It didn't. The electrical igniter wouldn't respond to the trigger. Swearing, I activated the backup pilot light and touched my Zippo's flame to the gas. A test squeeze later, and I was satisfied I had a mostly working flamethrower.

Replacing the lighter in my vest pocket, I jogged past the stairs my teammates had ascended. The corridor quickly devolved into a hard-packed tunnel, recently excavated from the looks of it.

With Boonsong's rediscovery of Meong Kal, at least some of the temple's basement levels must have been intact. Not so these lowest levels, where the statue to Akeila—and the original, intact heart stone—had probably been buried in the ages following the last war. I grimaced at the thought of Boonsong sending children down to dig the rooms out. Hell, it was bad enough just *being* down here.

Sweat dripped from my face, while the sharpening stink of bile curled my lips.

I remembered what Olaf had said about slaves entering the statue room and not coming back. But when the tunnel turned again, I found myself at a dead end. Edging forward, I pressed a hand to the packed earth and stone. Warmth radiated into my palm. After another moment I felt Boonsong's magic.

He'd sealed the room with an animation, but he wasn't here anymore to reinforce it.

Stepping back, I hefted the MP88 and unleashed a torrent of automatic fire. The exploding rounds ripped through Boonsong's lingering magic. The wall crumbled from the top and collapsed in a heap.

Using the settling debris as cover, I moved along the tunnel wall and peered through the opening. The room beyond was as large as an indoor football stadium. A single stone avenue snaked over a floor where boulders had been arranged into rows. The avenue proceeded to a temple at the room's far end.

A temple inside of a temple, I thought with the certainty that this was it. Even better, the coordinates I'd programmed into the transponder were on point.

I stepped inside for a better look. The room was clear. Even the stink of bile was gone, replaced by an almost pleasant aroma of wood smoke. I couldn't see any fires, though.

Leading with my weapon, I started down the avenue until I was facing the temple. It consisted of a large floor and several straight columns, but no ceiling. A massive statue rose from a pedestal at the temple's back half.

Like in the murals of the main temple, the goddess was depicted as a giant serpent with an attractive female face, the statue's detail almost as impressive as its sheer size. With the primitive technology of the age, it must have taken more than a hundred years and thousands of slaves to complete. The statue rose a good hundred feet into the air, its posture curved, poised to strike.

But it was inert stone.

"Akeila," I grunted. "The serpent goddess."

At her heart, a gem pulsed with purple light.

Jackpot.

34

"Abby is giving us her look," Daniela said.

"Hm?"

I raised my heavy lids. We were sitting in the corner of the leather couch, Dani nestled against my side. I must not have been dozing long, because the fire in the hearth was still burning with plenty of logs to spare. Beyond our propped-up feet—mine in thick wool socks, Dani's in Christmas ones to match her sweater—her Weimaraner stared at us, one brow arched. Abby's brother was starting to adopt the same expression.

When Abby saw us watching her, a whine rose in her throat.

I chuckled thickly. "You mean her 'If you don't let me out right now I'm going to turn your living room into a pond' look?"

Laughter bubbled from Dani. "Would you mind?"

I hated to move, but I didn't want a pond either. I kissed Dani's forehead and shifted out from under her. The walnut floor creaked underfoot as I stood and let the cuffs of my jeans drop back over my ankles. I stooped over to take Dani's empty glass of eggnog and my beer bottle from the coffee table.

"All right, let's go."

The dogs jumped up from their spots in front of the hearth and whimper-skittered around me. I ambled past our large, lit-up Christmas tree, where Dani had already piled an array of presents, to the back of the house. The pleasant scent of wood smoke and spruce thinned away.

When I opened the sliding glass door, the dogs shot across the deck and down into the yard. They'd need a good ten minutes to take care of all their business.

I lingered to breathe in a shot of the crisp night air before closing and locking the glass door again. I'd be switching the door out for something more durable soon. Just another on my long list of home-improvement projects. Not that I was complaining.

In the kitchen, I set the bottle and glass by the sink.

"Do you want anything?" I called.

"For you to come back."

I smiled and returned to the living room to find Dani standing and arching her back, one arm stretched overhead. In that position, I could see the start of her bump. *Our* bump, she was always quick to correct me. She straightened with a satisfied sigh. But as she turned, a sudden panic gripped me.

I felt over my face, heart pounding. Everything was as it should have been, though. No muzzle, no hair. I was still Jason Wolfe—and according to Biogen, I would remain that way. No more Blue Wolf.

They'd cured me.

Dani smirked. "Checking for crumbs?" She walked over and inspected my mouth before dropping her eyes to the neck of my flannel shirt. "You're clean—oh, wait." She picked something from the collar of my thermal layer and flicked it away. "You know, those cookies *were* supposed to last the week."

Cookies?

But how could I forget the plate she'd brought out after dinner, stacked with her homemade sugar cookies? They'd been a favorite of Daniela's growing up. A favorite of mine now too, apparently. The combo of sweet and salty had me popping the golden cookies into my mouth, one after another.

I gave an embarrassed laugh. "You might have to lock them up next time."

"Or I can just make another batch?"

"Better you don't," I said, "unless you want a hubby with a matching bump."

I rested my hand against the swell of her lower belly. She placed her warm hands over mine. The memories marched through my mind: the positive pregnancy test, our first visit to the doctor, the ultrasound, sharing the news with her overjoyed parents.

But like the cookies, the memories felt … late. As if they were being created in real time and slotted into place. When I started to pull my hand away, Dani pinned it against her belly and stepped closer.

"Wait another few seconds and you might feel—"

Something nudged the heel of my palm.

Her face lit up. "Did you feel that?"

"That's amazing," I said.

And it *was* amazing. With the next nudge, my heart melted a little more. Our first was going to be a boy.

"You're still doing all right?" I asked her.

The first trimester had been rough, but she'd weathered the storm of morning sickness and mood swings, and it had been mostly smooth sailing since.

"At least until the swelling really gets going." She lifted my hand to her lips for a kiss. "But they say it gets easier with each one." She winked and gave my knuckle a playful bite.

The logs shifted in the fireplace, sending up a burst of sparks. I squeezed her hand. When I went to release her this time, she let me.

"Where are you going?"

"Don't want the logs to spill out."

"Oh, they're fine," she said. *A little too insistently?*

Kneeling, I took the poker from the stand and pushed the crooked log back into place. Beneath the logs, a healthy bed of embers was forming. Flames licked up when I prodded them. *Fire. Heat. Intense heat.* Those had been the elements needed to destroy the heart stones in New Siam, I remembered.

I stopped, poker poised over the embers.

And how had that mission ended exactly?

I thought back to the moment I'd found the final heart stone. Using the statue's intricately carved scales as hand and toeholds, I retrieved the stone and radioed Takara and Kaito. With their combined power, they smashed the stone apart. Boom. Done.

But what had happened in the moments, hours, and days after?

The memory of Rusty succumbing to the poison lanced through me. Too much toxin. Right after, Takara had returned to Japan with her brother, leaving against our advice. Given that she and her brother had cooperated in New Siam, we hoped for the best. But word of her execution came two days later. The ache and guilt of losing Rusty and Takara still weighed like lead rounds in my heart. I remembered the small service we'd held at the Legion compound for them, everyone except Olaf taking a turn to speak.

But once again, the memories only seemed to be coming because I was looking for them.

"Jason?" Dani said.

I worked backwards. What was the last solid moment I remembered?

"You trancing out over there?"

The statue. That was the dividing line between the memories that flowed as naturally as a river and those that felt like someone laying bricks. And Akeila had commanded powers of possession and mind control, right?

An unsettling thought struck me. *Am I still in the statue room?*

When I sniffed, I detected the faintest sting of bile. Something gripped my shoulder.

I wheeled with a clawed hand and raked flesh. Daniela staggered back with a cry, her eyes huge. In an instant, the Weimaraners were at the sliding glass door. Above their frantic barking, I could hear their nails scrabbling against the glass, the dogs wanting inside to protect their owner.

"Jason?" she said, one hand cupping her belly, the other touching the abrasions at her throat.

"You're not Dani," I growled.

"Jason, *stop.*"

Though I was stalking toward her, a part of me wanted to reach out and pull her back against me, to beg her forgiveness.

"You're not Dani," I repeated.

She had recovered from the shock of the attack and was moving over to put the large coffee table between us. Blood beaded from her neck abrasions and began dribbling into her Christmas sweater. I noted the redness in the fibers, the awful way the blood spread out along the collar. So real.

Was I still in the statue room?

When I sniffed again, everything was back to wood smoke and spruce.

I angled my head like I was speaking into a radio. "Legion team. Do you copy?"

No answer.

"Does anyone copy?" I asked, the dry bite of panic filling my mouth.

The skin between Dani's eyes folded as she picked up her phone from the coffee table. She glanced between her device and me as she manipulated the screen. A faint tone sounded, and she brought the phone to her ear.

"Who are you calling?" I asked.

Don't go along with this, dammit. It's a hallucination.

"You were poisoned on the mission to New Siam," she said. "You told me about it, remember? You were cleaned, but some of the effects persisted. Memory loss. Hallucinations. You're getting better, though."

I did remember now.

The heart stones had been toxic. Yoofi was able to clean me to a point. Biogen got their crack when we returned to the Centurion campus. I spent a week at their facility going through a total fluid replacement regimen, which was as unpleasant as it sounded. They also reset the synaptic charges in my brain. Between the magical and the mundane treatment, I was about eighty percent cleaned. My transformation back to human had accounted for another ten. The rest would come with time, they said.

For a while, I'd struggled to recall *anything*. As my memory improved, the hallucinations began. Two episodes struck during my final month with Legion. Neither one on assignment, thank God. Three back home. The first was at night. I wandered around believing I was back in my childhood house. The second happened at Cantrell's Hardware when, for a few minutes, I thought I was on a battlefield in Central Asia. When that hallucination ended, I was crouched behind a stack of treated lumber, holding a large caulking gun like it was an M4.

With those two hallucinations occurring so far apart, I'd hoped they were done, but they weren't. And with this one, I'd hurt Dani.

"It's all right," I said, showing her a hand. "You can end the call."

She hesitated.

"I remember," I said. "You're calling Centurion Medical. It's what you're supposed to do after an episode. A tech comes over and injects me with a sedative that puts me in bed for two days. They say it helps with the hallucinatory aftershocks, but I think they just want to make it look like they're doing something."

I'd gone into the details to convince her that I was truly back.

Dani watched me for a moment, then gave a weary smile that punched me right in the heart. She set her phone back on the large ottoman.

Hadn't that been a coffee table a few seconds ago?

I silenced the voice.

"Dani, honey, I am so sorry. I—"

"Shh," she whispered, coming around the ottoman. Yes, it was an ottoman, and in the place we'd always had it.

"I'm going to get a damp cloth and some ointment," I told her.

Before I could pass her, she took my arm and pulled herself against me. As she clasped my back, the clean scent of her hair touched my nostrils, and I started to sob. I'd kept the Blue Wolf from her because I'd been afraid of hurting her, of making her fear me, and both had happened anyway.

"It'll take time, but we'll get you back," she whispered. "All the way back."

"I couldn't have done this with anyone else," I said through my tears.

"Well, you're stuck with me now."

I let her rock me for several moments before getting control of myself.

"Still, Dani. I should stay somewhere until the hallucinations are over."

When she looked up at me, moisture gleamed in her determined eyes. "We've already lost too much time. I'm not letting you leave again."

I dipped my face to kiss this woman I loved more than life.

"Wolfe, do you copy?"

I hesitated.

"What is it?" Dani asked, her lips inches from mine.

The voice had been dim, distant, but it belonged to Sarah.

"Nothing," I said.

"Your thermobaric bomb is on station."

Bomb?

I remembered the transponder suddenly. I'd put one in a grenade round and given it to Olaf to fire. The transponder carried two messages: one to medevac Rusty, one to put a bunker-busting thermobaric on standby. I cycled back through the events: destroying the third stone, emerging from the temple to find Centurion helos across the game court, one of them already lifting off with Rusty—I could see it all so clearly.

But if the transponder's message had gotten out, at what point had I called off the pilot carrying the two-ton piece of ordnance? That was a really big detail, and I had no clear memory of it. And now here it came ... I *had* called him off. I'd even made a dry joke about saving the company a few mill.

But I didn't buy it.

"Sarah!" I shouted.

Dani backed from my embrace. "It's happening again, isn't it?"

She retrieved the phone from the coffee table. It was a coffee table again.

"Wolfe?" came Sarah's voice, louder now. *"I can barely hear you."*

I'm still in the statue room. I have to be.

I watched Dani raise the phone to her ear. Hallucination or not, I wasn't going to strike her again. I couldn't.

Instead, I leaned back and released a soul-shattering roar.

And our living room came apart.

35

T he smell broke through first: an overpowering blast of bile
and reptile. Our cozy home fell away into a cavernous
chamber of death where only the warmth remained. But this
was a morbid warmth: humid, suffocating, and laced with
poison.

The statue room.

With the knowledge I was emerging, a part of my mind
scrabbled to pull the pleasant illusion back over it rather than
face the reality. It succeeded in restoring Dani's pregnant form.
She reached for me across the abyss.

Come back to us, she whispered, the other hand cradling her
belly. *Please...*

My heart lurched. Could I go back for just a little, return
again when I was ready?

But that was the poison talking.

I pushed more power into my roar until a rib-crushing force
squeezed it off. The vision of Dani disappeared. In its place grew
a massive diamond-shaped head with glowing albino eyes. A
mosaic of cracked gray scales covered the face. When the creature hissed, a noxious-smelling venom bubbled past its fangs.

Akeila.

She looked nothing like the femme fatale depicted on the friezes, but I could feel her ancient power, her mind-warping magic.

This was her.

Pain broke through my ribs as she squeezed again. My body, from shoulders to ankles, was trapped inside her coiled grip and suspended high in the air. I peered around with my returning vision. The hallucination must have begun the moment I'd looked into the room, because the grand temple was a ruins now. Regurgitated skeletons, some with scraps of clothing still attached, were piled over the temple floor.

And the statue to Akeila was alive and encircling me.

Boonsong animated the statue and made her flesh, I realized.

This was probably why Halia had trouble locating the statue through the Himitsu painting: Boonsong altered the statue by fusing Akeila's essence to it and bringing it to venomous life. The heart stone was now an actual heart. I could see it pulsing purple beneath the pale belly scales of her chest.

The piece of heart stone in the swamp had controlled the jungle, the one in the cavern room the city of Meong Kal. This last one held Boonsong's animating magic as well as the core of Akeila's own power.

Destroy it, and this ends.

I took stock of myself. My right arm was bent at the elbow, fist pinned to my chest. My pack had come off, and I was without my weapon. I tried to wriggle my arm free, but the muscles beneath Akeila's thick skin clenched.

"Wolfe, do you copy?"

"Loud and clear," I grunted.

"What's your status?" Sarah asked. *"We've been trying to reach you for an hour."*

"I'm in the statue room ... The last heart stone's here."

"*Should I send Takara and Kaito?*"

I hesitated. Even with Yoofi's protective magic still working inside me, Akeila was too powerful. I might have escaped her hallucination, but she probably hadn't tried as hard to maintain it once I was subdued and in her grasp. She would do the same to the others. Maybe that was the goddess's plan, to have me lure them all down here.

She watched me with her alien eyes.

"Is everyone out of the temple?" I asked.

"*Yes, we're in the clearing. Commo to the outside is still down, but the transponder got through. Rusty's been medevacked. We're triaging the survivors. Leej is organizing the snake people. There's a bomber circling, but we'll need to send a helo out of the zone to give the drop order.*"

That would mean a couple minutes between order and impact.

In an attempt to surprise Akeila, I bucked and fought to free my right arm again. The thick coils of her body simply tightened.

"*Do you need backup?*" Sarah asked.

I didn't have enough air now to answer.

Akeila brought me to her reptilian face, and I could see just how primitive a god she was. It explained why she used people as go-betweens. She couldn't speak to the masses herself—she was poison incarnate, her single-minded purpose to grow and spread. But she could reach into minds and promise people what they wanted most. For Boonsong that had been mass enlightenment and a future without wars or violence.

"*Captain Wolfe?*" Sarah said.

Something squirmed through my head, and I understood Akeila was still trying to marry my deepest ambitions to hers. I steeled my mind and pushed back. The serpent goddess stiffened as if I'd slapped her.

Her tongue flicked out—a dry lash that tore a swath of hair from my head.

Wincing, I attempted to free my right arm again. This time I managed to work my thumb and first two fingers out before she clenched tighter and tilted me to the side. Her next lash caught me across the neck.

"*Captain?*" Sarah repeated.

Biting back against the searing pain, I peered down. Where was my weapon?

Far below, close to Akeila's perch, I spotted the MP88. It must have fallen when she seized me. The fuel tank had separated from my patch job, and napalm covered the floor and part of Akeila's tail in a glistening jelly.

"*I'm sending a team down.*"

"No," I managed to squeeze out.

Another lash sent scalding pain across both shoulders. Akeila clenched her coils and rotated sharply so that I lost sight of my weapon. I was looking out over the large room now. About a hundred meters away, I could see the hole I'd entered by. My gaze dropped to the boulder-lined floor—only they weren't boulders anymore. They were giant eggs.

Hundreds of them.

This must have been what Sarah saw in Akeila's mind, because inside each craggy shell, a replica of the heart stone glimmered purple. It also explained why the final piece of heart stone had only compensated weakly for the other two following their destruction. Akeila had wanted to preserve that power for her babies. I flashed back to Boonsong telling me that he and Akeila were husband and wife. Lovers.

He'd meant that literally.

Akeila dipped suddenly and thrust her head out over the eggs. A noise like a loud exhaust sounded. I craned my neck. Akeila had dropped her lower jaw and was pushing out a noxious green gas between her fangs. She weaved back and forth just meters above the floor, fumigating her unhatched eggs.

When she finished, she reared up so that we were above the temple again. I craned my neck the other way and watched the mist settle around the eggs in a thick fog.

Before long, one of the eggs began to shift. The others followed until the entire floor was a sea of rocking.

Shit.

Akeila was moving up the time table on releasing these duplicates of herself. I had to escape her grasp before that happened, get out of the temple, order the damned strike. If I could just hit the spilled napalm with a flame...

I worked the talon of my freed finger under the flap of my top vest pocket. It released with a Velcro rip. I felt over the contours of the Zippo through the fabric and then began to push it up from the bottom.

Without warning, Akeila hissed and upended me. The lighter's metal casing flashed as it fell from my pocket. I lunged and caught the corner between a top and bottom canine, the grip tenuous and slipping.

Out in the room, the first egg didn't simply crack; it erupted in a geyser of steaming bile.

I brought my muzzle down and managed to grasp the lighter between my third finger and thumb.

More eruptions of hatching sounded. And now a growing chorus of hisses.

Blocking out the activity, I repositioned the lighter in my clasp and let gravity flip the lid. When I stroked the lighter's wheel with a talon, fuel caught spark and a finger of flame shot out. In upending me, Akeila had actually given me an assist. I now had a clear line of sight to the thickest concentration of napalm.

Much obliged, Mrs. Boonsong.

I released the lighter and watched the flame fall.

It landed dead center.

Akeila screamed as flames burst across the temple floor and over her tail. The shock rippled up her body in a wave that I used to thrash free. Air rushed back into my lungs and sensation into my body as I plummeted.

By luck, Akeila's writhing body struck me, knocking me clear of the flames. I crash-landed on the edge of the temple, regenerative abilities already knitting bone and tissue as I shoved myself to my feet.

Akeila withdrew her massive form into a recess behind the temple, tail whipping against the earthen wall in a frantic effort to extinguish the flames. If she was still screaming, I couldn't hear her. The space had become a wall of hissing.

Go! I shouted at myself.

I turned and fled, only stooping for my weapon, and bounded down the temple steps.

All across the room, naga hatchlings ten and twelve feet long were wriggling in the soups of their blown-open eggs and coming upright. I sprinted along the avenue I'd arrived by, aiming for the opening.

The nagas began orienting themselves to my movement. One launched itself at me. I batted it aside with my weapon. When I spotted another naga coiling to strike, I hit it with a blast of incendiary rounds.

I didn't know what was happening behind me at the temple to Akeila, and I didn't look to find out. Fifty meters from the opening, I caught a whiff of spruce and smoke.

Thirty meters, and I began to see snatches of our living room at Christmas time.

At ten, I could feel Dani's breath against my ear, begging me to stop running, to come back.

I bit down on my tongue until I tasted blood, and I was through the opening.

Only then did I turn. Beyond the flames, Akeila's massive form undulated back and forth, eyes radiating white through the smoke. She might have been pinned by the heat, but her children weren't. In squelches, they began slithering toward the opening. They would be a river soon. And if I let that river escape into the world, flowing off in every direction, it was definitely going to be game over.

"Sarah, do you read?"

"I'm still here."

"Give the order."

She hesitated. *"Now?"*

"Now."

I fired off another blast of rounds. The naga hatchlings reared from the explosions, but the protection afforded by their heart stones held. I used a few seconds of escape time jamming my remaining frag grenades into the earthen wall around the opening.

Sarah came back on. *"The helo's going up."*

"Estimated time to strike?" I asked, arming the grenades.

"About three minutes."

"I'll be clear by then."

"Jason, hurry."

She had a right to the concern I heard. We were talking about a two-ton thermobaric bomb. If I wasn't clear of the blast, the same 3,500 degrees that would incinerate the nagas and their heart stones would torch me too. That was if the pressure wall didn't kill me first. Even my regenerative abilities had their limits.

I sprinted up the corridor. Behind me, the grenades detonated, and I heard the rumble of collapsing tunnel. Enough to hold the nagas for three minutes? No way to know, but I'd settle for a delay.

As it was, *I* was going to be cutting it close. Damn close.

I hit the steps we'd come down, bounding up them ten at a time. *Need to lighten my load, hit an extra gear.* Arriving on the next level, I tossed aside my MP88, shucked my vest, and fell to my hands. I raced along my teammates' scent trail—up what seemed endless corridors connected by winding flights of stairs.

Breaths frothed from my muzzle as I demanded every last fiber of strength and speed from my supernatural body. My wedding band thrashed on the chain around my neck, still there. I hadn't lost it.

I'm getting out of here, baby, I thought as I panted. *I'm coming back to you.*

At last I heaved myself through the wall I'd blown open earlier. Cutting around pillars and broken casting circles, I leapt the bodies of fallen snake creatures and zombie mercs. The sides of the next stairwell streaked past my pumping wolf's head. When I emerged into the room above, I could smell the jungle.

One more flight, and I'd be out of the temple, emerging into night.

Still need to get clear a safe distance, I reminded myself. *Find cover.*

I was halfway up the stairs when the temple quaked. I had an instant to wonder whether it was bomb or serpent goddess or both when the pressure wave hit me from behind.

The force flung my four-hundred pounds the rest of the way like they were nothing. I landed hard, tumbling over the temple's ground level and toward an archway that framed the night.

The heat came a split second later. Though the blast had started more than a dozen levels down, the bomb was designed to combust in a superheated wave that stormed stairways and corridors like a demon horde from Hell.

I never saw the fireball that slammed into me. I just knew that by the time my body hit the steps that descended steeply from the temple, I was in flames and deaf, blood pouring hot from my ears.

As I tumbled down, I could feel the entire temple imploding from the bomb's negative pressure, trying to pull me back at the same time it was collapsing on itself.

I gripped my wedding band in a flaming hand and held on.

36

"Jason," a voice said.

The world was awash in fire, every flame a writhing naga. I couldn't raise my arms to stop them, couldn't make my legs run from them. When I tried to roar them back, my throat felt like it was tearing open.

"Jason," the voice repeated, more firmly.

The fire nagas thinned and disappeared. A woman stood over me, her figure bisecting a glow of plain white light. One of her hands was gripping my tensed upper arm. As I blinked her clear, I relaxed.

"Sarah," I managed from a raw throat.

She was wearing civvies and a white lab coat, her hair back in a ponytail.

I glanced around. "Can I assume we're not in New Siam anymore?"

"You're at a Centurion medical facility in Hong Kong," she replied in her clipped voice. "You were critically burned, your lungs all but destroyed. It wasn't until we induced a coma state that your innate healing kicked in. We weaned you from sedation this morning." She released my arm and pushed up her glasses. "How do you feel?"

I took closer stock of my surroundings. I was lying in a large hospital bed, arms and legs clamped down with metal shackles, lines running into both elbows. A ventilator unit sat dimly off to my right, no doubt what had been breathing for me. Explained why my throat felt so raw. Beeps and blips sounded behind me. When I inhaled deeply, a bruising ache opened in my chest and I began to cough.

"Try again," Sarah said.

I did. The aching faded with the next deep breath. I took several more without coughing.

"Not only did your body replace dermal and deep subdermal levels of tissue," she said as she released my various restraints, "but it had to replenish the lining of your lungs." I could feel my regenerative abilities prickling through my body, performing final repairs. My blue hair had even begun sprouting back through my skin.

As I stretched and flexed my freed limbs, I saw those final moments at the temple before I'd lost consciousness. My body on fire, skin blackening, fluids steaming—but now flaming nagas writhed through the memory.

I looked up at Sarah. "We destroyed them, right?"

"The temperatures in the enclosed spaces peaked at over five thousand degrees. Even collapsed, the lowest levels burned for days. Nothing in the temple survived, and nothing got out. Except for you. We recovered you from the edge of the wreckage."

"When was that?"

"Five nights ago."

"And the people of Ban Mau?"

"More than ninety-five percent survived their abduction and captivity. They're being treated, mostly for malnourishment and dehydration. The majority will return to their homes at the end of the week. And that includes Leilana, the girl whose journal we found. She never succumbed to Akeila's possession, apparently. She just played along."

"Smart girl," I said, but I'd already known that.

I gave Sarah a brief rundown of what I'd encountered in the statue room. When I finished, my thoughts went to my teammates, causing the beeps of my heart rate monitor to jump.

"Rusty," I said.

"Recovering, amazingly enough."

I released my breath with a "Thank God."

"He must have had prior exposure to venom," she added.

"Rattlesnakes," I said, remembering his story of the annual roundup.

"Well, without that buildup in immunity over the years, he would have succumbed."

And we would have lost a valuable teammate whom I'd come to consider a good friend.

"He's being treated back in the States," Sarah continued. "Olaf and Yoofi were flown out with him. Both are fine. Olaf's being held for observation. Centurion wants to make sure there are no lasting effects from the venom and possession."

"And Takara?" I asked carefully. "What became of that thing with her brother?"

Sarah went silent for a moment. "Because of their collaboration in destroying the evil at Meong Kal, Kaito granted her an alternative to execution: hara-kiri. Through self-disembowelment, she could die honorable."

"She didn't," I said.

"She started to," Sarah replied. "The blade had penetrated skin when Kaito stopped her. He said that in her readiness to perform the rite she had proven her penitence. She was freed from her bond to the clan."

"So she's alive?" I asked to be sure.

"Yes, and presently on personal leave."

The blips of my heart rate monitor slowed back down.

"You could have started out by telling me that," I growled.

"This brings up an issue, Jason."

"A bigger one than if she'd died?"

"Her willingness to take her own life raises questions about her mental fitness, not to mention her commitment to the team. In order to remain with Legion, she'll need to agree to a battery of psychological exams."

Knowing that was the surest path to pushing Takara away, I said, "Yeah, let's hold off on that. I'll talk to her when she gets back, see what's going on. Speaking of which, what's the timeline for heading home?"

"Forty-eight hours of observation and then you should be cleared."

I nodded before cracking a grin. "So did Director Beam crap a brick over the bomb?"

"No, which tells me he built a 'client responsibility for expenses' provision into the contract."

"Damn," I said, still smiling.

Sarah almost smiled back. Almost.

"Any word from Purdy?" I asked.

As she shook her head, her eyes flattened. I knew what that was about.

"Listen, I'm sorry for not telling you about his visit. I should have met with you to discuss it earlier."

"Well, he was wrong, anyway," she said curtly.

After what our team had just gone through, I wasn't so sure. Regardless, I curled a finger into Sarah's hand and gave it a squeeze. The important thing was we'd triumphed. She squeezed back, then withdrew her hand quickly and brushed her bangs.

"Jason," she said, "some things happened between us this mission..."

This was what she'd wanted to get off her chest, I realized, not anything to do with Purdy.

"And you were possessed," I interrupted. "There's nothing to explain."

"I believe you understand how Akeila's possession power worked," she pressed on. "For her victims' hallucinations, she took emotional desires and warped them to align with her own ambitions. She didn't create them."

She was referring to Boonsong, but I was thinking of my own hallucination of being home with Dani.

"In my adult life, there have been instances where my respect for certain men has triggered ... feelings, I guess you could call them. That was what Akeila exploited." Her voice had been turning increasingly formal as she spoke, and now it verged on robotic. "I respect you, Jason. But rest assured, any other feelings attached to that sentiment are purely incidental. They'll in no way intrude on our working relationship."

I looked at her for a moment, more perplexed than anything.

Had she just rationalized away the phenomenon of human attraction?

"Thanks for clearing that up," I said.

She returned a curt nod. "Oh, I have some things for you."

She left the room and returned a minute later with a stone spear, its dark wooden handle ornamented with colorful plumage. "It's from Leej's tribe," she said. "The spear represents individual sacrifice for the group. It's the highest honor that can be bestowed upon a tribe member. Leej wanted you to have it."

I took the spear, glad to have something to remember our alliance by.

"I'll accept it on behalf of the team," I said. We had all made sacrifices, after all.

Sarah reached into a coat pocket and emerged with a small plastic bag containing my wedding band.

"This was extracted from your hand."

I set the spear beside me and took the bag.

"Your skin had fused around it," she said.

I shook the gleaming ring out into my right palm, remembering how I'd grasped the ring before tumbling down the temple steps and into oblivion: my promise to Daniela. I grasped it again, forehead bowed to fist.

We made it out, baby.

"I'll give you some privacy. I assume there's someone special you'd like to call."

I looked up to find Sarah watching me, eyes unreadable beyond her thick lenses.

"Thank you," I said.

37

During the forty-eight hours I remained under observation, I followed the unfolding political developments in New Siam. King Savang suffered a massive stroke from which he wasn't expected to recover. Succession questions followed until Prince Ken and Princess Halia announced they were taking shared control of the kingdom. It marked only the second bloodless transition of leadership in the country's previous hundred years.

The new leaders video-called me as I was preparing to fly back to the States.

"We never had a chance to thank you for your help," the princess explained.

"Yes, Halia filled me in," her brother said. "I won't pretend to understand everything that happened, but it's clear that what you did was ... well, very brave. The kingdom extends its deepest gratitude."

"We all played a part," I said, "including your sister."

He smiled over at her, which surprised me almost as much as seeing them sitting shoulder to shoulder in the palace.

"So, how's the transition going?" I asked carefully.

Wearing a formal blouse and headdress, and with her hair combed to a midnight sheen, Princess Halia looked much different than the mystic we'd joined forces with in the jungle. "There's much to do, of course," she replied. "The constitutional reforms alone will take months, but we're very optimistic. I ... I learned some things in Meong Kal."

"Oh yeah?"

"When I told you the Himitsu painting hadn't anticipated the presence of the undead and that was why the divination came apart, I wasn't being entirely honest."

I furrowed my brow, the collar picking up the expression and integrating it into the holographic image of my face.

"No," she continued, "the blind spot was mine, not the painting's. I believed I'd mastered the art of Himitsu and that I could rely on that mastery alone. But if you and your team hadn't been there..." A shadow crossed her face. "I was wrong. Logic and modernity have their place, and that was as true in destroying the serpent goddess as it will be in reforming New Siam."

This time she was the one to smile over at her sibling.

"Thank you again, Captain Wolfe," Prince Ken said as a way of closing. "You always have a home in New Siam."

The princess leaned in. "And you won't have to enter under the cover of night."

"Sounds great, you two," I laughed. "Good luck."

———

Back at the Legion compound, I closed the door to my suite, dropped my pack, and started plugging devices into chargers. With the team fragmented, Director Beam was giving us the next two weeks to R&R—which meant I had an appointment with Biogen. The home inspection Dani scheduled was in two days, and I was going to be there.

Sarah was currently the only other team member on base. Intent on analyzing the samples she'd collected in New Siam, she planned to spend the two weeks in her lab. It was clear that despite whatever feelings she'd developed for me—incidental or not—her true passion remained her work. That gave me confidence that our co-management of Legion would survive any lingering awkwardness.

I'd attempted to reach Reginald Purdy a few times in the last days and was about to try again, when I realized I didn't have to.

"Here to deliver another collar?" I called.

A chuckle sounded from the living room. "Welcome home, Captain."

I followed his scent and found him sitting on the couch, eyes locked on the screen of a small tablet. He tapped it a couple times before sliding it into his pinstripe jacket and smiling up at me. I wasn't happy about him just dropping in again, but I wasn't going to let him leave this time without some answers.

He showed his hands. "Let me begin by admitting I erred."

"About the mission being beyond Legion or by failing to tell me anything?"

"Actually, I was quite correct about the mission—I think you know that. And didn't you receive my message? I called to persuade you to return home. Failing that, I wanted you to liaison with Princess Halia."

The corrupted message that had me thinking the princess was the secondary threat.

I felt myself tensing, ready to challenge him on the first point, but some key things had gone right in New Siam through no merit of our own. Had we run the mission ten times, chances were good we'd have failed the other nine.

"No," Purdy continued, "I erred in regards to the *proliferative* nature of the threat." He was referring to the naga's eggs. "So I'm here in part to thank you for your stubbornness. The consequences for nonaction would have been beyond just about anyone."

"You knew about the other team," I said, glaring down at him. "Their presence, their tech, that they'd been made undead —that was the secondary threat you mentioned. And you were right, they damn near took us down. But that means you're either spying on them or working for them. Which is it?"

Holding my gaze, Purdy pulled his folded handkerchief from his breast pocket and touched the corners of his lips.

"Well?"

"Neither one, Captain," he answered at last.

"Bullshit."

"This was the other reason for my visit. But it will require your discretion."

"How much discretion?"

"Nothing I tell you can leave this room."

I hesitated, thinking of my renewed promise to Sarah that I'd share everything.

"I'll understand if you can't abide by those terms," he added, "but they're the only ones I can offer."

"Go ahead," I grunted, thinking of future missions. I didn't want any more surprises for my team. I hoped Sarah would have done the same in my situation, even if it meant me not knowing.

"I'm not spying or working for the other team," he said. "Not exactly. No, I'm *coordinating* with them. Well, with a contact inside the organization."

"Why?"

"There are four major defense contractors in the world. Centurion is the largest, of course, but the others do respectable business to the tune of hundreds of billions per annum. We're competitors, yes. All the way down to our smallest divisions, including this one. Though I've pushed to expand, Centurion still considers the Legion Program experimental, practically an afterthought." He gave a dry chuckle. "You've been on the receiving end of Director Beam's nickel and diming to know that much."

"And, what? The other programs are getting ahead?"

"Oh, quite the opposite. They're lagging at best, especially now that one has been practically wiped out."

"So what's the problem?"

"Precisely that."

"I'm not following."

"Think about it, Captain. If there were ever a major Prod 1 attack, what would we do? Fire each small monster-hunting division at them like pellets from a slingshot until the four were spent and then hope for the best?"

"We'd coordinate," I said, following now.

He raised a finger and whispered, "Exactly."

"So you're sharing information with this contact in the event we'd have to work together?" It explained how Purdy would have known about the mercs in New Siam. It probably also explained why the security protocols on the device Rusty hacked had been so similar to ours. Purdy had shared them.

"Contacts, plural, Captain," he said.

"With the other monster-hunting divisions?"

He must have read my disapproval. "Yes, I'm committing some very serious breaches. That goes without saying. But the defense conglomerates are too blinded by their profit motives to appreciate the larger, looming picture. My vision—and fortunately the vision of several other individuals—are rather clearer."

Crossing my thick arms, I weighed everything he was saying. It all made sense ... except for one thing.

"Then why tell me?"

"Because if we *are* ever required to join forces, I'll want you in command."

Though the captain in me was honored, a foreboding swam through my gut.

"And what are the odds of that happening?"

Purdy touched his kerchief to his mouth again, this time smoothing his mustache.

"Well, not zero," he replied at last. "And that's high enough."

The End

But get ready for another full-length Blue Wolf adventure. Keep reading to learn more...

BLUE BLOOD

BLUE WOLF BOOK 5

WHERE THE DEAD WON'T DIE

Days from a cure for his lupine curse, Jason takes an urgent mission.

A medieval invader has returned to a remote corner of Eastern Europe. Backed by seven undead knights and a zombie horde, Lord Drago threatens the region's oldest province with ghastly force.

Drochia is like nowhere the Legion team has been before—a land of brooding ruins, savage wolf packs, mass graves, and secrets that lurk as quietly as the ever-present mist. Even their cheery client seems to be hiding something.

But as the Blue Wolf wages high-caliber warfare against Lord Drago, mysteries peel away, exposing monstrous truths. Is his team saving the innocent or sacrificing them to an even greater evil?

And are they too late to save themselves?

AVAILABLE NOW!

Blue Blood
(Blue Wolf, Book 5)

ACKNOWLEDGMENTS

This was a doozy of an installment, and I'm deeply indebted to those who helped out.

A huge thank you to my beta and advanced readers, with special thanks to Beverly Collie, Mark Denman, and Linda Ash for their feedback, and to Sharlene Magnarella and Donna Rich for final proofing. Naturally, any errors or inelegance that remain are this author's alone.

The inspiration for *Blue Venom* came in part from trips I took to Thailand and Laos this past year. Though I had no naga run-ins (whew), I saw several beautiful statues and explored a cave that would have made a great naga lair. The hospitality I was shown in both countries went above and beyond, and for that, I'm very grateful.

I also want to thank James Patrick Cronin for his superb narration of the Prof Croft series and now the Blue Wolf audiobooks. Those books, including samples, can be found at Audible.com.

Finally, thank you, intrepid reader, for continuing to explore this growing world with me.

Till the next one...

Best Wishes,
Brad Magnarella

P.S. Be sure to check out my website to learn more about the Croftverse, download a pair of free prequels, and find out what's coming. That's all at bradmagnarella.com

CROFTVERSE CATALOGUE

Shadow Duel

Shadow Deep

Godly Wars

Angel Doom

SPIN-OFFS

Croft & Tabby

Croft & Wesson

———

For the entire chronology go to bradmagnarella.com

ABOUT THE AUTHOR

Brad Magnarella writes urban fantasy for the same reason most read it...

To explore worlds where magic crackles from fingertips, vampires and shifters walk city streets, cats talk (some excessively), and good prevails against all odds. It's shamelessly fun.

His two main series, Prof Croft and Blue Wolf, make up the growing Croftverse, with over a quarter-million books sold to date and an Independent Audiobook Award nomination.

Hopelessly nomadic, Brad can be found in a rented room overseas or hiking America's backcountry.

Or just go to www.bradmagnarella.com

Made in United States
Orlando, FL
10 March 2024

44615523R00200